THE FAMILY AT NO. 12

ANITA WALLER

Boldwood

First published in Great Britain in 2022 by Boldwood Books Ltd. This paperback edition first published in 2023.

1

Copyright © Anita Waller, 2022 Cover

Design by Head Design Cover

Photography: Shutterstock

Every effort has been made to obtain the necessary permissions with reference to copyright material, both illustrative and quoted. We apologise for any omissions in this respect and will be pleased to make the appropriate acknowledgements in any future edition.

A CIP catalogue record for this book is available from the British Library.

Paperback ISBN: 978-1-83518-806-4

Hardback ISBN: 978-1-80415-306-2

Ebook ISBN: 978-1-80415-310-9

Kindle ISBN: 978-1-80415-309-3

Audio CD ISBN: 978-1-80415-301-7

MP3 CD ISBN: 978-1-80415-302-4

Digital audio download ISBN: 978-1-80415-303-1

Digital audio MP3 ISBN: 978-1-80415-305-5

Large Print ISBN: 978-1-80415-308-6

Boldwood Books Ltd.

23 Bowerdean Street, London, SW6 3TN

www.boldwoodbooks.com

To Livia Sbarbaro, my friend and my support, my cheerleader extraordinaire!

'Sometimes I know part of me is still a ghost, walking next to my mother, looking for something to make an offering to, holding her hand. Either this feeling means that part of me is dead, or that she's alive, somewhere inside of me.'

— TERESE MARIE MAILHOT, *HEART BERRIES*

'However motherhood comes to you, it's a miracle.'

— VALERIE HARPER

BOOK ONE

A HOUSE WITH NO BOOKS

May 1998 – January 2012

1

Janette Gregson always felt scared. Everything she did, most of what she saw or experienced, filled her with fear. Even going upstairs to the toilet made her worry that she might fall back down the narrow twisty stairs and hurt herself, and be lying there for days with nobody to assist her.

Her fear of the dark was helped by leaving the light on all night, a small lamp on her bedside table serving as her comfort blanket, until the night that the light bulb popped and went out. Now she had a light bulb in the lamp, and two spare ones in the bedside table drawer.

She had managed to pass her driving test, although she knew she would never understand how the driving examiner couldn't see how terrified she was; the buses as they pulled alongside her tiny car made her flinch, traffic lights at amber made her tremble as she had to make decisions as to whether to go or stop, and zebra crossings with people waiting to cross caused heart palpitations as she imagined her foot slipping as they got halfway across, and mowing them all down.

Fear. She hated this out-of-control feeling and blamed her mother for dying and leaving her to cope alone.

Cancer. The biggest fear of all, and her mother, the formidable Barbara Gregson, had been forced to tell her that she only had six months left when the inoperable tumour caused her stomach to reach massive proportions, but Janette would be taken care of because the house was paid for, and there was nobody else entitled to a share of it. Cancer. Fear. Panic that the stomach would explode and splatter her with blood and gore. Instead, Mother had simply faded away; nothing had exploded, she had merely died.

Janette had a job, of sorts. With the money from her mother's savings account, she became a dog carer. This, she decided, would save her having to go physically to work, be it either in an office or a shop, and she would only have to talk to the very minimum number of people. She'd had the concept of a small run of kennels in the back garden where she would house dogs for holiday periods when owners weren't able to take their much-loved animals with them, and she had built the little dog houses herself. To have somebody come into her home to do work for any length of time was unthinkable; Janette taught herself basic wood-working skills by getting books from the library. She coped with a gas or electric meter read, but nothing else.

Janette was simply terrified of life. She spoke only when she had to, with the exception of when quiz programmes were on television, and then she took pride in answering the questions, trying desperately to beat the *Mastermind* contestants. *University Challenge* was a bit more of a brain-hurting half-hour, but she enjoyed watching the struggles as the teams tried to work out the answers.

Neighbours on both sides of her house had given up trying to converse with her, and she was truly grateful for that. At twenty-four years of age, she had reached the decision that she simply didn't like people; she liked dogs. She enjoyed the seclusion of being on her own, and knew she wouldn't want her mother back to be part of her life again. She was happy when she was alone. The neighbours knew better than to complain about the occasional noisy barking of some unhappy animal who was missing his human parents, because she solved all problems by simply not answering the door. Even the milkman had devised a four-part knock so that she knew it was him calling to collect his weekly payment for the milk delivered to her doorstep.

So the day the man rang and asked if he could call to have a look at her kennels before committing to leaving his Cavalier King Charles Spaniel with her for a week was a worry, but everything was a worry, and when he arrived, on time and smartly dressed, she led him around the side of the house and to the back garden where the shelters were. He inspected them closely and agreed she had an excellent set-up. He liked the heaters she had installed for cold nights, and he was impressed by the leaflet she handed him with details of fees.

'That will be okay. I'll be bringing Bessie in three weeks, if that's okay?'

'That's fine. I will require a deposit to secure a place.'

'How much?' His eyes suddenly seemed hooded when he spoke.

'Fifty pounds.' Her voice was firm. She could do this, could take his money and then make herself a cup of tea to calm down.

'You can give me a receipt?'

'Of course. Please follow me.'

There was a tiny conservatory her mother had had built leading off the kitchen, which she had made into her office, and she took him there, to the desk where she kept all her paperwork. She pulled out the receipt book and felt a push on her back which catapulted her towards the kitchen door. It burst open, propelling her through to the kitchen, the momentum taking her down onto the floor.

Shock hit her and she tried to roll over but the man landed on top of her, his weight pinning her fragile frame underneath him with ease.

'Shut up,' he said, and dragged at her jeans.

She tried to fight, and he lifted her head, smashing it onto the tiles. Her vision darkened and she remembered nothing more.

* * *

When her brain began to surface, he had his trousers around his ankles; he had flipped her over, removed all her clothes and was raping her. She froze at the sheer horror of it, then saw the cast-iron cobbler's foot that had been the kitchen doorstop for as many years as she had lived there.

She felt him ejaculate into her with a groan, and collapse onto her, almost squashing the breath from her lungs, but she squirmed away, reached the cobbler's foot and swung it around, connecting with his head. She hit him three times with it, until he had no movement left in him.

Janette was sobbing as she extricated herself from the motion-less body on top of her, and she ran for the stairs, naked, trembling and crying. The pain between her legs was almost unbearable and she began to run a bath after locking the bathroom door behind her. While the water was filling up the tub, she swallowed three paracetamol tablets, and prayed they would begin to work quickly.

She stayed in the bath for over an hour, scrubbing herself furiously to get rid of the stickiness, the smell, all caused by the man she hoped had now left her home. She tried to clean around the large bite mark on her right breast, but that was a pain too far, and she dabbed gingerly at it several times.

Her skin felt raw as she wrapped a towel around her before putting on her dressing gown, and she sat down initially on the toilet seat, then slumped on the floor as she tried to find a comfortable, less painful way of sitting. She remained there for three hours, before venturing to open the bathroom door.

The pain had lessened, but she was sore, and she stepped cautiously down the stairs, listening for anything, any sounds from anywhere in her house. It was eerily silent, and she offered up a prayer of thanks that HE seemed to have gone. She hadn't even got his name, only the name of his bloody dog, and she wasn't convinced HE even had any sort of animal. HE was the animal.

The police? She trembled at the thought. No, she couldn't do that. She couldn't allow them into her home, her life. She had watched enough crime programmes on television to tell her what it would be like reporting a rape. It would be fobbed off as all her fault; she must have led the man on, she was probably wearing the wrong clothes. No, no police.

She stopped and sat on the bottom stair, listening. Still no sounds. Glancing at the clock in the hall, she saw it was almost five o'clock – surely HE would have gathered himself together and disappeared by now? She would lock the conservatory doors, lock the kitchen door and soothe herself out of the blue funk she was currently in. And she would cancel all bookings for the dogs she hadn't taken before. She would only take previously kennelled animals.

She felt as if she was re-taking control of her life, sitting there on the stairs, but she wasn't re-taking it to the extent that she wanted to move and do the actual locking of doors, face the carnage of the kitchen where it had all happened, clean up any blood. Her own head had bled from when HE had banged it on the floor to knock her out, so there must be bloodstains.

She felt comfortable on the stairs, in the enclosed and tidy hallway, away from the horror of her kitchen; her position on the bottom stair had allowed her to sit on one buttock, ease the pain inside her vagina. She wanted to stay there forever.

When the clock reached six, she knew that wasn't possible. She needed to heal herself, to heal the frantic workings of her brain, and that would begin with swallowing a couple of painkillers, removing her dressing gown and the towel and replacing them with proper clothes, taking control back. Yes, she was scared, but she couldn't sit on the bottom stair forever. She had two dogs in the kennels who needed feeding, and they had to be seen to, no matter what.

She slowly eased herself to a standing position, wincing at the sharp pain inside her, and tentatively stepped down onto the hall floor.

Pausing at the lounge door, she listened, but being convinced she couldn't hear anything, she slowly opened it, peering around the room. It looked exactly the same as it had always looked, simply furnished with only two armchairs, a small coffee table and a television on a stand. Her mother's sideboard held items that rarely saw the light of day, and had a lamp on top which was the only lighting ever used in this room. Now she switched on the large central ceiling globe. She needed the dark to go. She crossed to the curtains and pulled them back to let sunshine flood in; she normally kept them almost closed as she knew sunshine faded carpets and other fabrics. But now she needed the light, not the darkness.

HE hadn't been in there. She would have felt him. She hoped this meant HE had picked himself up when he'd come round from the battering, and simply disappeared. Her mind switched to thinking about security-proofing her garden – no more would she admit random visitors; it would be by appointment only, she would insist on names before they came, and she would damn well have to recognise those names as previous clients or she would tell them she was fully booked.

The dining room was equally free of his presence, and she sat on one of the dining chairs, relieved that HE hadn't contaminated her favourite room. This was where she sat when she wanted to draw. The table contained a small pile of items she used – pencils, rubbers, three drawing books, a twelve-inch-tall posable wooden figure. It would have been too much to bear if HE had entered this room, bringing evil into it.

She pulled her large drawing book towards her, opened it and stroked the paper. It soothed her. It didn't stop her pain, but it soothed her. She looked at the half-drawn figure of a child, sitting on a swing that was sending her high into the heavens, and remembered the day in the park with her mother when the world was good for both of them, the heights she had screamingly reached as the swing went higher and higher. She hadn't quite caught that delicious feeling yet in the drawing, but it would come, she knew it would. She closed the pad, and stood.

Time to face the kitchen. To feed the dogs then lock her doors. Tomorrow she would begin her recovery, but tonight she had to face the scene currently causing her so much distress.

The door was slightly open, just as she had left it as she had run headlong for the stairs. She pushed it open the rest of the way.

2

She could smell blood, smell it before she saw it. She felt herself begin to gag, felt the vomit rise from her stomach, but it wasn't as a result of the strange aroma, it was the sight of the man, still on her kitchen floor, still unconscious.

Fear, indecision, terror – all battled inside her head for supremacy. She turned her back on the scene, swallowed convulsively and returned to the hall, closing the kitchen door behind her.

'Think,' she said aloud, almost as if she didn't trust her thoughts on their own to give her the right answer. 'Think. Get dressed before HE comes round properly.'

She took her own advice and walked slowly towards the stairs, aware of pain and soreness with every step. She climbed, again with caution, reached her bedroom and left her thoughts switched off. She couldn't deal with him until she had sorted out some clean clothes. She put on five pairs of pants in the hope they would cushion some of the pain, added a clean pad to soak up any blood still left to flow out of her, then jeans. A bra and T-shirt soon followed, and she decided she would put on the bright yellow

Crocs she normally wore for cleaning out the kennels – they could be washed in the washing machine. The biggest problem was that they were in the conservatory. And HE was blocking the door through from the kitchen to that room.

She returned to the hallway, feeling more secure now she had shed the towel and dressing gown, but she knew she needed those Crocs. She put on her slippers, went through the front door and round the side of the house to the back garden.

Janette stepped into the conservatory and swapped her slippers for the Crocs. Only then did she glance at the open kitchen door. His eyes were wide, staring. She fixed her focus on his chest, and realised there was no movement. All movement had stopped in her mother's chest when she had breathed her last.

The two dogs in the kennels began to bark, as if to tell her it was walk time, and feeding time. She hurriedly grabbed food from her store in the conservatory, and ran outside to stop them barking; she tipped food into their bowls, checked their water, and spoke soothingly to them to calm them down. While she was looking after them, she wasn't having to deal with a dead body…

With the dogs happily eating, and the gates to the dog run opened, she left them and walked back to the conservatory, where she lowered all the blinds. She didn't know if the neighbours could see into her house, but she didn't want to take the chance.

There was a lot of blood. She tried to edge around it but the yellow Crocs soon became tinged with a thick deep red gunge. She filled a jug with water, walked back to him, and poured the liquid over his face.

'He's dead,' she confirmed to herself. 'If HE wasn't, he'd have moved. So, what do I do now?'

* * *

What she decided not to do was involve the police. After careful consideration, she realised there was no proof HE had been there that afternoon. She hadn't got around to entering his name in her bookings diary, hadn't even asked him his name, so she fetched a large piece of plastic sheeting that in an earlier life had been wrapped around bundles of wood used for making the kennels. She had saved it in case she ever needed it, and she really needed it now.

At only five feet in height, and very slim in stature, Janette wasn't the strongest person on the planet, so she began by tying her long dark hair into a ponytail, wincing as the hair tugged on the lump created by him smacking her head onto the tiled floor. She cleaned as much of the blood as possible from around the huge bulk of the man lying on her kitchen floor and carefully probed into his inside pocket, removing his wallet. His credit card confirmed his name as Philip Hancock, and she slipped the wallet into a kitchen drawer. She knew she would have to deal with it later, but currently she had a much bigger problem. The sixteen stones or so of man lying on her floor. She shuddered with horror as she thought of him on top of her, forcing himself into her, hurting her, bruising her, until it was almost too painful to move.

She placed an old duster over his eyes – she couldn't bear him to keep staring at her – then picked up the cobbler's foot and placed it in a bucket, checking that every part of it was submerged in cold water and bleach. Hadn't her mother always told her that bleach only worked effectively in cold water?

She returned to her final task, and stood for a moment, gathering her strength for the next part. HE didn't look half so scary with an old yellow duster covering his eyes, but HE still looked just as heavy. Before attempting to roll him, she headed to the point halfway down the hall where the door to the cellar was. She unlocked it and left it wide open. The rich earthy smell of the coal

remnants still down there flooded out, and she sniffed appreciatively. She had always loved the slight chemical smell of the cellar,
but her fear of steps kept her firmly grounded at the top of this
particular flight, and she knew once HE was down there, she could
continue to live her life. No police, and her own pain from the
attack would go.

She fetched a cushion from the lounge and used it to wedge the
cellar door open, then went back to the kitchen. She smoothed out
the plastic sheet, then braced herself against a kitchen unit and
attempted to move him by leaning against the unit and using her
yellow-Croc feet to roll him over and into position on the sheet.
She had already placed long pieces of garden twine under the plastic, and secured him inside the wrapping with them, in a very
clumsy fashion.

In all, it took her ninety minutes, and when she was finished
she felt exhausted. This wasn't how she lived her life; she would
never have dreamed of doing something so extraordinarily stupid
as killing someone, but here she was. A murderer.

And she still hadn't got this trussed up turkey-like thing out of
the kitchen.

* * *

Janette opened the door of her mother's sideboard and took out the
dark blue bottle of sherry, so loved by Barbara. She poured herself
a large tumbler of it, reflecting it was the first time the bottle had
been opened for a number of years, but she needed something.
She also had a further two painkillers, as she realised she would
really be hurting by the time she'd finished doing what she had
to do.

Sitting for half an hour and letting the alcohol and painkillers
do their work gave Janette time to recover, and to think through the

rest of her actions. She blessed the Victorians who had built her house, blessed them for the solid walls, the addition of solid locks on every door in the place, and knew she could get him into that cellar, turn the key, and nobody would ever stumble across him, not now, not in the future. And when she herself died, they would probably find him, whoever bought the house, but she would be gone anyway.

Her thoughts drifted towards leaving some sort of journal detailing what had happened, and sealing it into an envelope with the man's wallet, but her eyes were closing, and she had to shake herself awake, push herself to get up and complete the work.

She wedged the kitchen door open with the vacuum cleaner, and moved up to what she was desperately trying to think of as a turkey, and grabbed at the head. She tugged, she pulled, and it was only by going to the foot end that she made any significant movement. Pushing seemed to work better while in the kitchen, but once she actually had him in the hall, it seemed easier to pull him.

Deciding to take a rest from such physical back-breaking work, she left him for a bit and walked back into the kitchen. There were still spots of blood to clean now the body had been moved, so she filled the mop bucket and began to restore her domain to its previous pristine condition. The smell of bleach was almost overpowering, but she felt cleansed.

It was as she was rinsing the water down the sink that she heard a noise. In the conservatory.

She spun around, as the noise was followed by a knock on the kitchen door.

'Janette? You there?'

She cautiously opened the door. 'Oh, Mr Earnshaw. I'm sorry, I was just washing the floor...'

'No problem. We came home a day early, so I thought I'd pop round and collect Daisy. Are you okay? You look very pale.'

'I'm fine, thanks. I'll just get Daisy's lead, and you can take her. She's been fed.'

She stepped into the conservatory, closing the kitchen door behind her. Handing the lead to Ian Earnshaw, Janette followed him down to the kennels. She watched him and Daisy, bouncing around like a puppy, walk away, her breath expelling from her in short sharp bursts as she battled to keep control of her senses. If he'd come an hour earlier... That side gate had to be kept locked; it wasn't good that anybody could just arrive at her back door. She would see to it as soon as she felt well enough.

The body inside the plastic was almost at the cellar door, and she locked every possible means of access to her property before carrying on with what she was now beginning to think of as her punishment for battering him with the cobbler's foot.

She tugged, pulled, and got him half onto the small square space, the cellar head. She felt a little flummoxed by her next move, because HE was almost bent in two, but there was a stiffness creeping into the body now, and she knew rigor mortis was well on its way, making handling him so much harder.

She leaned her back against the door jamb and pushed with her feet. Slowly, inch by inch, HE began to slide, and suddenly to fall. She increased the pressure, pushed harder, and the large plastic bundle began to almost fold itself onto the steep cellar steps. She gave one last enormous push, and HE slid, the plastic helping the descent. Janette leaned over, unable to stop the vomit, unable to stop the shaking. She collapsed onto the ragged linoleum of the cellar head, and finally tears came.

She hugged herself tightly, wiped her mouth, and looked down the steps. HE had landed at an awkward angle, but that was it. His awkward angle for the rest of eternity, as far as she was concerned.

Had she saved other women from going through what she had gone through? She suspected yes, but she didn't really want to know. She wanted a cup of tea, a chat with her mother's ashes, and maybe she would bring in the one remaining dog for an hour in the lounge tonight. No more dogs were due for another week, so she would enjoy Candy for the rest of her stay and then she could give that dog-free time over to recovery.

She moved back out to the hallway, turned the large iron key in the lock, and slipped it into her jeans pocket. Tomorrow she would finish cleaning up the cobbler's foot and place it back in its usual place. Just in case.

3

Ten p.m. Tears. Janette's sobs became cataclysmic, and she grabbed for the paper bag that was always to hand for such moments as this. Panic attacks were a normal part of her life, a part she had learned to live with, but this one was bad.

She breathed slowly in and out, concentrating on making her actions steady and smooth, aware of her mother's voice echoing through her head. *Slowly, breathe deeply, Janette. You'll be fine in a minute.*

Except this time, it took fifteen minutes for her heart rate to settle, her breathing to slow to something approaching normal, and she had to deliberately steer her mind away from the body jammed halfway down the cellar steps.

She had another glass of sherry, emptying the last dregs from the deep blue bottle, and switched on the television to catch the last of the news. None of what she watched registered in her brain and at eleven o'clock she gave in, double-checked every door was locked and headed upstairs. At least HE hadn't contaminated anywhere above ground level in her home. She hadn't had the courage or the inclination to venture into the kennels to seek the company of what must now be a very lonely dog, but that was tough. She simply hadn't had the mental strength.

She ran her second bath of the evening, adding salt in the hope that it would help with the healing. She lay back and winced as the water touched the deep bite mark on her right breast. She knew it would make sense to use antibiotic cream on it, and that would accelerate the healing, but it hurt so damn much at the moment.

By midnight, she had taken further painkillers, smeared both breasts with the cream, and had put on her favourite nightie as she struggled to seek comfort from anywhere she could get it. She slept.

* * *

Sunshine woke Janette and she smiled. Then she stopped smiling as memories of the previous day washed over her.

She groaned as she swung her legs out of bed; there wasn't a part of her that didn't ache. She didn't wash, didn't brush her teeth, simply staggered downstairs in her nightie and dressing gown, stopped at the front door to collect the daily pint of milk from the step, then came to a halt as she reached the cellar door. She edged over to the left of the hallway, and almost ran past it until she was at the kitchen. Her mind saw the body, but the smell of bleach still lingered, and her floor and work surfaces were spotlessly clean.

After putting the milk bottle in the fridge, Janette cautiously opened the back door and breathed in the warm fresh air, the sunshine dazzling her. Candy, the little Jack Russell, barked as she spotted her carer, and a half smile touched Janette's face. At least she had nothing to fear from a dog. She went down to the kennels, put Candy's breakfast into her bowl, and renewed her water.

'We'll maybe go for a walk in an hour or so,' she said to the little dog, who wagged her tail in agreement.

She doubted if she would keep to that statement, but she knew that's what she would have done if she hadn't been brutally attacked the previous afternoon. Actions like that tended to change perspectives on normal routines. Despite a long restful sleep, the pain was still there. Maybe a walk today wasn't the best idea she'd had.

She opened the gate from the kennels to the run at the end of the garden, and knew Candy would find her own exercise – this particular little dog took great delight in running round and round in circles.

A dog. Because she looked after dogs of all breeds and sizes, she had resisted having one herself. It only now occurred to her that if she had had one yesterday, one who would protect its mistress, maybe things would have been a lot different. And possibly she wouldn't feel quite so alone. The three years without her mother had been an exceedingly long three years...

She stayed a few minutes longer, letting the sunshine warm her, comfort her, then turned and walked slowly back to the conservatory. She made a note in her diary that Daisy had been collected a day early, then closed the roll-top on her bureau. This small action was something she always did as she retired for the night, but the previous night had been something of an exception to her routine. Today she wasn't expecting any clients, and Candy was with her for a couple of days yet, so in theory, the bureau would remain closed. She stepped up from the conservatory into the kitchen, and felt her stomach lurch. Was this going to happen every time she came into this particular room? She took deep breaths, wanting no repetition of the panic attack of the previous evening, then clicked on the kettle. A cup of tea. Her mother had always made her a cup of tea after any sort of meltdown, and that was what she needed right now.

She popped a slice of bread into the toaster, and as soon as it was ready, she threw it straight into the bin. She couldn't eat. Not yet. The cup of tea was enough for the moment, her stomach would tell her when it was ready to accept food again, she figured. Going back into the hall was hard. The cellar door was simply there, and while it might be solidly locked, she knew what lay behind it. She needed to do something before it drove her mad.

A curtain. Mother had always insisted on a thick, full-length curtain against the front door – to keep out draughts, she had said. It was only when Janette had taken it down to wash it that she had realised she didn't like it, the front door looked much better without it, and the curtain had been consigned to the airing cupboard. She could put a curtain pole above the cellar door jamb, and hide the whole damn thing. If she couldn't see the door, it wasn't there.

Invigorated by positive thoughts and actions, and the sunshine, she headed back upstairs. This time, she only stayed in her salt bath for half an hour, then dressed and returned to the kitchen, clutching the door curtain. She shook it out and carried it outdoors, hanging it on the washing line. It would be freshened by a couple of hours in the sunshine, and she could spend that time putting the pole above the cellar door, the one saved from the front door.

* * *

She had to shorten the curtain by six inches, all of which helped to ease her mind. She would get over this. Mundane little jobs like hand-sewing a hem would calm her. One day, she would be able to walk past the door curtain and not go into a breakdown, one day she would forget his face, forget the hole in his head that she had excavated with her cobbler's foot. One day. Just not yet.

While there was still pain, she couldn't forget. Her breasts hurt, particularly the one with the deeper bite mark. Inside her, the pain had become intermittent, which she hoped was part of the healing process, and not a deeper indication of something going wrong that might require medical intervention. She didn't do doctors. The very thought of attending a surgery or an accident and emergency department caused shivers to run up and down her spine, and she knew that wouldn't happen. Visiting her mother at the hospice in her last few days had been traumatic enough, and since her death, Janette hadn't ventured anywhere near anything vaguely medical.

Having the curtain hanging in front of the cellar door changed everything. What was behind the door could now stay behind it, hidden for ever. She removed the key from her jeans pocket and placed it on the Victorian door jamb, hiding it completely from view. She had no reason to think anybody would come looking for him; with hindsight, she had no reason to think HE had a dog. HE had come to her home with the intention of raping her, not booking his dog in for a holiday. Questions raced around her head.

Had HE followed her at some stage? Had HE seen her walk back from the shops after she had put her card advertising her dog-sitting services in the newsagent's window and thought what a pretty girl she was? Was that where HE had gleaned her phone number from? Had HE thought HE could overpower her with no trouble? Because if HE had thought that, then his thoughts were spot on. She had been overpowered, but what HE had failed to realise was that possibly she might fight back. With a cobbler's foot. A cast iron, hundred-year-old cobbler's foot.

She made herself another cup of tea, but still wanted nothing to eat. She wanted to sleep, to be wrapped in a warm woolly throw that would surround her with comfort. Sleep on the sofa, in her cosy lounge that still bore traces of her late lamented mother. It had always been 'the front room', one rarely used. Now she used it for her relaxing times, for times when stress faded away, when she had no worries about anything. She needed that again, that trouble-free time, and 'the front room' gave that to her.

She fed Candy and brought her into the house with her. An hour of company would benefit both of them, and she felt able to cope better with an animal for a companion; it would have been unthinkable on that first night of pain. Her entire concentration had been needed for herself.

By nine o'clock, Janette had turned off the television, made the decision to sleep downstairs on the sofa, locked all doors, and settled Candy onto a dog bed on the floor, by her side. She left the small lamp on, and sat for a while drawing the little Jack Russell. She felt close to Candy; she didn't know why, but assumed it was because that's all she had had, her and the dog, on the most traumatic and difficult day of her life.

The drawing was good. She captured the way the little dog tilted her head when she heard a quiet human voice, and took care to make sure her brown markings were perfectly positioned.

'You're a good subject, Candy,' she said and smiled properly. She handed the dog a treat, and Candy accepted it with a slight woof. She showed the picture to Candy, who looked at it with disdain, and placed her paw on Janette's knee.

'You want more treats? Let's see what we can do.' She placed a few on her palm and Candy took them with some speed.

'Okay,' Janette said. 'Time to sleep. Come on, you need to wee if you're staying inside.' She led her to the back door, her eyes roaming everywhere to make sure it was safe. Would she ever feel it was again?

Candy disappeared, then a minute later was back by Janette's side. 'Good girl,' she said, and reached down to pat Candy's head. 'Let's go and make a glass of hot milk, take a couple of painkillers and go to sleep. We'll be over the top with milk, if I don't.'

Janette was aware she hadn't eaten for about thirty hours, and while the milk was heating, she pulled the biscuit barrel towards her. She glanced inside, then replaced the lid. 'Nah,' she said, 'don't want anything. Not yet, anyway. Let's get through tonight, Candy, and maybe I'll have something in the morning.'

The dog once again gave a gentle woof, and they walked together back into the lounge. Her comfort room, until she no longer needed a comfort room.

4

Janette woke at four, pushing back from the nightmare that had almost taken hold of her. The body she had dragged from the kitchen was the other side of the cellar door, knocking on it, demanding to be let out. Thankful she had left the small light glowing, she sat up, pulled the blanket around her, and realised Candy had left her own bed, and had climbed on the sofa to be with her.

Pulling the little dog towards her, she sat staring into space while she waited for her brain to normalise itself. 'Don't get used to this,' she murmured. 'You're back in your kennel tonight, I don't want to spoil you for your own home.'

Candy snuggled down and closed her eyes. Janette didn't. She didn't think she could trust going back to sleep, not yet. The nightmare needed to go; her mind needed to be at rest. She picked up the drawing pad, and once again drew Candy, this time snuggled beside her, the little dog's eyes closed. It was a quick sketch, and captured Candy perfectly. It brought a smile to Janette's face, and she turned over the page.

'Draw it out of you,' she murmured. 'Draw the damn thing out of you.' She closed her eyes for a moment and pictured her kitchen, then swiftly sketched the basic view of it, the cupboards, the table, the door through to the hall, before adding herself to the floor and him on top of her. It was a fast ten-minute drawing, and she knew she had captured it, the horror of it. She began to shade and fill out the strokes already there, and it was only when she heard the quadruple knock on the front door that she put it to one side.

Grabbing her dressing gown, she ran to the front door, picking up the money from the hall stand as she went.

'I'm sorry,' she gasped. 'I'm running late today.'

The milkman smiled at her, surprised to see her still in her nightwear. She was usually dressed, seeing to her dogs. 'No problem, I'd have waited. You've not missed your weekly milk money for the last few years, so you're not going to start now, I'm sure,' he said, and took the exact money from her, before handing her the bottle he held in his hand. 'Have a good week, Janette,' he said, and left her standing there with yet another pint of milk. Maybe cornflakes for breakfast then, she decided.

She closed the front door, and locked it, then went to find Candy, who was standing with her front paws on the bay windowsill, staring out at the departing milkman.

'Come on, Candy, let's go out the back and you can have a wee while I find us some breakfast.'

* * *

Candy was easily pleased with the dry dog food put down by Janette, followed by a small dish of milk.

Janette stared at her equally small dish of cornflakes and wondered if it would stay down if she ate it. She managed three spoonfuls, and decided it was enough; the rest she tipped into

Candy's bowl; the dog seemed hardly able to believe her luck. It was only as Janette bent over to tip the extra treat into the bowl that she realised she had been able to sit at the table, on a hard wooden chair, without discomfort. Her sigh of relief was heartfelt.

She decided to shower rather than sit in a bath, and walked into the bedroom, a spring in her step. She inspected the injury to her scalp, and carefully brushed her wet hair to hide it. She needed to go shopping, and on such a warm day she could hardly wear a hat to hide the lump, and the cut.

She played with Candy in the garden for a while, then locked her in the pound before getting ready to go to the shops. She unlocked the front door, and two police officers stood there, one of them with a hand raised and about to knock.

Janette froze.

'Sorry, ma'am. Hope I didn't make you jump.' His smile was infectious, and she gulped.

'Not at all, my fault. I was miles away. I'm just nipping out to the shops...' She knew she was waffling.

He held a picture out to her. 'Have you seen this man in the neighbourhood, or do you know him?'

Yes, he's dead in my cellar.

She took the picture and stared at him. 'No, I don't think so. Who is he?'

'His name is Philip Hancock, and his wife has reported him missing. He hasn't been home for almost three days. We've located his car in this area, so we're going door to door to see if anyone has seen him.'

She stepped onto the front step and closed the door behind her. 'Well, I go out very little, but I'll be sure to contact the police if I do see him. I do hope you find him alive and well.'

'Thank you, ma'am. We'll just tick you off our list, you shouldn't have anybody else call. Have a good day.' They left her at the garden gate; she turned left and they turned right.

She forced herself to take deep breaths all the way to the shops, went into the small Tesco, spoke to no one, and was back home within half an hour. She put her shopping away, took three tablets from the new pack of paracetamol, and went for a lie down on the bed.

She slept a dreamless, nightmareless sleep for three hours, then woke in a panic as she realised the sun had dipped lower in the sky.

* * *

Janette took Candy out for a walk, but saw no evidence of any further police activity. She had woken with good feelings and relief that most of the pain had gone, only to have her day ruined by the arrival of the two constables on her doorstep. She realised the issue wasn't going to go away, but surely the police wouldn't be granted search warrants for every home in the locality, just because he'd left his car there?

What puzzled her more than anything was that she had a desire to know if HE really did have a dog. If HE didn't, it meant HE had arrived with the intention of raping her. If HE did, maybe the kennelling query had been overridden by thoughts of easy sex, once HE spotted a pretty, slim female who was on her own, and available.

Except she wasn't available. She had never so much as kissed a man, let alone had sex with one. She had to know why HE had arrived in her back garden. It would almost be the worst thing if she found out HE had no dog – that meant HE had seen her at some point, and found out what she did for a living. Had tracked her down to her home, had invaded her space with the sole intention of forcing himself on her.

Janette needed to know where HE lived. She fastened Candy's lead, and they set off for the walk she had kept promising the little dog. The newsagent's shop was first on the list, and she bought the local daily paper, figuring there might be something in that. She hoped it wasn't too soon, but if it was, she would buy a paper every day until she got the information she wanted.

The walk around the park, with Candy zooming in all directions on the lead extension, brought Janette almost back to a feeling of normality. The police hadn't been in the least suspicious; it had been a few seconds of 'do you know this face?' and they had moved on.

So HE had a wife, apparently. Why couldn't that woman have been enough for him? She felt so tempted to open the newspaper and begin to search through it, but resisted. She needed either her kitchen or her dining table, where she could spread it out and not miss even the tiniest column. Candy was approaching a much bigger dog, a Labrador, and Janette called her name, beginning to reel in the lead extension, drawing the little dog closer to where Janette was resting on a bench. Candy ran towards her, and jumped up onto the seat, then onto Janette's lap to lick her face. Her breasts bore the full weight of the little dog, and Janette gave a whimper of pain. The bites definitely needed more healing time, and she stood, Candy now walking sedately by her side.

By the time they reached home, Janette had decided. She would ring the local animal rescue centre, who she occasionally helped out with boarding strays if they became too full, and check out availability of any older ones waiting for re-homing. She knew she would feel safer with a permanent animal companion; she would make the dog a part of her home and her life, and they would grow together. And he or she would keep her safe.

She made a hot drink, helped herself to a biscuit after taking Candy down to her kennel for a rest, and spread out the paper on the dining room table. She didn't turn any pages over until she had read every inch of the print. And then she saw it. A tiny version of the photograph the police had shown her. Philip Hancock. Missing. Police would like to hear from anyone who had seen him. His wife, Theresa, aged thirty-four, of Meadow Drive, had reported him missing when HE didn't return home after walking out on her as the result of an argument.

The police, it stated, weren't overly concerned about his welfare at this stage, but would like to hear from him, or from anyone who had seen him.

No mention of a bloody dog.

She cut out the small notification and placed it in her drawing book, now back in its rightful place on the dining table. She folded the paper, got out her street guide and looked up Meadow Drive. Time to put this whole episode to bed. She could do that once she knew what had prompted the attack. Once she knew if HE had planned to rape her anyway, or had simply taken advantage of the situation that had suddenly presented itself to him. Did HE have a dog called Bessie, or didn't HE, was what it really boiled down to, and she stuffed the newspaper in her kitchen bin. Tomorrow, early, she would take Candy in the car, travel to Meadow Drive, and see what she could see.

Tonight, Candy would stay indoors with her again, a complete reversal of Janette's earlier decision, because tomorrow she would be returning home. She was such a lovely little dog, and Janette knew she would miss her, but by the end of the day, Janette hoped to have her own, an animal who would grow to love her, and to feel loved in return. Animals were trustworthy; they didn't rape and molest without warning.

She pulled the sketch pad towards her and opened it at the

partly completed drawing she had created during the long hours of the night. She wrote the date of the attack in the bottom left corner, then paperclipped the newspaper cutting to the top right corner, before sharpening her pencil to begin shading the table. It almost fully concealed the image of her own head, and most of his head. It had been hard to draw her own naked body, but the exercise would have been pointless if she hadn't gone for complete accuracy. She could only see her right breast, but it required the addition of the bite mark, so she carefully drew it as near as she could get it to the exact spot. The picture was a depiction of the moment of rape, not the aftermath. Because of that, the only thing she hadn't added was the cobbler's foot...

5

Candy had been collected just after ten, negating any chances of an early morning trip to Meadow Drive, so Janette rang the dog rescue centre. She chatted with the woman in charge for a while, then asked what dogs they had in requiring re-homing.

'We have five,' Chloe Danvers said. 'Two of them need to be in a home without children, because neither of them have ever known children, and they're getting on a bit. The other three, we'd decide when we knew who wanted them. You're looking for one to live with you?'

'I am. There are no children here, so I want a medium-sized dog, doesn't have to be a breed, I'm quite happy to take a scruff, provided we like each other.'

Janette heard Chloe laugh. 'Then you're going to love Billy. He's definitely a scruff to look at, but all of us will be sad to see him go. Lovely attitude. He's lived for the past eight years, since he was a tiny puppy, with his previous owner, who passed away a couple of weeks ago. He went to live with the daughter but she has three kids, and they wouldn't leave him alone, so she's asked us if we can re-home him. Jump in the car, and come and have a look at him.'

* * *

Janette could see Billy had terrier in him, but what the rest was she couldn't even begin to guess. She played with him for a while in his cage, then took him for a walk around the yard. He walked to heel impeccably, and she knew his previous owner had given the dog the time and training he needed.

Janette went to find Chloe, and took out her purse. 'Can I take him today?'

'You can. He's vet-checked, fully vaccinated and good to go.'

'So how much do I owe?'

Chloe smiled at her. 'How much do I pay you if you have to take any overflow from us?'

'I don't ask for anything.'

'Then Billy is our payment. Enjoy him, Janette, but you'll be breaking a few hearts here, I can tell you. Proper charmer, he is.'

* * *

Billy explored the house, and she collected a clean dog bed from the storage cupboard in the spare bedroom. She placed it at the foot of her bed. 'This is where you'll sleep at night,' she explained, and the dog tilted his head to one side, listening carefully. He must have liked what he heard because he stepped onto the bed, and curled up.

'Good boy,' she said, and knelt down to stroke his head. 'Come on, let's go find out if you like the food I have in.'

He followed her obediently downstairs, and her face held a genuine smile for the first time in a couple of days. She headed for the kitchen, but Billy only followed as far as the curtain in front of the cellar door. He sniffed, moved the curtain slightly, then sniffed at the bottom edge of the door.

'Come on,' she said, feeling slightly panicked. She had thought earlier there was a strange smell, but decided to ignore it; she could do nothing about it except spray air fresheners everywhere. She filled a stainless-steel bowl with food, and the plastic bowl with water. Billy helped himself, having forgotten all about the odd smell for the time being.

She watched as he tucked in to his evening meal, and smiled. He clearly enjoyed the taste, and seemed to like her. Tomorrow they would go out – she had no clients due for almost a week, and Janette intended to bond with Billy over the next few days until she had to share herself with her guest dogs.

She opened the fridge and stared in. Nothing she had in there appealed to her, and she decided to have something simple. Her stomach warned her it didn't really want anything, but she couldn't keep refusing food; at some point, life had to return to what she thought of as normal. Pre-Philip Hancock.

Janette lifted her small radio down from the windowsill and tuned it in to the local radio station, guessing that if the police had anything to report, it would be on the station's next news bulletin.

She was right. They led with the story of the missing man, appealing for information from the public. Nothing in his car gave them any inkling of where HE might be, and they were getting increasingly concerned about his whereabouts. It had been a minor argument with his wife, nothing that would cause him to disappear altogether, and it was feared HE might have met with an accident. Nearby woods were being searched, but so far, police were baffled.

'And now on to football news,' the newscaster intoned, and Janette switched it off. She took the air freshener from under the sink and walked up and down the hallway, spraying liberally. Billy was still eating, so she had left him safely away from the chemicals. She returned to the kitchen and opened the back door leading into the conservatory. Billy popped his head inside, then waited for his mistress to tell him what to do next.

'Garden,' she said, and opened the conservatory door. Billy went through and headed straight for the kennels. He sniffed the full length of them, and returned to where she was sitting at the garden table, a bottle of water in her hand. He placed his head on her knee and looked up at her.

'You like it?'

He lifted his paw.

'Oh, good. I like having you here. I'm sorry your master's gone, but I promise I'll look after you. And I need you to look after me,' she said with a sigh.

Billy dropped down to sit by her feet, and she slipped off her shoe and stroked his back with her toes. 'Welcome to my home,' she said. 'There's only me here, so we'll make a good partnership, Billy.'

* * *

During the night, she heard Billy get up and walk around the bedroom, but she let him do it without speaking to him. She didn't want him to be frightened in any way by this strange environment he now found himself in; he needed to settle in his own time.

Her stomach grumbled at one point, and she realised she'd still had nothing to eat; she would make breakfast, she decided.

And she did. Beans on toast, just one slice, eaten out in the garden. Billy had his food outside with her, and she knew this dog had been well looked after, well schooled in how a dog should behave, and well loved. While he was eating on the patio, she had quickly sprayed the hallway once again with the air freshener; the smell was getting stronger and she was grateful that doors could be left open in the late May warmth.

* * *

Janette decided against having lunch; the smell was making her feel sick and she reckoned she could go out and buy some sealant tape, and seal the entire door until she was sure the smell had gone. She would also need to go to the library and find out how long that was likely to be – her knowledge of decomposition rates was limited. Her knowledge of rape had been pretty limited as well.

She slipped a lead on Billy, and they set off to walk to the shops. She bought two rolls of the tape, two cans of air freshener that announced they would dissipate any smell, and came out to find two children talking to Billy.

'He's lovely,' the little girl said. 'What's his name?'

Janette flashed a brief smile. She wasn't really used to speaking to children – in fact, she wasn't used to speaking to anyone except the milkman. 'His name is Billy.'

'He sits when you say sit,' the boy said.

'He's been well trained,' she responded.

'Is he old?'

'About eight, I believe. I only got him yesterday, so we're still getting to know each other.'

'Well, he's lovely.'

She unhooked Billy from the post to which he was secured, said goodbye to the children and carried on walking away from her home. It was a lovely afternoon, the sun was shining, and there were no obnoxious smells. And she needed to know where Meadow Drive was.

She headed in the general area of the small housing estate, and decided it might not be a smart move to ask somebody for directions – people tended to remember speaking to strangers, and the last thing she wanted was for somebody to pass information on to the police, saying a woman and a dog had been looking for

Meadow Drive. She wished now she'd brought her *A–Z* with her, but the decision to go looking for his home had been a spur of the moment thing, so she would simply walk around until she saw it. Which happened almost immediately.

It turned out HE had lived at 2 Meadow Drive before taking up residence in Janette's cellar, and that knowledge was brought to bear by the sight of a police car outside the first house on the road, number two.

A brick-built wall ran along the front of the garden, and a child of around ten years old was leaning with his arms along the top of the wall. He wasn't doing anything, just leaning and looking.

Janette scanned as much as she could, but carried on walking past the end of the road. She herself was on Meadow Avenue, and guessed, as it was an avenue, that the other end of it would be away from this small area. She didn't want the police to wonder who she was, she wanted them to think she was simply out taking her dog for a walk, so she continued at the same steady pace. Now she knew where HE had lived, she could park her car in the locality, and devise some plan for discovering if Bessie the dog was fictional or not.

It took her over an hour to walk back home, but she felt rejuvenated by the hike. Billy went straight to his water bowl, and she clicked on the kettle. The cup of tea was something she felt she desperately needed, before tackling the proper sealing of the cellar door.

She opened both the kitchen and the conservatory doors, then sprayed the new air freshener. She felt it did work better than the pretty lavender fragranced one she had previously used, and she wondered if she should write to the manufacturers and tell them it even helped conceal the smell of putrefaction caused by decomposition of a murdered body.

'Naughty Janette,' she said aloud. Billy pricked up his ears.

'Your new mummy is a very naughty girl. She accidentally bashed someone's head in, and now HE has to live in our cellar. Well, perhaps live is the wrong word.'

Billy tipped his head to one side, as if he understood what she was trying to say to him. She hoped to god he had never learned that skill with his previous owner. 'But don't ever tell anybody, Billy,' she said and stroked his head.

She finished her cup of tea, and smiled as the dog curled up beside her on the sofa. He was asleep very quickly, obviously worn out after the long walk.

Janette rinsed out her cup and brought the stepladder in from the conservatory. This time, she climbed it without pain shooting through her, and she took down the curtain. Then she began to seal everything around the door. Only after she was sure every part was covered did she repeat the action. No smell was going to escape through this area, that was for sure.

Once the curtain was re-hung and all the duct tape was hidden, she relaxed. She did a quick respray with the air freshener, returned the stepladder to the conservatory, and sat down by the side of Billy, who had slept through the entire thing.

'Fingers and paws crossed that will work, Billy.' At the sound of her voice, he gave a small wag of his tail. 'Glad you agree with me,' she said, and stroked his head gently.

6

Sunday dawned with bright sunlight, and Janette made a small, packed lunch with a flask of coffee, took water and some biscuits for Billy, and set off from the front garden to head towards Meadow Drive. It didn't seem like such a long journey now she knew the way, and she reached it in just over forty-five minutes. There was no police car there this time, and two children were out in the front garden, both leaning against the wall. The boy and his younger sister weren't talking, they were simply observing. They watched her as she walked past the end of the road, and the boy called out to her.

She stopped and turned towards the children. 'Did you shout me?'

The girl nodded. 'He did,' she called, as if negating any chance of being held to account for doing something wrong.

Janette and Billy walked a few steps towards them. 'You have a problem?'

The boy looked a little sullen. 'I asked if you'd seen my dad.'

'I don't think so,' she said. 'Who's your dad?'

'He's missing. He's called Philip Hancock. He's been in the papers and on the news.'

'Oh, I'm so sorry,' she said. 'Of course I've heard of him. I didn't know where he lived, though. I don't know him, so if I saw him, I wouldn't realise I'd seen him.'

'You going to the park?' This time the little girl spoke.

'Yes. We've had a long walk, and I've brought us a picnic.' Janette felt slightly panicked. She didn't know there was a park.

'We sometimes go to the park with Mummy and Daddy,' the girl continued. 'Your dog's nice. What's he called?'

'He's called Billy. Do you have a dog?' Janette held her breath as she waited for the answer.

'No, Mummy's allergic to cats and dogs. She has asthma.'

'I'm sorry about that. I hope they find your father soon,' and she turned and walked away, hardly able to control the shaking in her body.

No dog. Therefore HE had seen her somewhere, found out where she lived and planned the rape. The bastard had visited her with every intention of having sex with her. HE deserved to die, to be entombed forever in her cellar.

* * *

The park, Janette discovered, was only five minutes' walk away, and she entered the gates, Billy walking sedately by her side. She could see there was a pond, and made her way towards it, hoping there was a bench. She wasn't totally convinced she could sit on grass and not feel residual pain from the attack.

She could see several empty benches, so she made her way to one that was partly in shade. The sun had become a little too hot, and Billy went underneath the bench without any encouragement from her. She had a little sip of the water from his bottle before tipping the rest into his dish, then opened her flask and poured a coffee. She placed a few of his biscuits into a smaller dish, and he was quite happy to sit and enjoy his own doggy picnic.

Janette didn't even open her sandwich. She needed to think. When had HE seen her? When had HE decided she had been a good target for his perversions? Why her? Her mother had always told her not to tart herself up with make-up, she was beautiful without it, but that was through her mother's eyes, not a stranger's. She accepted she had a good figure, but disguised it by wearing jeans and sloppy jumpers, baggy tops, trainers. She was happy on her own, she didn't need to attract anybody, whatever sex they were. So why had this awful man looked at her and thought he'd like to fuck her? Because that's what it had been. HE hadn't made love to her, he'd fucked her. He'd worked his way into her home under the pretext of needing a dog kennelling, and he'd changed her life. Now she was stuck with his body in the cellar, a smell of something awful as his body rotted, and she would have to implement new rules with regard to continuing her business. That was going to take some figuring out, because she couldn't have people signing forms in the back garden, she would still have to let them come into the conservatory.

She allowed her brain to wander, and realised she could reconfigure the layout of the furniture in her little conservatory so that when she was dealing with people, the kitchen door could be closed, and her back would be to it. She could change the bureau to an ordinary desk, take control of her life and her future. The bureau would go into her dining room, she could use it for her art supplies, and things would stop feeling quite so wobbly, more levelled.

Billy had finished his biscuits and most of his water, so he placed his head on his front paws, and closed his eyes. Someone walked close by, then sat on the other end of the seat, taking out a newspaper to read. Billy stood, instantly on the alert, and moved to stand in front of Janette. She patted his head, and he looked up at her. She felt inordinately pleased that the dog had reacted in that way, and knew they would become close friends.

The man at the other end of the bench never spoke, and eventually Billy settled down once again, but his eyes remained open, his ears pricked upright.

* * *

Janette packed everything back into her bag, and stood. She shortened the extension lead until Billy was right by her side, and they walked along the path that she hoped would take them to the far side of the lake, and out of an exit that wasn't so far from home. Gradually she lengthened the lead, pulling it in and out when necessary, as she judged Billy's reactions to other people. He seemed to accept most of them, whether they were male or female. He didn't seem to appreciate children. Smart dog, she decided, and smiled.

The walk home was pleasant, if a little warm, and she was pleased to open her front door and enter her home to the slight fragrance of the air freshener, and not the decomposing body.

On the mat was a picture of that decomposing body, although not in the state it was currently in, but the state it was usually in. A smiling face, short brown hair, slightly chubby cheeks that made him look overweight. HE had definitely felt overweight when his body had been crushing her into the kitchen floor, and she had had his weight confirmed when she had to drag his body to the top of the cellar steps.

Her first inclination was to screw up the piece of paper and throw it in the bin, but she changed her mind. It would go into the back of her sketchbook, the one she would leave for whoever needed to see it once she was dead.

It seemed the police had canvassed the area once again, this time leaving leaflets asking for the public's help in tracing Philip Hancock. She almost had a rush of importance as she realised she was the only one who had any information at all; proving that HE had no dog had convinced her that HE would definitely have told nobody else that HE would be visiting her. It had been an exercise on his part in finding out information about her, realising she lived alone, and taking advantage of what HE had discovered. Why? Had HE known her at some point, had HE been an acquaintance of her mother's? Why her, little miss timid mouse? And had HE done this before?

She froze for a moment as that thought hit home. Had HE? She could hardly put an advert in the newsagents, or the local paper, asking women to get in touch with her if they had been raped by an overweight thug of a man.

Billy followed her through to the kitchen, and she put fresh water in his bowl before pouring herself a drink from the jug in the fridge. It was icy cold, and she relished the taste. The walk had been tiring, but she felt she now had answers.

His two children were clearly desperate for his safe return, but there was nothing she could do about that. She briefly wondered how his wife was feeling, but dismissed the thought pretty quickly; she wouldn't feel anything except anger if she knew how HE had died and what HE had been doing to cause that death.

She walked slowly upstairs, deciding to shower and put on some shorts before spending the rest of the day in the back garden with Billy. Then she could almost foretell an early night; she ached from the long walk.

Her body was now turning a brownish yellow where the purple bruising was changing colour, and she decided not to wear shorts in case anybody should see her, but then laughed. She only ever saw the milkman, really, and he definitely wasn't due on a Sunday afternoon.

She put on the white shorts almost as an act of defiance. HE wouldn't win. Billy waited patiently for her as she dressed, then ran downstairs in front of her, waiting in the hall for his next instructions. She smiled as she realised how quickly they had bonded in such a short space of time, but knew the true test would come when she started taking in her next kennel lodgers.

They sat on the patio, and she began to sketch. Her mother had never encouraged her to read, and she had never enjoyed living in somebody else's imaginary world; her escape had been her sketchbook, and the only book she possessed was her *A–Z*, a book inherited from her mother.

But her sketchbook filled her with satisfaction. She felt she came alive at school when it was the art class, and had stayed one evening a week to attend an art group. And her talents had grown.

She quickly sketched Billy, then settled down to make the drawing more detailed. She laughed. 'My god, Billy, you're a scruffy dog.'

Billy wagged his tail, almost as if to concur with her.

'You been told that before?'

He gave a gentle woof, and she tossed him a dental stick. He pounced on it, and settled down to enjoy his treat.

She continued to draw, noticing how the changing light altered the colour of his coat, making him look a much darker grey. She tried to imagine him as a puppy, and knew his scruffiness would have been what drew his previous owner to him. He had clearly been loved, but in an adult world. She hoped the old man was looking down on them and seeing that Billy was happy in his new home.

'Next time we go out, we'll buy you a new collar and lead,' she said, but this time she was ignored. The dental stick was so much more important than a new collar.

As the sun dipped lower in the sky, it put the patio into shade, and she stood, gathering her drawing equipment into a pile. She headed back into the kitchen, followed closely by Billy, and she locked both the conservatory and the kitchen door.

Her fortress was once more her sanctuary.

7

It was 14 August 1998 when Janette bought a pregnancy test from a pharmacy she had never entered before. She wanted nobody to know anything, except Billy. He had become her confidant, alongside her mother's ashes, neither one of which could verbalise any comfort to her, or advice, but she told them her worries anyway.

On 18 August, after a heavy bout of vomiting following catching a whiff of coffee, she used the test.

* * *

Janette bought a new notebook, left Billy in one of the garden kennels with plenty of food and water and two lodger dogs for company, and drove to the large Central Library in Sheffield.

She pulled out several books and began to make notes on childbirth. She had a cover story just in case anybody said anything – she was considering midwifery as a career and wanted as much information as possible before taking a leap into the unknown. She had a very tiny bump of her own, which didn't show at all; her gipsy-style top, loose and floaty, hid everything.

Nobody could know about this baby. Nobody. When it was born, she could throw it down the cellar with its father, and she could get on with her life. She would learn as much as she could absorb, deliver the child herself, and let nature take its course once she had got rid of it.

The notebook had page after page of notes. She swiftly copied diagrams, read pages of words and pulled out relevant parts that she knew she would need, then transcribed it into her notebook.

She recognised she would only have this one opportunity to do her research; she would begin to expand, and she couldn't take the risk of leaving home when visibly pregnant.

The milkman... she would have to start to leave his money every Saturday morning under a brick or something. She would speak to him this week and organise it, saying she was expecting to expand her kennels, and wouldn't necessarily hear him at the door. It was only a small lie – it was her waistline that was expanding, not her kennels.

She would also have to contact her clients to say she was temporarily closing her business as she had health issues that meant she couldn't look after animals in her care for the moment, but when things were resolved she would be in touch.

Janette had to go into hibernation. Because of him.

She wrote in the back of her notebook the words 'milkman' and 'clients', quickly flicked through the books once more, then returned them to the shelves. She had been in the library six hours, and needed to go home.

* * *

Janette's car radio was tuned into Radio Sheffield, and it seemed the police were having yet another push on the missing man, Philip Hancock. They were appealing for any sightings, any information at all that could help. His wife and children were desperate to hear from him, and they gave out a special number for callers to ring.

She smiled as she thought of what she could tell them, but continued her journey homewards, keen to get back to Billy, to make sure all the dogs were okay.

And they were. Candy was back for a two-day visit while her owners went to a conference in Ipswich, and Billy, in the next kennel space, was lying stretched out next to her.

'Well, you two are getting on, aren't you.' She smiled, and both dogs jumped up to greet her. The other lodger, a large German Shepherd of indeterminate years, was snoozing, and merely opened his eyes to see who had arrived.

She freed Billy out into the garden, and Candy into the dog run, then went inside to sort out food for all three of them. She thought she might make some fresh chicken for them, as a special treat, so began to prepare it.

It suddenly hit her that she had a problem. She needed food, probably to last her until the end of January. Basics she could get from the milkman as she did now, such as butter, milk, eggs, and chicken, but that was his entire range of deliverable items. She had to plan.

* * *

The large chest freezer was delivered the next day, and once again, Janette had to reconfigure the layout of the conservatory to accommodate the item. She plugged it in as instructed, and left it to stand.

She sat at her desk for what seemed like a lifetime but was actually a couple of hours, and sent letters to all her clients advising them of the changes in her life; as soon as she was physically fit, she would contact them again. She blessed the day she had acquired the laptop and printer; it made life so much easier than having to handwrite everything.

The following day, she put Billy back in a kennel, and apologised to him for Candy not being there; her owners had collected her, and she had handed them her letter. She had been forced into some sort of explanation because they had opened it immediately and expressed concern, so she had glossed over it saying she had a couple of operations coming up, and she needed time to recover quietly. They had left amidst words of concern, and offers of help if she needed it.

Can you get rid of a body and a baby?

She left Billy and Bruce, the German Shepherd, and headed off to a supermarket, where she scurried around like a mouse looking to escape from a trap, following her list of requirements, and missing nothing. She made sure she had enough dog food for at least six months – that was one worry off her mind. She bought several loaves of bread, but backed that up with a few bags of strong flour, and dried yeast. She had always enjoyed baking bread with her mother, and knew she would never be stuck for the basics. Then she began to stock up on individual meals, just in case she wasn't well at any point, and slowly filled her basket with everything to see her well into the new year.

It seemed to take her forever, and she drove home feeling odd twinges in her head as she tried to think of anything else she might need. Unloading the car was a nightmare, and it did briefly occur to her that such strenuous activity would surely have an effect on the baby, maybe cause her to abort it...

But it didn't.

Janette made a further two trips over the next few days, stockpiling everything she could think of, knowing that in a couple of weeks, she would have to hide herself away. The bump seemed to grow daily.

She sat for hours transcribing her notes onto her laptop, leaving spaces for her to draw her diagrams, and in the end, it became a passable manuscript. It also refreshed everything she had discovered in the library, and she hoped it would be enough to see her through the delivery of this object inside her.

The milkman arranged to leave her a note every Friday with the amount she owed, and he would collect her envelope containing the cash every Saturday morning, from under the brick by the front doorstep.

By the end of September, Janette hoped she had every eventuality covered, and that night, she told her mother's ashes and Billy of her plans.

'When it's born, I will put it in the cellar with him. I can't kill it, but it will die down there, I suppose. Maybe it won't draw breath. I shan't help it to; it will have to breathe on its own if that's what it wants to do.'

Billy wagged his tail as if in agreement.

* * *

Janette felt as if, finally, she had organised everything that needed to be organised. She just needed to get over the constant vomiting, the inability to be within fifty yards of a cup of coffee, and the constant craving for a full English breakfast for every meal.

She was missing her boarding dogs, and had received several letters requesting that she inform her clients as soon as she was able to take in their pets again. Billy never left her side, almost as if he knew she had things on her mind. He listened with one ear cocked every time she told him of the problem, and she did rather think that it was a good job he couldn't understand or repeat what she was saying.

The house was full of food, most of it frozen, but she also had lots of tinned items. Sausage casserole became something of a speciality, and she made lots of different meals, packaging them in some plastic cartons she had found in a pound shop before freezing them.

It occurred to her that wartime would have been a lot easier if they had known about freezing food at that time. She felt as if she was at war in many areas of her life, and the one person – dog – keeping her sane was Billy.

She began to look like her mother had as she'd reached the end of her life; the swollen belly, however, didn't contain a tumour as it had with Mother, it definitely contained a child. She could feel it moving, kicking, as it grew its way into a world where it wasn't wanted, and she grew more and more scared as time seemed to fly by.

Janette spoke to nobody for months. She didn't bother to consider whether it might be a boy or a girl, whether it would be healthy, or anything else about it. It would die very quickly, if indeed it ever drew breath, once she had tossed it down the cellar. Then she could re-start her life, re-start her business and try to forget the evil thing lying at the bottom of her cellar steps.

Christmas was a nothing time. She didn't bother with a tree, ordered a chicken and fresh vegetables from the milkman, and had a non-celebration with Billy. She did buy him a new winter coat from a catalogue for when he went out to tear around the garden, but she couldn't take him out for long walks; it was important nobody saw her.

She made one Christmas card. It was for the milkman, and she knew she had to send him one. She did it every year, always putting inside it a five-pound note. She decided it would be smart to continue the practice, so sat one night and drew a picture of some penguins playing 'follow my leader', then used her watercolours to paint them. Just for that small window of time, when she was being creative, her world felt so much better, so much smaller.

She put the card, along with her money for her Christmas goods, under the brick the week before Christmas, and to her horror, he knocked on her door. She froze, and ignored it completely. Then she heard the rattle of the letterbox and his card came through.

Have a lovely Christmas, love Michael x.

She felt tears prick her eyes, and stood the card on the mantelpiece. It was the only card she had; neighbours had stopped bothering years earlier, when they realised their cards didn't get a reciprocatively delivered one.

That evening, she put a Christmas programme on television, and sat with her drawing pad. She made a card for Billy, a drawing of him with a Father Christmas hat on his head, his front paws laid across a sack full of toys.

Janette took care painting it, and smiled at the finished picture. Signing it with a simple kiss, she handed it to him. He sniffed at it, then placed a paw on it.

'You like it?'

He pushed it towards her, as if wanting her to look at it as well. She stood it on the mantelpiece beside Michael's card, and Christmas suddenly didn't feel like such a lonely time.

8

5 JANUARY 1999

Janette had been uncomfortable all night; her back ached, she felt sick intermittently, and throughout the long dark hours, she kept getting out of bed to pace backwards and forwards in the bedroom. Billy watched every move, as if unable to understand what she was doing.

Dawn started to make itself apparent, and the rain came down incessantly. Janette crawled downstairs, wishing the whole situation could be over, and she could be normal once more. This thing inside of her wasn't due for two more weeks, and if she had to put up with this for that length of time, then the two weeks were going to seem like a year. She headed for the kitchen, with Billy at her heels, and she reached down into the cupboard for the bag of dog food. She would see to Billy, then decide if her sickly stomach wanted anything at all.

Her waters broke as she heaved up the bag of dog food, and she stared with something very akin to horror at the sight of the liquid puddling around her feet. She grabbed some cleaning cloths and scattered them around, steering Billy away from the kitchen and into the lounge, before heading upstairs to get in the shower. She had to get clean, before she could think about anything else. It was while she was standing under the shower spray that she felt the first contraction, nothing bad, just a tightening, and she knew it would be an early baby. Maybe it wouldn't be alive.

Everything was prepared, and to stop any last vestiges of her waters, she placed a pad inside her larger sized pants. That small act put her back in control, and she put on a clean nightie and a dressing gown that had seen better days. She intended to throw both items away after everything was over. When she could get back to her life of just her and Billy.

Billy was still in the lounge, so she mopped the kitchen floor, then brought him back to the kitchen for his breakfast. Her own breakfast was a glass of water.

She had prepared. Leaning up against the back of the sofa was a blow-up mattress. She intended to give birth on it, then puncture it and throw it away. The pile of old towels were taken from the cupboard, with an exceptionally large bath towel used to cover the mattress. She brought in a new washing-up bowl, and her kettle, filled with water, and set them up ready for her to switch it on when they were needed for cleaning her up after the event; she didn't want to think of it as after the birth, it was merely an event.

She heard Michael deliver the milk, and went to bring it inside. She didn't want it to still be there the following morning; Michael would immediately think there was something wrong with her, and then all secrets would no longer be secrets.

Billy stayed with her through the long day. As the severity of the contractions increased, she took paracetamol; when things really began to get serious, she took co-codamol. And she waited.

She reread her notes. It was the cutting of the cord she was most scared about, and she read that section several times, until she felt she could qualify as a midwife with no difficulty at all. She had prepared small pieces of string for tying off the cord, and everything was placed on a table that was close to the mattress, ready for immediate action if required.

What she hadn't been prepared for was the intensity of the pain. The books she had read in the library extolled the virtues of gas and air, epidurals and such like, all of which were denied to her by the brutality of Philip Hancock, the shame HE had created in her, the inconvenience of his death...

She groaned as another contraction began, and she realised she had no idea how long this could carry on for. Every birth was different, but hospitals would step in to help if things dragged on too long. She would have to soldier on until this thing was expelled by her body in its own good time.

She walked around the ground floor intermittently – the books said walking around helped. She couldn't go upstairs; her fears of falling, of lying undiscovered for days, kept her at the bottom of the stairs only, where she knew she had nowhere to fall to.

Through that long January day, Billy never left her alone, and when she eventually accepted it was time to be on the mattress, he settled by her side. She removed her pants, then dropped to her knees to get on the mattress. She could sense a change, the child moving lower, an increase in frequency of the contractions, and she moaned through the pain.

Her natural instinct was to open wide her legs, and she reached down to touch herself; the head had crowned, and she screamed as she pushed. She tried to pant, but things were happening too fast and with one last yell, she expelled the child.

She took hold of the baby and lifted it, the horror of everything that was happening overwhelming her to the extent that she automatically pushed out the afterbirth without really noticing it. She began the task of cutting the cord, and the baby whimpered. Then cried.

Billy came over to look then moved towards the window,

leaving Janette to deal with it all. With the cord finally cut, she lay back, exhausted. The baby was on Janette's chest, making little mewing noises. She grabbed a towel and wrapped it around the child, then placed it at the foot of the mattress. She could deal with that later. In the meantime, she needed to clean herself, so she switched on the kettle and took half an hour to wash herself thoroughly before putting on a clean nightie and her usual dressing gown. The child, disregarded up to this point, was becoming noisier and she knew she would have to do something about it. Janette didn't want any nosy neighbours hearing baby cries, not at this late stage, not when she'd gone to so much trouble to hide any evidence of the rape for the last six months.

Janette knew she needed to get rid of the mattress so stabbed it with the scissors she had used to cut the cord, those couple of minutes a blur in her mind. She couldn't actually remember the action, just the relief that she had done it.

She lifted the baby and the towel enclosing it up onto the sofa and managed with some difficulty to roll up the mattress and stuff it into a black bag ready for disposal into the bin. She placed it out of sight behind the sofa, and surveyed the normality of her lounge with a feeling of relief. She wanted a cup of tea but wasn't sure if travelling from the lounge into the kitchen was such a good idea at the moment.

'Billy,' she said, 'why didn't I teach you to make cups of tea?' The dog laid his head on her knee, then moved to look at the child at the other end of the sofa.

'Don't get used to that,' she said, 'it's going. We'll be back to our usual carry-on tomorrow.'

The child whimpered, and Billy touched it with his nose.

'Leave it alone,' she said, and closed her eyes, exhaustion finally washing over her.

* * *

Janette slept for half an hour, then felt Billy nudging her legs; the baby was about to go into full-throttle screaming.

She stared at the towelled bundle just a couple of feet away from her, and pulled it closer.

'Shut up,' she said.

The baby ignored the instruction and increased the volume. She leaned it on her chest, and the screams became tiny whimpers. Janette knew she had to do something to stop it crying, so she unbuttoned her nightie, freed her left breast and her mind brought up the feeding instructions from the library book. How to make the baby latch onto the nipple, with the nipple fully inside their mouth, how to hold them so they felt safe... and the baby stopped crying. She just needed it to shut up while she built up the energy to remove the duct tape from around the cellar door. That had been the last thing on her to-do list, but the early arrival of the baby meant it hadn't been done. Yet. Then it could join its father, and she would be free.

The baby suckled for two minutes on each breast and she felt that the towel was damp.

Janette stared at the tiny face, its eyes now closed in contentment. Could she see anything of Philip Hancock there? Anything of her?

She needed to get a different towel, she could feel the dampness of this one – and then she remembered the tiny nappies in the sideboard. A client had brought them when their bitch had been in season and was leaving droplets of blood everywhere. She thought there was half a pack left. She replaced the sleeping child at the far end of the sofa and opened the sideboard cupboard. Seven. Seven nappies. Well, she'd only need one. She took it out and it was indeed tiny. The bitch had been a Jack Russell called Milly, she recalled.

There were also three newborn-size vests, still in their packaging. They had suggested she might want to use them to hold on the nappies, eager to placate her as they felt guilty for leaving her for two weeks with an on heat Milly.

She took them out, opened up the disposable nappy and worked out how to use it on a human child as opposed to a bitch who was bleeding. She hadn't needed the vests, so had left them there in case she ever did.

But why would it need a vest if she was going to dispose of it? Her head was buzzing. She could throw its naked body down the cellar steps and just leave it. She recognised she couldn't kill it first, but she could leave it to simply fade away.

Nobody, absolutely nobody, could ever know about this child, because in knowing about it, it would in all probability lead to the discovery of who the father was, which in turn would lead to the discovery of his body.

Maybe the baby wasn't viable? What if it was underweight? It soon would be, as she had no baby milk in storage. Only in her breasts. The breasts that the baby had already stimulated into activity. The breasts that in three days' time would be producing the nutrients the baby would require to get it through the first months of its life.

She felt she needed to weigh it, to stick a nappy on it, to follow the rules of the library books she had pored over on that long day. Weighing the child was the first thing to happen, before anything else followed. Her brain had slipped into automatic mode. She picked up the still sleeping bundle, and walked very carefully into the kitchen. Her large kitchen scales, normally used for measuring out dog food portions for boarding dogs on diets, would certainly be big enough to weigh the child.

She spread out some kitchen roll in the base of the scales, and turned to take the towel off the child.

Billy watched with some interest, wondering if the action involving the scales meant he was going to be fed. It didn't.

Janette stared at the child, now nakedly lying on the damp towel.

'For fuck's sake,' she said, feeling horror at her use of profanities. Mother would never have allowed it, no matter what the exceptional circumstances.

'For fuck's sake,' she repeated. She stared at the child's genital area, the area her eyes had previously glossed over while trying to deal with the trauma of cutting what she had thought of as his cord. 'You're a bloody girl.'

9

Janette hadn't considered for one second that it would be a girl. This brought plan B into play.

Except she didn't have a plan B. There had only ever been plan A; have the kid – in her head it had always been a boy – then throw him down the cellar steps to join his father. But she couldn't do that to a girl. Mother had told her girls were special, boys thugs.

So she couldn't throw away this child. She would have to be hidden, to hide the fact that her mother was a murderer. She had years to perfect plan B, it was just a bit muddled at the moment.

Her first job was to weigh Child, which would wake her, then she would have to feed her again probably. Janette frantically tried to remember the part of the books she hadn't digested properly, knowing the baby wouldn't be living anyway. She would have to feed on demand, rather than the stricter every four hours, because she couldn't risk the baby crying.

She laid her in the large scale pan, and saw she was six pounds three ounces. *Good enough*, Janette thought, then ran some warm water into the washing-up bowl. She washed the baby, who temporarily opened her eyes before drifting back to sleep, then dressed her in a nappy and one of the tiny vests. Even the newborn size was a little bit large on her.

Mother's shawl was in the sideboard, and Janette took it out of the tissue paper in which she had carefully placed it after it had been washed following Mother's death. Mother had crocheted it in white and cream, giving it an almost pearlescent glow, and Janette wrapped it around the baby.

She placed the baby back on the sofa and sat down. Now what? Why couldn't she have been a boy? Life would have been so much simpler. And why the fuck had she never considered it might be a girl? Profanities again, she thought, and felt relieved she hadn't spoken out loud this time.

She had to come up with a plan, whatever capital letter might follow it, and get something organised for having a child that nobody could ever find out about.

* * *

The wardrobe in the front guest bedroom was pine, and large. The drawer in the base was the biggest drawer Janette possessed, and she removed it, took out the contents – Mother's nighties – and placed a pillow in it. She took a white sheet from the airing cupboard and cut it into six pieces, covering the pillow with two of them.

She dragged it downstairs one step at a time, knowing her strength was fading. She also felt as if her blood loss had increased and a quick visit to the downstairs toilet confirmed it. She packed herself with pads, then placed the still sleeping baby in the drawer. They would sleep in the lounge, she decided, for one night. Then she would have to sort out more regular sleeping arrangements. There would be no bonding with the child; she had given it life, she wouldn't give it love.

Ten minutes later, she was feeding the child again, and wondering how she could get items she needed without leaving her home. A cot could wait until she was well enough to go and get one, but she needed nappies urgently. The local shop was a five-minute walk, but could she manage ten minutes away from the security of her home after just giving birth? Did she have a choice?

The baby had latched on to her nipple with no difficulty at all, and was making strange little noises as she drank. After two minutes, Janette swapped her over to her other breast and waited until the child fell asleep before removing her. She laid her down in the drawer, and slowly forced herself upright. She felt sore, although not as sore as she had felt on the day nine months earlier that this long journey of childbirth had begun.

She walked slowly to the kitchen and made herself a pot of tea, before checking that Billy had enough food in his dish. He had been by her side throughout the entire day, almost as if he understood what was happening.

She wanted nothing to eat, but the tea was most welcome. It revived her somewhat, and she stared down at the child. She knew then that it would never have a name.

It would be Child.

And she would be Mother.

* * *

Child was a good baby, but there were times in the first three weeks that Janette almost gave up. Her breasts became horrifically sore, but the alternative to breastfeeding was buying baby milk powder, bottles, steriliser and other such bits and bobs, all of which could lead to questions being asked, suppositions made.

Her blood flow finally settled and her worry on that score dissipated; she now had a good supply of nappies bought from a large supermarket where nobody knew her, and even some clothing for the tiny girl which she had found at a charity shop. Janette knew some decisions had to be made – the baby wouldn't stay a baby for ever, and this little girl would be brought up not knowing that other people existed. She would be in a locked room once she began to walk, but she would think it was normal.

This house without books, as designated by Janette's own mother, would remain so. There would be no education; Child would learn to behave quietly or face consequences. Just as she had faced consequences. She had soon discovered that she must not speak of anything that happened in her home to any teachers; she had told her teacher when she was five years old that she couldn't go home with any books because Mother wouldn't allow it, and the teacher had actually visited their home to find out why, as it was a curriculum requirement.

Mother had angrily explained to the woman that it wasn't her place to teach Janette because that was down to the school to do, and when Janette was old enough to do her homework without the help of an adult, then she could bring home the work. Until then, she couldn't. That night, Barbara used a slipper to smack her daughter's bottom, leaving raw marks on her skin that took days to disappear. Janette couldn't scream, or even cry – she knew the punishment would double if she did so.

Barbara Gregson had never explained to anyone that she couldn't read, although the teacher who had bravely faced up to her did suspect it was the case. Janette was, as a result, given extra tuition, but it was only when her mother was dying that she discovered the truth.

Mother had to explain the finances and how she dealt with paying bills. Janette had to know, so that she could continue with the routine. Janette had bought a small notebook and begun to list the few items that needed to be remembered, but she wanted

Mother to check what she had written, in case anything was wrong.

Barbara had tried, but in the end had to confess she understood nothing of Janette's notes, because she had never been able to read and write, other than sign her name.

Power of Attorney solved the whole situation, and a will basically leaving everything to Janette made the transition easy once Barbara had gone, but by then, Janette had become accustomed to living without books, which was why she had physically taken herself off to the library to research childbirth instead of buying books on the subject.

This had always been a house without books, and would continue to be so. Child would have to behave in her own room, and would certainly never be allowed out of that room.

* * *

Janette got used to timing her visits to the shops for immediately after feeding time. Child slept after a feed, so Janette left her alone while she went to buy food, or baby things she might need.

She no longer used the local shop, preferring the anonymity of shopping in a large supermarket where whatever was in her trolley wouldn't be scrutinised by anyone who might recognise her. Driving the car still scared her, but it had now become even more of a necessity, as she needed to be out of the house for the minimum amount of time.

She spoke very little to Child. It wasn't something she needed to do, she felt. She hadn't asked for this burden, nor indeed for the burden down her cellar steps, so while she was allowing Child to live, it would be without contact and without parental bonding. Just like her own childhood.

She didn't project her thoughts forward to a future that was by no means certain – after all, cot death was a thing around the twelve-week mark, wasn't it? She only ever ventured into Child's room if she heard a whimper on the monitor – a purchase on day one of this nightmare. Every time she heard a tiny sound, she knew Child was alive, and she had to stop the sound escalating.

She began to fill her evenings with knitting cardigans and jumpers for Child, and even pulled out the old sewing machine that Barbara had used to make skirts. It was a treadle machine, stored in the cloakroom in the hall, and Janette spent an hour cleaning it out, and trying to remember what she had seen when watching her mother make a skirt for her.

In the drawer of the table, she found some patterns, and realised her mother wouldn't have needed to read; patterns were self-explanatory, really. Had her own mother been just as ashamed of her child as she was of Child? Janette knew she hadn't been shown love, but had Barbara really not wanted her at all? Could it have been for the same reason that Janette didn't want Child? There had never been a father in the offing...

She sat down on the sofa to look at the patterns, and knew that with a bit of adjustment, she could make some tiny dresses for Child for when summer came around, if she lived that long.

She ran upstairs to collect the suitcase full of fabric from the top of a wardrobe, and brought it back downstairs. She removed a remnant, brought a kitchen chair into the lounge and sat down, her feet resting gently on the treadle plate. She checked everything was okay, then pressed on the footplate, while pulling the side wheel towards her.

It worked perfectly and she gasped aloud. The line of stitching meandered slightly because of her shock that it actually worked, but she carried on, trying to remember the lessons from school on the electric machines. The shuttle eventually ran out, and she had to work out how to refill it, but it was simple enough.

For the first time in weeks, she felt like smiling. She lowered the machine into the body of the table, and wheeled the entire thing over to the bay window. It would need a cover over it, she decided, to protect the highly polished surface from the sun, but it wouldn't be hidden away any longer. She would teach herself to sew.

The suitcase was a treasure trove of fabrics. It was only when she reached the bottom that she found the quilt. It wasn't complete. The top was a kaleidoscope of pretty cotton fabrics, joined together to form pinwheel designs that almost seemed to dance across the surface. It was cot-sized, and she knew Mother had made it for her. The top was complete; underneath that was a layer of wadding, and under that a complete piece of pale green fabric. All three layers were tacked together, and the central pinwheel had hand-quilting worked on it.

Beautiful tiny stitches, holding all three layers closely together. Janette knew she would finish it, and wondered what had stopped Mother from doing that all those years ago. The quilt was undoubtedly cot-sized, but something had stopped Barbara Gregson from completing it.

10

The needle was threaded into the quilt, waiting to be picked up to continue the journey of the stitches, currently on hold. Janette had never quilted in her life, yet somehow knew the basics – had it been something at school she had covered, then forgotten? Or a long-ago conversation with a clearly incredibly talented mother that Janette could no longer remember?

Janette could vaguely recall watching a film, possibly three or four years earlier, that was about a group of women who were quilters in America, and the way they had treated each and every stitch as if it was the most precious thing on earth. It had been before Mother had died, because Mother had made comments about the quilting throughout the film. It was a memory for Janette to treasure, because Barbara rarely became animated about anything. That night, her enthusiasm had bubbled out of her. Shortly after, she had been diagnosed with the cancer, and everything had gone back to the normal morose lifestyle.

Janette knew she would never find out why this quilt was unfinished, but she also knew she would make the time to continue with the delicate quilting, then learn how to bind the edges.

Billy, by now sitting by her side on the sofa, laid his head on her arm, and she smiled at him. 'Look at this, Billy boy,' she said. 'I think my mum started it, but me and you are going to finish it. All you have to do is be a good boy, and learn how to make me cups of tea.'

The dog woofed as if he understood every word.

* * *

Child was bathed, fed and asleep by nine, and Janette sat on the sofa with a deep sigh. She felt tired. Life in general had been a nonstop whirligig for the past few months, the baby being the biggest issue of them all. Child was clearly here to stay, but she couldn't imagine what the future would hold when Child became able to think for herself. That was many years away, but the problem would also sit in her mind for all those years.

She pulled the quilt towards her, and ran her fingers over the section already quilted in exquisite tiny stitches by Mother. The texture was superb, and she allowed her palm to caress it one more time before lifting it closer to her eyes. Quite apart from the intricate design of the pinwheel quilt, the careful matching of colours, and the shimmering effect of the design, the stitches were a separate design. She placed the quilt on the coffee table and brought the suitcase over, placing it by her side on the sofa. She hoped she would find something else, some detail that would help her with the design she needed to follow. She needed to go through everything in the suitcase with a bit more care, and if she couldn't find her mother's plan – which she suspected was probably all in her head – she would have to draw one.

It was after midnight before Janette climbed into bed. She hoped Child would sleep, but suspected she would be awake and ready for feeding within a couple of hours. It had become routine to go to bed as soon as Child went to sleep after her last feed, but the quilt had captured her heart.

Initially she had been unhappy with the size of her stitches – so much longer than the ones already decorating the centre panel – but she pulled them out and started again, taking it much slower, checking each individual one, until her rhythm settled and she was happy to continue.

She didn't fall asleep immediately, but stared at the plan she had found in the suitcase. There were no words on it; Janette recognised now that it would have been beyond Mother's capabilities, but the plan was a detailed one. Each segment was carefully drawn, with dotted lines showing where the quilting should travel.

Taking more time to go through the suitcase had revealed other items, not least of which was a carrier bag full of tiny pieces of fabric, plus lots of newspaper hexagons carefully cut out, ready for the fabric off-cuts to be tacked to them. Mother had clearly made a start on this quilt, which also came with its own plan.

This plan wasn't about quilting, because that was simply quilting around the edge of each hexagon, but it was all about colour. The quilt, when finished, would resemble a rainbow, each stripe blending into the next one with graduated shades.

It almost took away Janette's breath as she studied it. Now she understood exactly where her own artistic talents came from. Mother couldn't read, but she was an absolute master of the arts.

As she gave in to sleep, she vowed she would finish everything Mother had left in that suitcase to be completed, everything.

* * *

Child woke around three, and was actually crying rather than whimpering by the time Janette came to her senses. She panicked slightly and ran into Child's bedroom to pick her up to soothe her. Nobody must hear any baby sounds.

She sat in the old nursing chair that hadn't been used since Mother had used it to nurse her, and freed her breast. Child latched on hungrily, and twenty minutes later was placed back in her drawer.

Janette stood in the bedroom doorway and looked across at the sleeping child. She was getting too long for the drawer, and it was time to be thinking about going into the attic and looking at the cot. She might have to do some repairs, but she was confident they would be manageable. She could remain in this room until a single bed was required, and then changes would have to be made. She would have to move into the guest bedroom, giving up her own room with its tiny en suite for Child. Then she could be locked in, and live her life in there.

Janette didn't want to think about a future, didn't want to contemplate her own mortality and what would happen once she was dead. It was irrelevant. She hadn't wanted to think about what would happen once her own mother died, but life had continued to evolve once that event had occurred, and she had no doubt things would work out one way or another when she herself passed over.

* * *

Once Child was fed and asleep, Janette stood at the top of the stairs and stared up at the loft hatch. She hadn't been up there for years.

'Come on, Janette,' she said quietly. 'Time to gird up your loins. You can't be a coward for ever. You're not going to fall back down the loft ladder, it's perfectly safe, you've done it before...'

She turned the Victorian handle attached to the wall and

watched as the loft hatch slid back, freeing the ladder to descend towards her. She took a deep breath and began to climb.

The light switch was easily reached and she switched it on, feeling relief that it actually illuminated the loft space. She still had a thing about the longevity or otherwise of light bulbs.

The loft was remarkably clear. It did seem as though most of Janette's childhood had found its way into the area, and she moved across to the cot. Dragging the wooden frame across the floor, she balanced it across the top of the ladder, leaving herself room to navigate around it and get both feet firmly on the flat rungs. She took a deep breath to calm her nerves, then slowly lowered the cot down the ladder until both she and it were safely at the bottom. It was considerably easier carrying it down the main staircase and into the lounge.

She returned to retrieve the plastic-encased mattress, but that was much easier to manoeuvre, and she sat for a few moments on the sofa, slowing down her heart rate. In that moment, she felt a very unfit twenty-five-year-old, and guessed it was all down to her six-month imprisonment while she awaited the birth of Child. No exercise, no dog-walking, and she now felt as though she needed to lie down just because she'd brought a cot down from the loft.

She made herself a drink of tea before continuing her search for anything that could prove to be useful, and then headed back up to the loft. The highchair she brought down with her, not sure how soon she would need it, but it might require a bit of repair work. She discovered a walking toy, filled with bricks. She moved it nearer to the hatch so she wouldn't have to go into the loft when the time came for needing it; she could simply reach from the top of the ladder. There was a large plastic bag tied at the top with string that looked as though it might contain cot bedding, so she took that downstairs, and closed the loft.

The bag contained four cot sheets, two pink blankets, and a cot bumper with lambs gambolling along the length of it. She gathered it all up and put it in the washing machine before unwrapping the mattress. It was in perfect condition, and she exhaled slowly. She wouldn't have to go out and buy a new one, risking being seen carrying it from her car into the house. Her paranoia about the discovery of Child was escalating, and she was aware of it but didn't know what to do about it.

Once she had fully inspected the mattress, she carried it back upstairs, leaving it on the landing until Child woke for her next feed, then it could go into Child's bedroom ready for when the cot was built. But first she had to inspect that item, judge what, if anything, needed repairing, and hope that nothing was beyond repair.

It was immaculate, and she tried to think back to her childhood. She had no memories of ever sleeping in the cot, but realised that memories started later in life, around four years, when she would have been in a single bed anyway.

She flinched as she remembered Mother hitting her so hard that she had fallen onto the single bed, the momentum carrying her over the bed, off the other side and into the wall. She had been too afraid to cry, too scared to speak, and had simply laid on the floor, trembling. She couldn't remember why, what she had done to cause such an eruption of anger in Mother. But she could remember no food for two days, and having to use a bucket in her room because she was locked in and couldn't get out to go to the bathroom...

Janette shook her head to clear it of looking backwards; she wanted no further memories of her own childhood infiltrating her brain; it was already frazzled from the past few months.

She carried the separate parts of the cot into the kitchen and diligently washed every section before transporting it to the top of the stairs. Once Child woke, she would feed her and place her back in her drawer, but this time in a different room, so her own room could be turned into a proper nursery containing the cot.

* * *

The room looked and smelt clean; the bedding was almost dry, and the cot had gone together remarkably easily, considering its age. For the first time, Janette opened the window slightly to allow some fresh air in, knowing it would have to be closed as soon as Child was back in the room. She couldn't risk anyone hearing her cry. And the drawer could now be returned to the wardrobe, making her home once more her fortress, with everything back in its rightful place. A body in the cellar and an unwanted and disliked child in the nursery – but apart from that, all would be well again.

That night, she worked for an hour on the tiny quilt that she somehow knew had been intended for her when she was in the cot, and listened to some music. It had been a traumatic day, but all was now good.

11

ONE YEAR ON – 31 DECEMBER 1999

Janette spent some time oiling the lock on Child's bedroom door, making sure it worked perfectly. She could sense it wouldn't be long before Child would be walking, and she had decided that from today the room would be locked at all times. Just in case.

Child already walked from one end of the cot to the other, and Janette had noticed she occasionally let go of the rail, balancing on her legs carefully before attempting a step.

She made beans and toast for Child for her evening meal, cutting the toast into bite-size pieces. She lifted Child out of the cot, and placed her into the highchair, strapping her in. Janette put the small plastic dish and a sippy cup of water on the tray, said, 'Eat,' and left the room.

Child stared as she disappeared through the door, then without making a sound picked up a piece of toast and ate it. She carefully scooped beans onto the plastic spoon, almost managing to get all of them into her mouth. The ones that dropped onto her bib she picked up with her fingers and popped them on her tongue. At almost one year old, she had already learnt that being quiet was the way to be, and she silently worked through her meal, having the occasional sip of water.

Then she simply sat and waited until Mother returned with a small dish of chopped banana. While eating that, she watched carefully as Mother changed the bedding on her cot, then held out her hands to be wiped as Janette tucked in the newly finished quilt. Although Child didn't know it then, it would be the only gift she would ever receive from Mother.

Child went to sleep at seven, and Janette sat quietly in the lounge, reflecting on how much easier life was now that she didn't have to keep offering her breasts to Child. She had routine mealtimes, definitely on the dot of seven bedtimes, and she slept until 6.30 in the morning.

Billy always accompanied her when she went into Child's bedroom every morning, waited until she had changed and dressed the little girl, then accompanied her downstairs as she prepared Child's breakfast.

The dog would then repeat every journey upstairs with his mistress as she visited Child's bedroom at set times during the day – he too had become a slave to routine.

Janette looked at her watch, and sighed. She really wanted to go to bed, but as this was such a special New Year's Eve, leading the whole world directly into the first day of the new millennium, she had decided to make the effort to stay awake until midnight, welcoming the day in with a small glass of her mother's sherry.

She had also made another decision. Tomorrow she would remove the curtain from the cellar door, rip off the duct tape sealing the decomposing smells inside the cellar and allow her life to reach a degree of the normality she had once enjoyed.

The door would remain locked, the key on top of the jamb. Never again during her lifetime would it be opened.

Then she could proceed to handle the various developmental

stages of Child; the girl had to be taught, above all else, the sensibility of obedience at all times, just as she had been taught by her own mother. Barbara Gregson had indeed been a hard taskmaster, never afraid to use a slipper on her, or her hand when required, and Janette felt she had come through that upbringing with some credit. She would pass those same rules on to Child, and they could maybe at some point learn to live in the same room as each other, when Child reached her late teens.

Until that point, she would remain locked in her room.

* * *

The fireworks started at one minute to midnight, and she listened in horror to bangs that seemed to last for ever. The countdown was happening simultaneously on the television, and Janette began to shake. She stood and walked towards the curtains in the bay window, pulled them open slightly and stared out at a sky that was aglow in all directions with cascades of light.

Billy, standing as close to her leg as he could possibly get, also began to shake and whimper. She knelt down, putting her arm around him.

'It's okay, Billy. It's silly people wasting all their money on fireworks. We'll be okay as long as we stay inside.'

There was a brief lull as new fireworks were lit, and Janette heard the cry from upstairs. She ran, closely followed by Billy.

Child was standing in her cot, shaking from head to foot, crying, rubbing her eyes.

'Shut up,' Janette said, but Child continued to cry. Janette pushed her back down into the sleep position, pulled the covers around her and waited. 'I said shut up.'

Child gave a huge hiccup, continuing to sob but much quieter.

And then the loudest bang so far erupted in a flash of sparks into the night sky, and Child screamed.

Janette grabbed her and the quilt, carried her across to the wardrobe and laid her inside it.

'Sleep,' she commanded, and locked the door.

* * *

She didn't wake until almost nine on that first day of the millennium; the fireworks had continued until the early hours, and had made sleep impossible.

She entered Child's room, and heard a gentle humming, a drawn-out tone that bore no resemblance to anything musical, but was a hum for all that. She opened the wardrobe door, and Billy put his nose in to nudge Child.

The little girl stared up at Janette and stopped the hum. She stroked Billy's head and Janette slapped her hand.

'Don't touch the dog.'

Child waited, instinct telling her not to move, and Janette picked her up to return her to her cot.

'You smell,' Janette said. Child stared, having no idea what *you smell* meant.

Janette cleaned her up, then sat her in the highchair. Without further words, she left the bedroom and headed downstairs to make Child's breakfast.

* * *

Child found eating Weetabix difficult. It fell off the spoon, didn't always end up in her mouth, and generally made her hands very sticky indeed. She stared at the almost empty dish and pushed it to one side. She was licking her fingers as Janette opened the bedroom door.

'Dirty child,' Janette said. 'You can stay in that chair now, and think about what you've done wrong.'

Janette closed the bedroom door, an inexplicable anger washing over her. Why her? Why had that man chosen her? What had she done so wrong in her life to merit being punished like this? She did not want this child, couldn't bear to think how life would be when Child grew older, became mobile under her own steam.

She grabbed a kitchen chair, found a screwdriver and unhooked the heavy curtain covering the cellar door. She began to unscrew the curtain track, and let it drop to the floor. It didn't take long to remove all the duct tape, and finally she stood back and surveyed what she had demolished in ten minutes.

Sniffing the air around her convinced her there was no lingering rotting smell, and she heaved a sigh of relief. Would HE be only bones now?

She washed down the door with bleach, and put everything away before taking a cup of tea into the lounge. Billy climbed onto the sofa, and laid his head on her knee.

'Why can't she be like you?' Janette asked the dog. 'You don't upset me, do things you shouldn't do, and now I've got to punish her by not taking her any lunch.'

* * *

Both mistress and dog slept for three hours, and she woke with a sense of shock. She didn't sleep in the afternoon, because that was for old people. Then she remembered the fireworks of the previous night, her lack of sleep, and the bad behaviour of Child – all of it enough to make anybody have an afternoon nap.

There was no sound from upstairs, so she went into the kitchen and chopped vegetables into small pieces for soup. She couldn't face the thought of doing anything more complicated than that, and soup was easy enough for Child to eat on her own without needing assistance from Mother.

Just after five, she and Billy ascended the stairs, food for Child carefully balanced on a tray. She hadn't given the cellar door a second glance as she passed it, which was a deliberate act on her part. She unlocked Child's bedroom door and the little girl was slumped over in her high chair, her cheek flattened onto the tray.

Just for a moment, Janette thought Child was dead, but then realised she was also having an afternoon nap. She probably hadn't slept well locked inside the wardrobe.

She shook Child awake, and the little girl stared at Mother with bleary eyes, eyes that had clearly emitted tears not so long before.

'I didn't hear you crying.' Janette's tone was accusatory towards her daughter. Child looked at her, then snuffled before wiping her nose and her eyes with her hand.

Janette reached for a baby wipe and cleaned Child's face and hands, and Child gave a tentative smile. It wasn't returned by her mother, who was busy trying to analyse her feelings from when she had thought Child was dead. She had had feelings of denial, of horror, then of thankfulness that Child was only sleeping.

'Child.' The baby looked up, recognising the word. 'Soup. Eat now.'

* * *

Janette finished her own soup, not really enjoying it. It had been a strange couple of days, and she felt that it had been rammed home to her that Child was growing up. In four days' time, it would be the anniversary of her birth, and she would probably noticeably improve as a human being every day.

She clearly recognised her own name already, and Janette concluded that she should start to use certain words that would give them a modicum of communication. She didn't particularly want to talk to Child, but sometimes she would have to give her instructions and she really would need a basic vocabulary, picked up in exactly the same way as any other child.

'Billy,' she said to the dog as he followed her around, 'we have to do something about the child upstairs. I will give her ten minutes every day for the moment, but when we start to get her out of nappies, we may have to stay upstairs with her until she gets it right. I'm going up in the loft to get that walking toy down, because she seems to be steady on her feet in the cot, and I shall start saying a few words to her. She will become much more controllable when she understands what I'm saying.'

Billy gave a gentle bark of agreement, and she patted his head. 'And when it gets warmer, we're going to get rid of all those kennels. Now Child has managed to live this far, I don't think she's going to die, which means I won't be able to board dogs any longer because I can't walk them. So I'll close it down; we can manage on what we have.'

Again, Billy gave a gentle bark of agreement, then pushed his food bowl with his nose. She laughed. 'Sorry, I forgot to feed you! I'm a bad mother, aren't I?'

Once more he gave a small bark, without really knowing what his agreement was.

12

Everything Child learned she learned by brutality and bullying. Potty training had been the most difficult part – Child understood how to recognise when she wanted to wee or poo, but she found it impossible to clean herself. Every time there was a mark in her pants, she was made to take them to her tiny sink and wash them herself, then she would feel her mother's slipper across her bottom. She learned not only to scream silently inside herself, but also to cry silently, something that happened a lot when Mother wasn't there because the pain of constipation could be traumatic. If she didn't poo, she didn't mark her pants; she didn't feel the slipper.

She now lived in a different bedroom. Mother had moved into the guest bedroom, giving up her own room so that Child would have the en suite and would never need to leave the room.

It was kept locked as a matter of routine, and it never once occurred to Child that other people lived differently to the way that she lived. She had a small table and chair for when she ate her meals, but any other time, she was expected to sit on the edge of her bed. She woke at half past seven, and went back to sleep at seven. At five years old, she was told she could no longer have afternoon naps, and Child obeyed the instruction.

She was never bored, because she knew no other state than staring into space. She couldn't risk being anywhere else other than on the edge of the bed; to be anywhere other than on the bed or in the toilet risked pain.

She spoke in a soft, almost ethereal tone, and knew a few words. Mother, dog, thank you, and most of all, sorry. Every slipper stroke brought the words out of Mother's mouth – 'Say sorry, say sorry.' So she did.

And she hummed. She hummed most of the day, but stopped the split second she heard the key turn in the lock of her room door.

She began to live in her own tiny fantasy world – another Child sat at the side of her, they held hands and smiled at each other. And the other Child cried with her, but Mother couldn't see her; Child Two never had to feel the pain alongside her.

* * *

Janette didn't bother with a coat. The day was gloriously hot, and she decided to walk down to the doctor. The pain in her chest the previous evening had scared her enough to send her off to bed by eight o'clock, and she had woken determined to make an appointment.

'Billy, let's pop you in the kitchen.'

The dog stood and followed her through to the kitchen; he immediately went back to his bed. She looked at him for long moments. He was now around fourteen years old, and she wondered how much longer she would have him. He had been the one redeeming quality about this whole period of her life, and she was under no illusions about what a godsend he had been.

'Okay, Billy. I'm going to the doctor. You've plenty of food and water, and I won't be long.'

Billy wagged his tail.

* * *

The walk to the doctor only took five minutes, but by the time she reached the surgery, she was breathless. The receptionist looked at her with some concern.

'Are you okay?'

'I will be. I just need to sit down. Janette Gregson.'

The receptionist pulled up the list of attendees waiting to see Dr Carmichael and rearranged the order they were to go in. Janette Gregson was grey and clearly in discomfort.

The buzzer sounded for the next patient. She hurried through to explain the situation to Carmichael, and he nodded. 'Well done, Anna. I'll see her now.'

* * *

'My receptionist explained you were breathless when you arrived here. How far had you walked?'

Janette felt woozy, and tried not to show it. 'I live about five minutes away.'

He paused while he looked through her notes. 'I haven't seen you for fifteen years, and then it was for tonsillitis. So tell me what's causing this breathlessness.'

'I don't know. I had a pain last night, so I went to bed early. It was still there this morning but nothing like as severe as the one last night.'

Carmichael picked up his stethoscope and stood behind her.

He lifted her T-shirt and listened carefully. He walked around to face her. 'Just lift it at the front, please.'

She did so, feeling embarrassed. He listened, then returned to her back before sitting down to face her.

'I suspect you have angina. Your heartbeat is certainly irregular, and I'm going to give you a spray which you direct under your tongue, in case this happens again. In the meantime, I shall refer you to the cardiac unit at the hospital and they will do more tests. You're not even thirty yet and this is unusual but not unheard of at your age. Do you lead an active life?'

'Not really. I have a dog, and we go out for walks, but that's about it.'

'No running? No sports of any kind?'

She gave a small laugh. 'Definitely not. I've never been the slightest bit interested in physical activity.'

'Then for the moment, I suggest you keep up the walking, until we know more about what's happening with this heart of yours. I'll make sure my letter goes off today, so you should hear from cardiology within the next week or so. If you haven't heard from them in two weeks, I want to see you back here. Okay?'

She nodded. 'Thank you very much.'

'And call at the chemist on the way home and get this spray. Until we know more, this may just save your life.' He handed her the prescription form, and she walked away, seeing nothing of the other patients, but watched all the way by the receptionist. Anna had doubted she would make it in to the doctor, so bad had Janette seemed when she arrived.

Janette sat on the low stone wall surrounding the car park, and fished in her bag for her sunglasses. She felt more than panicked; what if she required a stay in hospital? Who would feed Billy?

And Child would be one problem too far. An image of the cellar door flashed into her mind, but she knew that after six and a half years of teaching Child to be something resembling a human, she couldn't simply throw her down the cellar steps and forget about her.

She sat for half an hour, then felt a tap on her shoulder. 'Are you okay?'

She jumped in fright, then forced a smile when she recognised the receptionist.

'I'm fine, Anna. I was sitting here enjoying the sunshine, and thinking things through. The pharmacy seems to close for lunch but it opens in five minutes, so I'll wait until it does.'

Anna smiled. 'That's okay then. I've just finished my shift, and saw you sitting here. I didn't want you to be in pain, so I thought I'd better check.'

'No, I'm good. I thought it was silly to walk all the way home, only to have to come out again.'

'Okay. I've done the urgent emails, and your letter has gone to cardiology, so you should have an appointment very soon. Take care, Janette.'

Janette watched her walk away, then stood and moved across the road. She collected her medication and set off for home, keen to get out of the hot sun and read through the leaflet that she hoped was included with the spray. She needed to know things now.

* * *

Billy was asleep and there was no sound from upstairs. She made a sandwich and took it up to Child, along with a glass of orange juice.

Child was sitting on the edge of the bed in her usual position, and she looked up as Janette came through the door, carrying the tray.

'Thank you, Mother,' she said in the dreamlike way she had. Her voice had an abstract quality to it that seemed to float around her small body. Although tiny, she was a beautiful child, with long golden curls that reached below her shoulders, blue eyes that sometimes seemed to cloud to grey when she recognised certain signs in Mother that did not bode well for the little girl, and a heart-shaped face that spoke of a stunning woman at the end of her childhood years. If she survived.

'Sit at the table, Child,' Janette said.

Child obeyed instantly. She was hungry and didn't want to risk having the meal removed for any minor transgression.

She waited, as always, for Mother to leave the room before she lifted the cover to reveal the 'yellow sandwich'. She had no idea what the filling was called; she hadn't heard the word banana at any point, but Mother had sometimes told her to get out her yellow dress, the same shade as the filling of the yellow sandwich. She loved yellow sandwiches, and for the first time that day, she smiled.

* * *

Janette took her sandwich into the conservatory along with her current year's sketchbook. The pile of pads was growing as she sketched out her life – everything of any importance was drawn without words in these precious books.

She felt scared. The future was suddenly getting out of hand, and she knew that if the cardiology people started talking operations, she would have no choice. She would refuse one. She couldn't leave her home for any length of time, so they would have to manage whatever condition she had with medication.

She sketched a heart, then drew a ragged line down it to show it was broken. Not through love, through disease. Then she drew

Anna and Dr Carmichael, and a tiny sketch of her angina spray at the bottom of the page.

She smiled at the quickly drawn page, then began to put more details in, to level it up to the same standard as her previous artwork. Billy watched her, but didn't join her.

'Billy, go get a drink of water. It's too hot.'

The dog stood and ambled across to his drinking bowl. He looked old, and she stifled a panicky hiccup. Should she book a vet's appointment? He didn't seem to be in any pain, but he was slowing, and life without him would be unbearable. Just her and the nonentity upstairs.

Janette put down the book and closed her eyes. It felt frustrating to have problems that she couldn't do anything about, and she had no idea what to do. She dismissed the idea of a vet's appointment – if Billy had reached the end, she didn't want it to be by a vet's hypodermic, she wanted him to go peacefully at home, with her.

The sweltering day dragged on, dozing, waking, drinking ice-cold water, occasionally adding bits to her sketch. She took Child's meal up at six, then went to collect her dishes and check she was in bed just before seven.

All was quiet and peaceful, Child was almost asleep, and Janette left the room, locked the door and headed downstairs.

* * *

Child waited. Child Two was sitting over by the wardrobe expectantly. Fifteen minutes later, she climbed out of bed, went to join Child Two and they played with the building bricks from the old walker rescued from the loft five years earlier.

Child loved these times with Child Two, and knew Mother had no idea about Child's other self.

Child felt she wasn't so alone now, and she reached out to stroke Child Two's hair. It was just like her own, and she loved the feel of its silky smoothness.

After an hour, Child stood, took one last look into the wardrobe mirror and climbed back into bed. Child Two was going to sleep now, so she would too.

'See you in the morning,' she whispered with a smile.

Child Two simply smiled.

13

Janette was confirmed as having angina, and she breathed many sighs of relief that it could be managed with medication. She occasionally had to use the spray, and she stopped being quite so brutal when she was forced to use the slipper on Child. It didn't take so much effort to use her hand as it did anything else, including the leather belt her own mother had used on her.

Walking Billy became problematic; he no longer had the joie de vivre he had shown when he first came to live with Janette, and she kept their activities to playing in the now cleared garden. She had removed the dog kennels, freeing up a considerable amount of space that had been grassed over for convenience.

Sometimes Child could hear him, and she wondered why he was barking. Mother expected her to be quiet at all times, but on the odd occasion when Billy had wandered into her room, he had barked. And Mother always said *Be quiet, Billy*. Child had an image in her mind of the slipper, or the belt, being used on the dog, and she shivered at the thought of it.

* * *

Time moved on, and Child gathered more scars from the treatment dished out by Mother. Child came to realise that sometimes she was punished just because Mother felt like punishing her.

The worst scar was the one on her arm. Mother had thrown a knife at her because she had spilt some water on the quilt, and she happened to have a small, very sharp knife in her apron pocket. As if by magic, it had appeared in her hand and she threw it with a degree of accuracy that could only have been a lucky throw, and it pierced Child's forearm. Child bit on her lip to stop the scream, and Mother then drew the knife further down, opening up the skin even more. Child didn't know it then, but it was a physical scar that would be with her for the rest of her life, as would the mental trauma.

It had never healed properly, and the puckered, raised line of flesh stood proudly red against the paleness of Child's skin.

* * *

The day that Billy died saw Child go without food for the entire day.

Janette rose before seven and showered, heading back into her bedroom to decide what to wear. It was hot outside, even at that early hour. She opened her wardrobe door, and stared at the clothes that had multiplied since she had started to make them for herself.

'Shorts or a skirt, Billy?' she said to the dog. The usual wag and thump of his tail didn't happen, and she turned to see if he was okay. There was no movement, his eyes were closed, and he had simply drifted away in his sleep.

'Oh no, Billy,' she whispered, feeling tears come into her throat for the first time in many years. She dropped to her knees, her towel pooling around her. She pulled him to her, and she hugged him, feeling the stillness in the animal.

She sat holding him for a while, then gently laid him back on his bed. She dressed quickly in jeans and a strappy top, then spent the next hour in the garden, digging a large deep hole to take Billy's body.

By lunchtime, she had placed Billy inside a sturdy cardboard box and had lowered him into the hole. Tears came intermittently, and she wondered how she would exist without him. She would draw the burial scene, and it would be a form of remembrance for him. Although nobody had been sure about his age, it had been felt he was around eight when he had come to live with her, which made him around eighteen or so now. Old, but he had had a good life and he had been... Janette hesitated over where her thoughts were going. Had she loved the dog? She thought so but wasn't too sure what love was.

She had a cup of coffee and sat by the open grave, building up her strength to shovel the soil back into the hole. The pain was bad in her chest, and she fished in her pocket for the spray. A quick burst of it soon brought the stitch-like pain under control, and she sat quietly until the palpitations disappeared.

The sun was hot on her face as she rested, and she wondered if she should make an appointment with the doctor. The pains were becoming more frequent, but she knew it would mean hospital visits and that simply couldn't happen. The sun was soporific, and she closed her eyes.

By the time she woke, her face was burning and she prepared herself both physically and mentally for shovelling the earth over Billy.

It took half an hour to get it looking good, and she placed large stones along the length, promising a plaque with his name on it, and the date of his death. Then she wiped away the last of her tears and went back inside the house, to search feverishly for after-sun cream to cool down her glowing cheeks and nose.

Janette pulled her latest sketchbook towards her and swiftly drew the preliminary strokes that would turn into a carefully crafted picture showing this latest development in her life. No Billy, it was unthinkable.

* * *

Child was hungry. She tried to think what she had done wrong but couldn't remember anything. She had been in bed by seven and pretending to be fast asleep by the time Mother came in half an hour later, so all had been good at that point. If it hadn't, Mother would have made it clear. Child felt uneasy.

Breakfast time had come and gone – Child had heard Mother having her shower, then nothing. No breakfast, no sandwich for lunch, only water to drink obtained from Child's en suite.

She continued to sit on the edge of the bed, not even wanting the company of Child Two. Her worries were starting to over-whelm her, and she hoped with everything in her that it wouldn't be the belt that was used on her. The slipper she could stand, but the belt always drew blood and then she got into even more trouble if the blood stained anything.

And it was so hot. She was unable to open the window – indeed, unable to open the curtains that were nailed all along the bottom and stitched up the middle – and the air felt stagnant and overpowering. She had dressed in shorts and a T-shirt, but even that felt too much.

'Please, Mother,' she whispered in her soft tones, 'please bring me some food. I feel so hungry. My stomach is hurting.'

She thought about walking to the door and listening to see if there were any sounds but knew she couldn't get back to the bed quick enough if Mother suddenly unlocked the door. That had once resulted in six swipes with the slipper, so Child had never risked it again.

She stood and walked to the en suite, sitting on the toilet just for something different to do. She could get away with doing that. Standing, she splashed cold water on her arms and her face, then reluctantly walked back to sit on the bed.

The endless day dragged on. Child went to bed still without having eaten anything, sleeping fitfully.

* * *

Janette pulled the sketchbook towards her and began to fill in the shading on the drawing started earlier. She had a large glass of sherry by her side, and worked on the picture for a couple of hours before feeling happy with it.

'Stop,' she told herself. 'You'll do too much to it and spoil it.' She wrote *RIP Billy, 4 July 2010* and followed it with a tiny heart. The sketchbooks, one for each year since 1998, were stacked on the dining table, some of them full, some half empty, but each one acted like a diary in pictures. Why had she started filling the pages? She had no idea, but one day she expected to show them to Child.

Throughout all the books, she had only drawn two pictures of Child – the first one had been a week or so after the birth, and the second had been after she had cut Child's arm. She had no intention of drawing her any more, because she always had it partly in her mind that one day Child wouldn't be allowed to live any longer. The day would come when she didn't know what to do with her. She wasn't official; her birth hadn't been recorded anywhere, so nobody would miss her; she was invisible.

She took out the new quilt, a complicated one using the New York Beauty patterns, and spread out the completed blocks on the dining table. She needed twenty-four blocks for a double quilt and had already completed half of them. She checked out the colours required for block thirteen and picked up the skilfully drawn diagram she needed for the paper-piecing. This one was going to be hand-pieced for the quilt top, then the machine would be brought into play for the bringing together of all three layers. She was some way off that, but the pleasure she gained from every part of the process was enough to make her forget she hadn't eaten all day until she went to bed.

She settled down, pulling the single sheet over her as it was much too humid for any other bedding, then thought about Child.

Had she fed her? Had she even seen her? She mentally shrugged, then closed her eyes. She would take her a dippy egg with her toast, and that would shut her rumbling stomach up, for sure.

* * *

And it did. Child was sitting on the edge of the bed when she heard the key turn in the lock. She exhaled slowly, wondering if it meant further punishment or food.

Janette carried the tray into the room. The egg was balanced inside a white eggcup, and she placed it on the little table. 'Come on, Child. Dippy egg and toast for breakfast. And orange juice.'

Child stood and quietly walked to sit at the table. 'Thank you, Mother,' she said.

Janette turned and walked to the door. With her back to Child, she spoke. 'Oh, by the way, Billy's dead.'

She slammed the door behind her and turned the key.

Child stared at the door, half expecting her to come back in. When she didn't, she dipped her toast in the soft-boiled egg, and smiled. She loved dippy eggs. The toast was soft, thick with butter, and memories of the previous day with her constantly rumbling stomach began to fade.

Billy's dead. What did that mean? Once she'd finished her breakfast, she began to think about Mother's words, unsure what to make of them. Was it something she'd done? Was that why there had been no food? What did dead mean, anyway? And why hadn't Billy been at the door, or even in her room? She liked the dog; he didn't bully or beat her.

She walked across to where Child Two lived in the mirror. 'Am I dead?' she asked. Child Two simply smiled. Child reached across and touched the mirror. Child Two responded by touching hands.

Walking back to the table, the young girl put her egg cup, plate and beaker onto the tray, then went into the en suite to brush her teeth. Mother always checked, and Child didn't want any more food restrictions because she hadn't followed routine.

The key turning in the lock had her confident she had done everything she should have done. Mother inspected her mouth, then picked up the tray to take it downstairs.

Child risked speaking. 'Mother. What is dead?'

Janette stared at her. It hadn't occurred to her that Child wouldn't understand the word.

'You'll find out one day, Child. You'll find out.'

14

Janette's smile was huge. The new quilt was spread across her bed and looked wonderful. The twenty-four blocks consisted of six lots of four designs in assorted fabrics, spaced haphazardly, and in glorious colours. She had edged the block section with a border of navy blue, followed by a cream border, and bound the whole lot with the navy blue. She had kept the actual quilting simple, sewing in the ditch, which turned out not to be as simple as she had originally thought because she kept wandering away from the seam and having to unpick it. 'In the bloody ditch,' she had muttered constantly, but the extra care she had taken had certainly paid off.

The quilt with the many thousands of hexagons had been on her bed prior to the completion of the New York Beauty, and she decided to take it downstairs to be washed. It would then go on Child's bed – the little cot quilt did look a bit small just sitting in the middle of the double bed.

She sat down in her rocking chair and looked across at the bed. The smile was huge on her face, and she knew her 2011 sketchbook would have a new page started tonight. The quilt had been an ambitious design and not for the faint-hearted, but it was worth every needle stab, every stitch removed that was in the wrong place, and she couldn't ever remember smiling so much.

Already her mind was moving onto the next project, and she was considering actually buying a book that would teach her how to make an heirloom quilt using silks and satins. It occurred to her that she had never bought any sort of book in her whole life, so this would be a first. The New York Beauty had been copied from a book in the library, but Janette knew if she were to consider this project, she would have to work from the book all the way through.

She moved across the landing to Child's room and unlocked the door. 'Have you changed your bedding as I asked?'

Child nodded, sitting on the edge of the newly made bed. 'Yes, Mother.'

'Good. I'll take mine down and put it in the washer, then come back up to get yours.'

Janette locked the door, and returned to her own room, picking up the pile of laundry consisting of her bottom sheet, duvet cover, two pillowcases and the hexagon quilt. She felt the familiar quiver of her heart as she gathered the items into a manageable bundle, and walked along the landing, the bottom sheet trailing. The pain ripped through her as she struggled with the cumbersome wash load and she trod on the edge of the quilt as she stepped forward onto the top stair. She catapulted down the stairs, unable to scream because of the intense pain coursing through her chest. She hit the newel post at the bottom with a thud.

Silence.

* * *

Child heard the noise and assumed Mother had dropped something. She felt relieved it was nothing to do with her; she couldn't possibly be to blame for whatever it was, because Mother was taking her own laundry downstairs. Not hers.

She remained sitting on the edge of the bed, wishing she still had her imaginary Child Two with her, but as she had grown older, she had come to realise it was just an image of herself. She had wondered many times if she would ever be like Mother, who seemed to know 'stuff', and she didn't. When would Mother start to tell her about what she called 'stuff'?

Did everybody live in one room as she did? Mother must have more than one room because she brought food to her, so Child guessed that one day when she was older, she would have more than one room as well.

Child needed to wee, so she went to the toilet, expecting Mother to come and collect the laundry, but it was still waiting there when she returned to the bed. She sat once again and waited.

She waited all day and went to bed when she judged it to be seven o'clock. She was hungry but having had porridge for breakfast, she wasn't stomach-rumbling hungry.

It was an uncomfortable night for Child. She was worried that she had inadvertently done something to upset Mother, and was being punished by her food being withheld, but she was more worried that it might mean she would receive physical punishment. She still had a black eye from the last punch into her face.

She gave in at six and quietly got out of bed. She showered and chose jeans and a sweatshirt to wear. It was still wintery weather, and sometimes Mother would turn off the heating, so it was best to be prepared in case she did that. She sat on the edge of the bed, not sure whether she was dreading the arrival of Mother or looking forward to the arrival of food.

* * *

Michael was feeling his age. It was cold, and despite twenty-odd years of delivering milk on this round, he had been relieved to be handed a redundancy notice along with his Christmas payslip. 'Folks are buying their milk from the supermarket now,' his boss had said, 'so we're stopping doorstep deliveries from the end of March.'

Michael's smile had shown his true feelings. 'I'm sixty-five next, boss. Happy to go.'

And he was. He would miss his customers, though. He pulled up outside Janette's house, and walked to the front door, her daily pint of milk in his hand. He stopped, feeling a sense of foreboding. Yesterday's milk was still on the doorstep. Never, in the last twenty-something years, had she left her milk outside. Neither her, nor her mother before her.

He put down the milk, and knocked at the door using the special knock from all those years ago when he used to chat with her. There was no reply, so he knocked again, lifted the letterbox and called her name.

'Janette. It's Michael. You there?'

He waited a moment, then bent his back carefully, aware of pain that usually accompanied such an action, and lifted the letterbox again. This time it was to look through it.

He saw her straight away.

* * *

The police arrived within ten minutes, and were careful about how they got in following Michael's warning that he believed she had a dog. Eventually they broke through the door with an Enforcer, and DS Lavers went immediately to check Janette's pulse. She looked up at Alan Jenkins, her colleague standing by her side, and shook her head.

'Is she...?' Michael stared at the woman, who looked too young to be dead.

'I'm afraid so. We'll need a statement, so can you leave your name and address with DC Jenkins, please? I know you have deliveries to make, so I suggest you contact your dairy, tell them what's happened. They might even send somebody out to complete your round so you can go home. You knew the lady?'

'Kind of. I knew her mother for years, then she died and Janette carried on having the milk delivered. She's called Janette Gregson.' He looked around. 'Looks as though she might have tripped on this lot and fallen down the stairs.' He waved his hand towards the pile of laundry squashed underneath and around Janette. 'She was a lovely woman. We always exchanged Christmas cards. Never missed paying me for her milk, every Saturday morning.'

'She lives here alone?'

He nodded. 'Just her and the dog, but Billy doesn't seem to be here now. I thought she might be ill and needing help, but this is a proper shock. She's not very old.' He pursed his lips while he thought back. 'I would say she's maybe thirty-five, that's all. My memory's not what it was, but I reckon her mother died ten or eleven years ago, and she was twenty-four or -five then. I'll nip outside and sort somebody to come and take over the round, I don't feel right just carrying on as if nothing's happened.'

Fleur Lavers nodded. 'Thank you. I think the ambulance has just pulled up, so we need to all get out of the way and let them do their job. Forensics won't be far behind, although it does look pretty clear what's happened.'

Michael left them to it, and they could hear him on the phone for some time, telling the tale of his morning so far.

Fleur stared at the woman, who was around the same age as herself, and wondered what had happened. She suspected she had tripped on a dangling item of bedding as she carried it all in her arms, but the post-mortem would reveal anything else that might give them some clues.

She stepped aside as the paramedics came through the door, and she joined her colleague in the lounge.

'Anything?' Fleur asked.

Alan shook his head. 'Not in here. Very tidy, no sign of a dog, but there was one because she drew him.' He pointed to a picture in a frame on the sideboard. 'It says Billy on the back, then the date he died a couple of years ago.'

'She drew it?'

Alan Jenkins nodded. 'She signed it. I've had a quick look in the dining room, and there's a load of sketchbooks in one of those slider things that people used to keep books in before we had bookcases. It looks as though she has a sketchbook for every year, but I only looked at the current one. She's very good. Was very good,' he corrected himself.

Fleur felt a frisson of unease. 'Alan, nip next door and see if they know anything, if she was ill or something. Try the neighbours both sides, find out who she was friends with around here. I don't like just assuming it was an accident when we know nothing. I'll have a quick look at those sketchbooks, and I think they'll be starting to clear up by the time we're done. Then we'll check the entire house, make sure we haven't missed anything. I'm sure it's simply an accident, there's a small amount of blood on that newel post and blood on her head, so I think it's safe to say she hit her head on it, but let's be thorough.'

'Okay, boss,' Alan responded, and Fleur watched through the bay window as he walked down the path, heading off to the right to visit the neighbour.

Sitting at the dining table, she pulled the open sketchbook towards her. It was open at the second page and bore a date at the top of the page of January 2012. It was a picture of a sewing machine – Fleur presumed it was the treadle machine standing in the bay window of the lounge. A quilt with a detailed design was under the needle, and it was clearly an unfinished picture, because the pencil crayons used to colour in the quilt were standing in a jar on the table. It was unsigned, and Fleur felt a small shiver go through her as she realised it never would be now.

She flipped back to the first picture in the book, again dated January 2012, and this one was complete. It was a picture of a young girl, a beautiful child with long curly hair cascading down around her shoulders, and a black eye. Fleur stared thoughtfully at it – was the sketch a forgotten memory suddenly appearing of an earlier part of the dead woman's life, a memory of a much younger Janette Gregson? The child bore a definite resemblance to the adult.

She took a couple more of the books out of the slider and it slowly dawned on her that these were diaries of Janette's current life. Whatever happened to her she drew in pictures, not words. This creative woman wasn't a writer, she was an artist. Was the quilt now finished and on a bed? She suspected it was, in view of the quilt that had landed at the bottom of the stairs with her. Janette had clearly changed her bedding, and was probably bringing it downstairs to wash it.

'Fleur?' She heard David Fenwick, the pathologist she easily recognised by his Welsh accent, call her name.

'David? I'm in the dining room.'

He popped his head around the door. 'I've told them they can take her. I'll do the post-mortem tomorrow, but it looks as though she tripped and tumbled downstairs. She certainly bashed her head on the newel post. I'll know more after tomorrow, but as it stands at the moment, it's looking like an accident.'

15

Fleur moved back into the hall and waited respectfully to one side while the body of Janette Gregson was lifted onto a trolley in the sealed body bag. A black bag containing all the bedding was also taken, but David told Fleur that would be handed to her for return to the house as soon as his post-mortem results were validated.

David's team left with him, and Fleur moved to the lounge to watch as the ambulance pulled away. She glanced at her watch. Two hours. The two of them could take two hours to go through this house looking for next of kin, and find something of Janette's story other than her obvious creative talents.

Alan gave a wave as he walked up the path, and she met him in the hallway.

'They know nothing of her,' he said. 'She kept herself to herself, they occasionally saw her go out in her car but only on shopping trips, and they think it's a couple of years since her dog died. That's about it. She has no visitors that they're aware of. They knew her mother a bit better, but it seems as soon as she died and Janette inherited the house, that was it. She used to have a dog-boarding business, built her own set of kennels in the back garden, but even that's all gone now.'

'Right, look at these sketchbooks. These tell us much more than the neighbours can.'

He looked puzzled.

'These are her diaries. If something happens in her life, she draws it. And surely she must have some relatives somewhere. I don't intend working on this beyond today because I think tomorrow we'll get confirmation that it was accidental death, but I can give her today. We'll have a couple of hours here, then a bit of Internet trawling to see if anything shows up, then hope she's left a will. There's some value in the house, and it seems to me she didn't go out to work, so her mother must have left her okay for money. She stopped her dog-boarding business, so she clearly felt she was okay financially.'

They sat at opposite sides of the table, and Fleur pulled the first sketchpad towards her. It was the only one that was a pad, the others were spiral-bound sketchbooks. 'This is 1998, so if you take the following year... make notes on anything that may be helpful. If it takes longer than we've got here, we'll take them back to the station with us. This one says May to December ninety-eight.'

Alan looked at his spiral-bound book. 'Good quality book. Mine's dated the full year, says 1999.'

Fleur spun her sketch pad around so that Alan could see the first picture. 'A graphic portrait of a rape in progress, and if I'm not mistaken, it's in the kitchen here.'

Alan pulled it towards him. 'Look at her face. She definitely isn't in agreement with what's happening.' He stared at it, studying it for any clues as to who the rapist might be. Then he lifted the picture to look at the second one.

He passed it across to Fleur, who felt the blood drain from her face. It clearly showed the man's head with something embedded in it.

'What's that in his head?' she asked quietly.

'It's a cobbler's foot, or a last, which I think is the correct term. They're usually used nowadays as door stops because they're heavy and made of cast iron. Hang on.' He stood and left the room, returning a few seconds later with the implement. 'She still uses it as a door stop.'

'Thank god you put a glove on. Put it in an evidence bag, Alan. Maybe this isn't quite the accidental death we thought it was.' She lifted the page to look at the next drawing.

Silently she pushed the book across to Alan. 'Is this a cellar? Are these cellar steps with a body on them?' She stood. 'Let's find out.'

They walked into the hallway and looked at what they assumed must be the cellar door. Fleur pulled on nitrile gloves, and turned the handle. Nothing happened. There was no key in the lock, and she ran her hand along the door jamb. The key clattered to the floor, so she scooped it up, inserted it and for the first time in years, the door was opened.

She stepped carefully through onto the cellar head and looked for a light switch. The feeble glow from the low-wattage bulb illuminated a plastic-encased bundle halfway down the stairs.

She stepped back. 'Get the forensic team back here, Alan. Tell them we've possibly found a body, but aren't going near it.'

* * *

Fleur and Alan collected a black bag from under the kitchen sink and loaded the sketchbooks into it. They needed to have them back at the station where each one could be photocopied and a timeline noted, easily established because Gregson had dated each picture.

David was the first to arrive, and Fleur explained what they had discovered in the artworks that had led them to unlock the cellar door. He covered his clothes with his white suit, and edged carefully down the cellar steps until he reached the obvious bones and cracked plastic covering.

He looked up to see Fleur at the top of the steps. 'Think you can borrow a light bulb from somewhere else in the house that's a bit brighter than this one? We can set our lights up, but this isn't bright enough to see anything.'

'Give me a minute,' she said, heading towards the kitchen. In one of the drawers, she found a huge assortment of light bulbs, and chose a 150-watt bulb. She swapped it over, and it turned the bleakness into instant daylight.

'Thank you,' David said. 'It certainly looks as though he died from a blow to the head; there's a massive dent in the skull, but I'll know more when I get him on the table. You want to find me any more work for tomorrow, Fleur?'

'Sorry, David. I wasn't looking for this one. I was actually looking for next of kin, because I need to notify them before this reaches any news outlets. Accidental deaths usually do, and I was hoping I could avert any issues. Now I'm on a back burner with everything. I don't think we'll be looking too far to find his killer, her confession is in shades of black and white in her sketchbook, but the crime he committed to find himself dumped on the cellar steps is pretty graphic as well.'

'It's self-defence? Why the hell didn't she call in the police?'

'My impression is that she's a loner. She doesn't seem to have had any contact with anyone since her mother died. The neighbours don't know her at all, see her very rarely. She would probably have been too scared to go to the police.'

She left David to discuss with his newly arrived team what they needed to do, and went to find Alan, who was checking through the next couple of pages in the first sketchbook. 'You have to see this,' he said, his face ashen. 'She delivered a baby. Was there a child on the cellar steps?'

'Come with me,' she said, her pale face now matching his as she stared at the picture he had turned towards her. 'We haven't ventured upstairs yet, and I suspect...'

'The child?'

She nodded. They both took the stairs two at a time and stopped at the door that had a key in the lock.

* * *

Child was dressed and sitting on her bed. She was so hungry, and wondered what she could hear. Voices. She had never heard anything other than Mother. She felt scared. Was this some other form of punishment? Wasn't the slipper and the belt enough for Mother? And her eye, although fading to yellow, was still painful.

She thought about going to get another drink of water in an effort to appease the hunger pangs, but decided she didn't want to be anywhere else other than sitting on the designated bed spot when Mother came through that door.

So she waited.

* * *

Fleur turned the key, then the round doorknob. There was a slight squeak as the door opened. They both hesitated in the doorway. If there was someone in the room, this was their private domain, and they were infiltrating it.

The little girl stared at them.

'Hello,' Fleur said. 'My name is Fleur, and this is Alan. What's your name?'

The delicate tones of the girl's voice flowed from her. 'My name is Child. Is Mother bringing breakfast? I am very hungry.'

'Does Mother always bring your breakfast?' Alan said gently, kneeling down so he was on the same level as her.

'Yes, unless I am being punished.'

'And lunch?' Fleur asked.

'Yes.'

'And tea?'

'Yes.'

Fleur shot a quick glance towards Alan. This child was clearly fragile, and with, she suspected, an extremely limited vocabulary. 'Alan, we need to make a phone call.'

Alan understood what she was saying without vocalising, and headed downstairs to ring Child Protection Services. But first he needed to feed her. Feed Child. He felt angry that she didn't even have a proper name, and wondered how she would cope with the massive lifestyle changes that were heading her way. He went into the kitchen, popped two slices of bread into the toaster, then buttered them before carrying them back upstairs.

Fleur was sitting by the side of Child, but as soon as Alan walked through the door with the toast, Child stood and moved to the table. 'Thank you, Mother,' she said.

Alan smiled at her. 'You're very welcome. But I'm not Mother, I'm Alan.'

He returned downstairs to put into motion something he had no idea how to deal with, leaving Fleur to sit with her young charge. He filled David in on what was happening upstairs while waiting to be connected with Child Protection, and then told the whole story once more when he finally spoke to the right person.

He could hear the noise from down in the cellar as people tried to pass one another on the steps in the limited available space, and heard David call a halt. 'Have we got all the photographs we need?'

Someone said they had, so David said, 'Let's get everything into a body bag and transported to the morgue. We can't work effectively here.'

Fifteen minutes later, David stood looking down the steps. 'Everything's gone,' he said. 'I'm just going back down with my torch to make sure we haven't missed anything, then I'll get out of your hair before Child Protection arrive. That little girl won't want to see us here.'

Alan thanked him, and moved into the lounge to keep a watchful eye out for the arrival of somebody who could take care of the girl. He couldn't bring himself to call her Child.

Suddenly he heard, 'For fuck's sake,' coming from the cellar and he went back to the cellar door.

'You okay, David?'

'Well, I am,' David said, 'but there's another one, been tied to a chair for I don't know how many years, and covered with a sheet. He's been here a lot longer than the first one, that's pretty obvious. He's not very well, that's one thing I'm certain of. I need to get him back to the autopsy suite and find out why he's here.'

BOOK TWO

MARTA'S STORY

January 2012 – November 2016

16

Child finished her toast, moved to the bathroom to wash her hands and brush her teeth, then returned to sit on the bed.

'Was that good?' Fleur asked, smiling at the young girl.

'Yes, thank you. Where is Mother?'

'I'm sorry, sweetheart, she won't be coming home.'

Child looked at the stranger at her side, a puzzled look on her face. 'No more food?'

'Yes, you will have food. Are you still hungry?'

'No, thank you. I had toast.'

'I can get you more toast if you want more.'

A simple shake of Child's head gave Fleur her answer.

Fleur took hold of Child's hand, and the little girl flinched.

'I won't hurt you,' she said. 'I need to tell you that some ladies are going to come and talk to you, and then they will look after you. They won't hurt you either. You can trust them. Shall we go down-stairs now?'

'I have to sit here.'

'All the time?' Fleur couldn't keep the shock out of her voice.

'Yes. Was that my breakfast?'

'I suppose so.'

'I will go to the table when lunch arrives, then I sit here again until tea arrives. I go to bed when Mother shouts "bed" through the door.'

'When do you play?'

There was a lengthy pause. 'I don't know what you mean. Please don't hit me.'

Fleur wanted to cry. 'I promise you, nobody will hit you. These people who will be here to talk to you are here to help you. Would you like to go in the garden?'

'Garden?'

'Where the plants and the grass grow.'

'I don't know what you mean.'

'Sweetheart, have you never been out of this room?' This young girl desperately needed a name, they couldn't expect everybody to call her sweetheart.

'No.'

It flashed across Fleur's brain that they could have a potential problem when it came to removing this youngster from her surroundings. Thirteen years of never knowing anything different on a day-to-day basis would terrify even an adult when it came time to take those first steps down the stairs.

There was a knock on the door, and then it was opened by Alan, who stepped back to allow a man and a woman to enter.

'Lorraine. Lovely to see you again.' Fleur turned to Child. 'Listen, sweetheart, this lady is called Lorraine Lowe, and this gentleman works with her. He is called Rob Owens. Will you be okay if Rob stays with you for two minutes while I talk to Lorraine?'

'Yes.' Child folded her hands together, and rested them on her lap.

Rob knelt down. 'Hi, what's your name?'

'Child.'

'Well, that's a bit boring. You can choose your own name soon, but can I call you Blondie for now?' He touched her hair lightly, and once again she flinched. He ignored it. 'Because you're a proper blondie. Beautiful curls. So, you had something to eat, Blondie?'

His words faded away as the two women exited the bedroom, and moved into the one across the landing.

The quilt on the bed was stunningly beautiful. Fleur reached down and touched it. 'I think this quilt is possibly the cause of her mother's death. She appears to have changed the bedding, replacing one quilt with this newly made one, then tripped as she carried the laundry downstairs. Luckily, she had milk delivered by a long-standing conscientious milkman, or she could have been at the bottom of those stairs for months, and that child, who it seems is permanently locked in that bedroom, would have died anyway. She would have been too scared to try to escape. She has no concept of anything – god, Lorraine, I don't know how you'll manage this.'

'Let's start with her name. I know nothing.'

'She hasn't got one, not a real one. I told her my name straight away, not my rank or anything, so she doesn't even know I'm a police officer, but I'm not convinced she would understand the word police anyway. I asked her name, and she said Child. She doesn't appear to have had any form of learning, her vocabulary is definitely limited, and, just for the record, I could never do your job, Lorraine. I'd want to adopt all these waifs and strays we keep finding for you.'

Lorraine smiled. 'She's a beautiful child. I am guessing, in the absence of a name, that she was never registered at birth. That will have to be a priority, then we can start to treat her, to teach her about the world we know and she doesn't.'

'Janette Gregson, her mother, gave birth to her in the lounge, on her own, with only the dog for company. We know this because she sketched everything that happened to her from the afternoon she was raped onwards. She dated her drawings, signed them all, very detailed. I think to understand anything about this young one, you're going to have to look through these sketchbooks. I'm taking them back to the station with me, and I'll get one of the younger officers to stand at a photocopier for a bit and copy the lot of them. Then I'll have one complete set sent to you. It seems Janette killed the little girl's father after he raped her. We found what we believe to be his bones down the cellar, but I'm not sure what's going on because there was a second set of bones down there, and our pathologist thought they were much older than the first set he found on the cellar steps.' Fleur gave a sigh. 'And I anticipated this being a couple of hours to complete, because it's pretty obvious what happened to Janette, but it's now turned into certainly one murder, possibly two.'

'That poor lassie,' Lorraine said. 'Okay, I'm getting the gist of it. Was any violence towards her involved? I'm booking her into the Children's tonight, I want a doctor to check her out, but they have a special room for situations that require special attention. I've already spoken to them, and they're preparing for her arrival. I said I'd bring her in the car as she isn't injured; I don't want to frighten her with an ambulance.'

'I'm sure violence was used. She has a black eye at the moment, and that was no accident because she doesn't do anything except sit on the bed, or sit at the little table. And she flinches if you go near her. She's never been outside that room, so what the hell did her mother find that required punishment?'

'Okay, let's go and see how Rob is getting on with her,' said Lorraine. 'If she has never had any schooling, then I shall be the one to have most time with her.'

'I guessed that. Your teaching qualifications for her age group are exactly what she needs right now, because one thing's for sure, she can't go into mainstream education yet.'

'She seems quite small for her age. You said she was thirteen?'

Fleur nodded. 'She is. Born 5 January 1999. She looks around ten, but I suspect poor diet has a lot to do with that. She had food withheld as a punishment many times, from what she told me.'

They reached the bedroom door, and Lorraine knocked before opening it. She smiled at Rob and Child.

'Okay, my love, we're going to pack you some clothes, and tonight you will be staying in a smart little room at the Children's Hospital, where nurses and doctors will take care of you until I come by tomorrow with a more permanent home for you.' Lorraine moved towards the wardrobe, and saw two dresses. The drawer revealed two nighties, five pairs of pants and a few white socks. Lorraine pulled a carrier bag from her handbag and began to fill it. She realised with a jolt that there was no coat, and was glad to see that Blondie, as she had heard Rob call her, was wearing a thick cardigan with a pair of jeans and a flimsy top.

'Okay,' she said, 'time to go. I need to have you settled in. Then we can begin to sort out your life.'

Child stared at her, her eyes glistening with unshed tears. 'Will you hit me?'

'I promise, nobody will hit you.' Lorraine placed her arms around Child and pulled her towards her. She felt the girl freeze, and she immediately removed her arms.

'I'm sorry,' she said, 'I just thought a cuddle might help.' Child was crying properly. 'I didn't hurt you, did I?'

'No,' Child sobbed, hiccupping with the distress of the moment.

'Would you like me to hold your hand while we go to the car?'

Child stared at Lorraine. 'Car?'

'Blondie has never been outside of this room,' Rob interrupted.

'Not for anything. She knows nothing of the rest of this house, its garden, or the fact there is a car parked outside belonging to her mother.'

'Then Blondie is going to have to be a brave girl and trust us.' Lorraine gently took Child's hand, and didn't tug on it, simply let the girl get used to the feel of it. After a few minutes of waiting for the tears to dry, she stroked the hand, such a tiny one.

'Will you come with me now?'

'Mother says I have to sit here to wait for lunchtime.'

'Mother isn't here. She won't be coming back to look after you, so I'm going to find you a new mummy.'

'Mummy?' The name puzzled her, and she stared at the woman still holding her hand.

'It is a different name for mother,' Lorraine explained.

The three adults waited expectantly; the air felt electric with tension, and then slowly Child stood, turned towards her bed and picked up the cot-size quilt. 'You hold my hand?' she asked Lorraine.

'Always,' Lorraine answered. She didn't believe for one minute that Child understood the word, but Lorraine herself did.

* * *

Lorraine leaned over to fasten the seat belt across Child, and was suddenly aware of a change in the young girl's breathing. She clicked the seatbelt into the holder, and paused.

'Are you okay?'

Child didn't say anything; she was trying hard to breathe, with not a lot of success. Lorraine reached into her handbag and fished out a paper bag. She made a rosette of the opening, and held it to the girl's mouth.

'Breathe slowly into this, deep breaths. This will pass, sweet-heart, you simply need to take deep breaths.'

Lorraine was aware of Rob climbing into the driver's seat, but she ignored him. Her concentration was all on getting an estab-lished breathing pattern, and when it appeared to be returning to normal, she gently eased the bag out of Child's hands.

'You'll be fine now,' she said with a smile of encouragement. 'I'm just going to put my seat belt on, but I'm sitting by your side, so you'll be okay. I'm going to put this paper bag into your carrier bag with your clothes. Snuggle into your quilt, and we'll be in your own little room before you know it.'

Child pulled her quilt into her arms, rocking from side to side and showing Lorraine how much terror was inside her; she looked back towards the house in which she had spent the first thirteen years of her life. It meant nothing. As yet, she couldn't comprehend time and distance, but something inside her was telling her that her time for living was approaching. She would understand things Mother had dismissed as 'nothing to do with her'.

The car began to move and Lorraine heard a small squeak of fear from the seat alongside her, so she reached across and grasped Child's hand.

'Don't worry, sweetheart, and one day you will come back to this house, even if it is only to sell it, because I do believe it prob-ably belongs to you.'

17

Dr Paula hurt her when she stuck the needle in her arm to take some blood, but Child smiled through her tears. She was given chocolate to help get through it.

Child had never had chocolate buttons before, and she sucked each one, enjoying the taste until it disappeared down her throat. Nurses were in and out all afternoon, chatting and smiling, bringing her juice, water, anything she wanted.

Lorraine stayed with her, and Rob went back to organise an urgent meeting for the following morning to decide where this unbelievable case would go next.

Lorraine's notepad was filling fast as she asked questions, initially receiving monosyllabic answers that progressed to responses with a little bit more detail as Child got used to her.

A nurse, her dark skin causing absolutely no reaction in Child, brought in a jigsaw with only fifteen pieces, and a couple of board books with more pictures than words.

'Thank you, Mother,' Child said, and the nurse's white teeth flashed brightly as she smiled.

'I'm not your mother, honey, but I sure wish I was.'

Child tentatively reached for the books.

'Books, sweetheart,' Lorraine said. 'They're called books. You've never seen one?'

'No. Will they hurt me?'

'No, they're to look at, and one day you will be able to read them. Then the world will become much better. I'm going to help you to read, and to know your numbers.'

She watched as a look of puzzlement flashed across Child's face.

The girl bent her head to look at the front covers of the books. 'Is this me?'

'No, but she looks just like you with your blonde curly hair, and those beautiful blue eyes.'

'Who is she?'

Lorraine took the book and opened it at the first page. 'She is Marta, and she lives in a country called Poland.'

'Will I live in Poland?'

'No, you live in a city called Sheffield, and your country is England.' Lorraine decided not to expand on the whole UK bit, time enough to learn such convolutions in the future.

'Marta,' Child repeated. 'I like it. Can I be Marta?'

'Of course. It is a pretty name, and it suits you. You look very much like this Marta.' Lorraine tapped on the book. 'Marta Gregson. And if you would like another name to go after Marta, you can have one, but I don't need to know for a couple of days. Okay, Marta Gregson, shall we start right now by calling you Marta?'

Child grinned and nodded, and Marta was born.

* * *

They changed the name card outside her door to 'Marta G' instead of simply 'Gregson?' and Lorraine moved her chair so that she was no longer facing Marta, but sitting alongside her.

'Okay, Marta, lesson number one.' Lorraine turned to the back page in her notebook. 'This is a biro, or a pen, and it makes marks. What I have been doing since I saw you is called making notes, and everything we have spoken about, or the doctors and nurses have said, has been written down. Maybe you would like to write?'

Marta looked terrified. 'Will it hurt?'

'I promise you it won't. Okay, watch me.'

Marta shuffled around so that she could see what Lorraine was doing, and watched as Lorraine wrote M.

'This is the first letter in your name. See,' and she pulled the book towards them. 'This is Polish Marta, and her name, and yours, looks like that.' She returned to her notebook.

Carefully spelling out M-a-r-t-a, she pronounced the letters, then counted them through to five.

She handed the pen to Marta, who stared at it. 'It just does it?'

'It does,' Lorraine laughed. 'Nothing magical, it just works.'

Marta placed the tip on the page and attempted the M. It looked like a U, so Lorraine held her hand as she tried again.

This time it was less wobbly, and resembled an M much more closely.

'Oh, Marta, that's lovely. When you get used to holding the pen, it will be much easier. Did you ever see Mother doing her drawings?'

'Drawings?'

'Pictures. Like this picture in the book of Marta. That is a drawing.'

Marta's forehead creased in thought. 'No. I only saw her when she brought food.'

Lorraine felt sick. Thirteen years of childhood lost beyond

redemption, leaving a much-damaged child who thought everything was going to hurt her.

Lorraine looked up as the door opened, to see Fleur, a huge smile on her face, a teddy in her arms.

She handed it to Marta. 'This is for you. It's to say sorry, because I have to put a stick in your mouth.'

Instantly there was stiffening in Marta's attitude. 'A stick?'

'I promise it won't hurt,' Lorraine said gently. 'It takes a few seconds, and then you'll never have to have this done again. And after it, you're allowed some more chocolate buttons.'

Marta thought this through, then nodded. 'Don't hurt me,' she said.

Fleur collected the DNA sample as quickly as she could, then dropped it into an evidence bag. It had been an urgent request from David Fenwick, as he attempted to conclusively prove who was who with all three bodies he appeared to have lying on tables in his laboratory.

'Is it okay if I stay for a bit, sweetheart?'

Lorraine laughed. 'We don't have to call her sweetheart any longer. Our beautiful princess has chosen her name, and she is now Marta.'

'I can have another name if I want.' Marta's voice hovered like a cloud in the air, and Fleur wondered if it had that floaty sound because she rarely used her vocal cords.

'And how many will you have then?' Lorraine interrupted.

Marta's eyes clouded as she thought about it. 'Two?'

'Good girl.' Lorraine clapped her hands.

'I have two names,' Fleur said. 'My first name is Fleur, which means flower, and my second name is Beatrice because my mum wanted to keep a family name going.'

'Has Marta in the book got two names?' Marta asked. Already she was starting to react to a different world, and Lorraine absolutely knew she wouldn't have dared to ask questions of Janette Gregson.

'Let's have a look,' Fleur said, and pulled the book towards her, scanning it so that Marta could see it. 'She does! Look, in this little bit, her mummy is calling her to come and eat. She is shouting "Marta Rose".'

'Rose. Is it pretty like Marta?'

Lorraine couldn't help but smile. 'It's pretty enough for me to want to be called that rather than Lorraine Alice.'

'Marta Rose. What is my last name again? Do I use that?'

'It depends what comes back from that stick you've had in your mouth, but I think you are a Gregson. You are Miss Marta Rose Gregson, and I shall be making it legal tomorrow.'

'Legal?' Again Marta was puzzled by a word.

'Every country has rules, things you have to do. One here is that when a child is born, they must be registered. That means the parents tell somebody they have a child with a name they have chosen, and they get a birth certificate, a piece of paper, to say the child's name. I shall get one of those for you.'

Marta pulled the book towards her, and began to look through it, this time drawing over the letter M with her finger. Fleur stood and left the room to fetch coffees for her and Lorraine, and Lorraine caught up on her notes.

Her heart was aching for the young child now in her care, and she knew at the following day's meeting, she would move heaven and earth to have charge of her education. And to get her placed with the Needhams. Wendy Needham, with her gentleness and nurturing nature, would be the one who could get through to this young girl, and who always worked well with everyone in Child Protection Services. Stewart Needham, his kindly actions and words ever-present when with his family, had already proved his worth as a father, and the biggest bonus would be Ellie Needham, their thirteen-year-old daughter.

Marta would mature in the company of a child of the same age, would catch up on the missing years and hopefully be a friend for life.

* * *

Fleur rang David to tell him she had the DNA sample, and she would drop it off at his laboratory before heading home.

'Good, I'll set the test going tonight. I'm going to be here late. I've already obtained enough DNA from our two cellar bodies, but their deaths aren't at the same hands. The one hidden round that wall and sat in a chair was a good twenty or twenty-five years earlier than the second one, found on the cellar steps. That's not going to make for an easy investigation, Fleur.'

'Well, my heart's breaking for our young girl. She's got a name now – Marta Rose Gregson. I've written it on the evidence bag. She's really bonded with Lorraine Lowe, so hopefully there's a brighter future for her.'

They disconnected, with Fleur promising to see him shortly. She headed back to the room where Marta and Lorraine were, said goodnight to them and was delighted to see Marta eating chips and fishfingers.

Lorraine walked with her to the exit, telling her that Marta had never had that meal before.

'It seems she lived mainly on toast, occasionally an egg, and usually porridge for breakfast. No wonder she's so underweight.'

'She'll be sorted if you can manage to get her with that family you have in mind. They take long-term children?'

'Yes. Their daughter was placed with them, and three years after we took her there, they adopted her. I'm not saying that will happen here, but Ellie, their adopted daughter, is used to children being placed there. They've had several from us, so I think she'll welcome another girl of the same age. However, there's a world of difference between them. Ellie is doing really well at school, and I suspect Marta hasn't even heard the word before today.'

'If she's discharged, will you let me know? If she isn't, I'd like to pop in and see her tomorrow afternoon.'

'Certainly. I'll be here after our meeting to discuss her tomorrow morning, and as it's an eight o'clock meeting, I should be here by ten. I'll know for definite that the Needhams can take her before I come back here, so it will be just a matter of waiting for the doctors to discharge her. I'll let you know as soon as I know anything.'

Fleur wished Marta goodnight, and Marta waved a fishfinger on the end of a fork in response. 'Fishfingers,' she said, in explanation.

'They're good?' Fleur asked.

'They are,' was said with some fervour.

* * *

As Fleur walked down the corridor, heading towards the car park, she reflected on the future for the child, wondering how Marta would react to being out in this strange world. Someone who had seen nothing of it would find it a frightening place, and she hoped everybody involved with the recovery of Marta's spirit would be up to coping with any fall-out.

Handing the DNA sample in at the laboratory took no time at all, and David acknowledged his thanks through the window with a wave of his hand. She walked back to her car, sank into the leather upholstery of the old Jaguar, and laid her head back.

She went over everything in her head that had happened

during the day, and thought about the house that held so many secrets. Tomorrow would be a day of going through those sketch-books, creating a timeline of what had happened and when. It would be a discovery journey of what was possibly the most dysfunctional family she had ever come across in her entire career.

18

The meeting didn't last long, and everyone was in agreement. Lorraine would make the education of Marta a priority, and she would see to the birth registration. She would liaise with the police as their key contact, particularly in view of the two bodies found in the cellar, and there would be a whole army of experts on hand to help with the intricacies of leading this unique child into a world she had never known. They appreciated that Marta would have no knowledge of this, but the police would presumably want to speak with her at some point, and Lorraine should be there when that happened.

'This young girl is happy with her new name?'

Lorraine smiled at Kathryn Browne, her supervisor. 'She chose it. Marta Rose is a character who looks like her, with long blonde curls, blue eyes and a pretty face, and she was in the very first book Marta ever saw. Can you imagine living in a house with no books? When I left last night, she made me write Marta Rose out on a piece of paper I tore out of my notebook, and she was going to try and master it. She didn't even know what a pencil or a biro was...' Lorraine felt her voice break. 'But she will.'

'You're going to the hospital now?'

'I am, and I'm going to contact Wendy Needham later and go through everything with her. She's agreed – all of them have agreed – that they'll be delighted to take Marta, but I've only skimmed the surface with telling them Marta's background. I've still to get to the bottom of everything with Marta herself. She has such a limited vocabulary. She seems to understand orders. And she is well schooled in sitting still, not moving without permission, that sort of thing. The doctors are documenting all the scars. I haven't seen everything yet, but as I walked out last night, one of the nurses was visibly upset. She said Marta's back and her bottom were a mess. Old scars, she said. And there's quite a bad one on her arm caused by Janette Gregson throwing a knife at Marta, then dragging it down her arm. It didn't heal well.'

Kathryn touched her colleague's arm. 'Stay strong. We've seen some awful things in this job, and we can handle it. When she's settled with Wendy and Stewart, I'll go with you; I'd like to meet this child. There is a need to get her into mainstream schooling as soon as possible, but we simply don't know how fast she will learn. It's dreadful to think that if her mother hadn't fallen down those stairs, she could have gone through her whole life never learning anything.'

'I honestly don't think she realised there was stuff to learn,' Lorraine said. 'I'll be starting with reading, obviously, and basic number work, but she seems bright enough.'

Kathryn nodded. 'Okay. I suggest you have set hours with Marta, because you still have your other visits to fit in. It'll mean a complete re-jig of your diary but if you find it becomes impossible to complete visits, then come and see me. On the plus side, once Marta is in school, we can get back to our normal routine, so this overload of work won't last for ever.'

* * *

Marta smiled as Lorraine opened the door. 'Look what I did!'

She held up the piece of paper on which Lorraine had written Marta Rose, and the third version handwritten by Marta was almost a perfect copy. What was more impressive was the drawing underneath her name. It was a roughly copied picture of the fictional Marta Rose, replicated from the front of the book, instantly recognisable.

'Did you trace this picture from the book?'

'Trace?' Marta frowned, not understanding the word.

'Like this.' Lorraine placed the picture over the girl on the front cover, and shook her head. 'Of course you didn't. This picture is smaller than yours. You drew it. You obviously have your mother's artistic skills, so well done. Let me show you what trace means.' She removed another sheet of paper from her notebook, and placed it over the picture. The image wasn't clear at all. 'You would then go over the lines with a pencil, and the picture would be the same as on the front of the book.'

Marta's eyes opened wide. 'I didn't do that. I just looked at the book and I used the pen. Did I do wrong? I'm sorry...'

Lorraine saw tears glisten in the young girl's eyes and pulled her towards her, hugging her tightly. 'You did nothing wrong. Everything you do from now on will be teaching you how to live in the true world, not the way you have lived so far. Your name is beautifully written, and this drawing is wonderful. May I keep it?'

'Yes.'

'Thank you. And I'm going to make sure you have lots of drawing paper, pencils, felt tips, whatever you need, because this will be for your time. Whenever you feel you need to be alone, and you will because that is all you know so far, you can draw. Your mother did the same, which is how we know what sort of life you've had. But it's over now, Marta, and soon you'll be with two people, Wendy and Stewart Needham. They have a daughter called Ellie who is the same age as you. You'll also see me every day for quite some time, because I'm taking on your education, your learning. Reading will come first, because without reading, you have nothing else. Already you can recognise your name.'

She handed the newly removed piece of paper to Marta. 'Let's see if you can write your name without copying it. It's not a test, I just want to see how your memory is.'

Marta flashed a small smile, picked up the pen and carefully, slowly, wrote Marta Rose. She pushed the paper back towards Lorraine. 'Show me Gregson, please.'

Lorraine printed it, aware of the concentration on Marta's face as her eyes followed what the pen was doing. She pushed the paper towards Marta, who picked up the pen, holding it much more expertly than she had the previous evening.

'That's better,' Lorraine said. 'Does the pen feel more comfortable in your hand?'

'Yes.' Her tongue slipped out between her lips as she focused on 'Gregson', and she slowly formed the seven letters. She stared at it for a moment, then did it again. The second time was slightly large, but the letters were perfectly formed. The third time produced Marta Rose Gregson.

'Brilliant, Marta. There are...' Lorraine hesitated while she counted the letters, 'nine letters from the alphabet in your name. All names begin with a capital letter, and the smaller letters are called lower case. When we begin our lessons, we will mainly look at lower case, but you have to know English has twenty-six letters in the alphabet. Don't let that frighten you, you'll soon get used to seeing them all.'

They both looked towards the door as it opened, and a smiling doctor walked in. Lorraine barely caught Marta's words, but she knew she said *don't hurt me, please don't hurt me*.

'Hi, Marta. Love the name. I've just come to check the dressing on your back.' He turned towards Lorraine. 'We're looking at keeping her overnight, but if she continues to improve, I'm sure we can let her go tomorrow.'

Lorraine felt a surge of happiness at the news. 'Marta, turn onto your stomach so the doctor can see your back.'

Marta turned over slowly, and Lorraine watched as the doctor opened up the back of her hospital gown. Across the top of her buttocks was a padded dressing, quite large, and with the addition of micropore tape to hold it securely.

The doctor carefully peeled it away, and Marta made no sound. Lorraine sucked in a breath.

The wound was open, although appeared to be clean and healing.

The doctor bent closer to inspect it. 'Looking much better, Marta,' he said. 'When we send you home, I want you to continue with the antibiotics, we don't want this getting infected, and in a few days, the dressing can stay off. I would advise not wearing trousers until it is healed, we don't want a waistband aggravating it.'

He attached a fresh dressing, and as she rolled back to sit up once more, she thanked him. 'Thank you' seemed to be the phrase she used most often.

He blew her a kiss and waved from the doorway, and Lorraine swallowed to release the lump in her throat.

'How did it happen, Marta?'

Marta's head dropped. 'I spilt a glass of orange. Orange juice is expensive, don't spill the orange, Child. You'll be on water for a week, Child.' Marta's head didn't lift. 'She took off her belt. It cut me.'

'She hit you with the buckle?' Lorraine tried to keep her voice calm.

'Yes. Blood on the sheet, so she hit me in the face. That's why my eye turned this colour.'

Slowly Marta raised her head. 'If anybody hits me now, can I hit them?'

Lorraine wanted to say you certainly can, but chose her actual words more carefully. 'It's never right to hit somebody else. Marta, do you understand that you'll never be in that position of feeling threatened, of being scared, again? Your mother is never coming back. Do you understand death?'

'I do. Mother told me Billy had died, and that she had buried him. I never saw him again. Is that what dead means?'

'It is. Marta, later today I'm going to meet with the police lady who sat with you after you were found. Is there anything you need bringing from the house?'

Marta reached for the quilt on her bed. 'No, I have it.'

'This is the only thing you have?'

'Yes. Mother made it, but she said her mother started it. This is the word you said.'

'The word I said?'

Marta screwed up her face as she tried to recall what was obviously on the tip of her tongue. 'Flam something,' she said eventually.

'Well done. I think you mean family. And yes, it is a family thing. Your mother's mother is your grandmother. Most children would call her Nan, Granny, something like that. We will make a family tree when we have more information. Information means stuff that we know is right.'

'A tree like Marta's in her garden in the book?'

'Forgive me, Marta, I forget how little you know. No, a tree in a garden is grown there. Sometimes trees grow apples or pears in this country. You understand apples?'

'Yes. Sometimes I had one for a treat. I don't really like them. They make my mouth tingle.'

'That would be a sour apple, but some of them are sweet and taste very nice.'

'They grow on trees?'

'They do.'

'So my family tree, will it grow apples? I like bananas best.'

'It won't, my lovely girl. A family tree is a chart that we will write on as we find out more about where you came from, because your grandmother must have had a mother and a father, so we will add them into it. Everybody needs to know who they are, Marta, and over the next five years, you will find out from working on your family tree. Would you like to do that?'

Marta stared at Lorraine. 'It won't hurt me?'

'I promise it won't hurt you. You will enjoy discovering who you are.'

The door opened once again, and a nurse walked in, smiling, carrying a sandwich, a carton of milk, and a banana. 'Lunchtime, Marta,' she said.

Marta gave a huge smile. 'Did my family tree grow this banana?' she asked Lorraine, her eyes twinkling.

'Probably,' Lorraine said with a laugh. 'Eat your lunch, I'm going to pop down to the café to pick up something to eat and a coffee. I won't be long, but I'm going to find the newspaper kiosk and see if they have a sketchbook of some sort for you, so we can keep a record of what we do at this early stage. Do you know your colours, Marta?'

Marta picked up the banana. 'I know a banana is yellow, like my dress,' she said. 'I called banana sandwiches yellow sandwiches, until Mother said the right name one day. I like yellow best.'

19

The timeline created by the sketchbooks of Janette Gregson was fairly simple. The actual books had now been packaged up, and several copies had been made of the entire fourteen years. One set was in an envelope bearing Lorraine Lowe's name – Fleur wanted Lorraine to have all the information they had, as she believed Lorraine had a mighty task in front of her with the thirteen-year-old daughter of Janette.

She loved Marta's new name, and felt sad that Marta had seemed to pay the price for her mother having been raped. Locked into a room all her life, the youngster had known no happiness, had endured painful punishments, and love wasn't even in her limited vocabulary.

The first year of the sketchbooks, 1998, began in May, with vividly depicted drawings of a rape and a murder, although Fleur knew that if only Janette had dialled 999 immediately after hitting the rapist over the head with the cobbler's last, it would have been classed as self-defence. But she hadn't. The pictures told a story of a man being taken to the cellar, of him tumbling down the cellar steps, of the cellar door being sealed, presumably to stop the offensive odours from permeating the entire house, and a pregnancy test. They also told the story of a dog, Billy, who was sketched into almost every scene, and as 1998 drew to a close, the ever-expanding stomach was revealed inch by inch.

Fleur guessed that the diaries had only come into effect because of the attack and the massive change to Janette's life following the rape. Prior to that, Janette had produced work, but not the plethora of drawings evident post-attack. And drawings in her earlier life were nature studies and views, not rape on the kitchen floor.

The leaflet showing a missing Philip Hancock was attached, and in her mind, it confirmed their assumption of who the dead body was, although DNA results hadn't yet said yes or no.

Fleur had numbered each page in her copy of the books, and by the end of that first year, she had ten sheets. The second year had twelve, and three pages had been used to depict the stages of the birth. Then it moved on to building furniture, finding the half-finished baby quilt, the meticulous planning used to complete it, and a wonderful picture of the sewing machine that had been used for the final construction of the three layers of the quilt.

By the time Fleur had worked her way through 1999, she was itching to make a quilt herself, and wondering if she had enough of any fabric to make a start.

Her sheet of paper listed the contents against the sheet numbers, and she knew it was going to take some time to complete it, but in the absence of any DNA results, they were very much in limbo as to where to take the investigation next.

She hoped the following day would bring a little more enlightenment, and she lifted her eyes as she heard the gentle knock on her office door. She waved Lorraine through, and immediately stood to make the social worker a coffee.

'So how's our girl?'

'Doing well. They seem to be treating her like a princess in the hospital, and are hopeful they can release her tomorrow. There's a really nasty wound on her back, and they'll not let her go until they're satisfied that's getting better. That evil bitch hit her with a belt, the buckle end, then blacked her eye for bleeding onto the bed sheet. And it was all because she'd knocked over her orange juice.'

Fleur leaned across her desk and handed the envelope to Lorraine. 'These are your copies of the sketchbooks. She was an absolute cow through and through. I've not looked at them all yet, I'm working through them from one page to the next, and most of them are making my blood boil. It seems the only thing that merited any love from her was Billy, the dog. I've created a timeline so I know what she was doing and when, but whatever she's done, she's got away with it. That child will never recover from the abuse in her childhood, she has no idea what love means – such a fucking mess, Lorraine.'

'It is. We're going to try and build a family tree as part of her education programme, because I feel she needs to know who she is. She had no idea what a tree was, let alone what a family tree was. I tried to explain, but until we actually sit down and try to make sense of her background, I don't think she'll really under-stand. Bright kid, though. She'd never held a pen until yesterday, and now can already write her name, including the Gregson part. And she can definitely draw. She wrote her name, then tried to replicate the picture from the front cover of the Marta Rose book. Much better than I could have done. I guess she gets it from her mother.'

'And her grandmother. Her grandmother drew up plans for that quilt without being able to read or write. I'm looking forward to investigating her backstory, but Marta is very much at the bewildered stage, and still thinks that everything that is suggested for her is going to hurt her.'

Fleur handed Lorraine a coffee, then sat down, clutching hers. 'I'm hoping we'll have some answers by tomorrow. David said as soon as he has any test results, he'll contact me. We had a man go missing in May 1998. Nothing's been heard of him since, and I reckon David's going to announce the body from the cellar steps is Philip Hancock. His wife has had him declared dead, because there's never been any sight of him, he's never withdrawn any money, and I believe she has a new husband now. Both her kids are grown up and none of them ever really came up with any theory as to what might have happened to him. I think they always thought he must have fallen into a river and been swept away, but that was a bit of clutching at straws, they really had no idea. If it is him, it will put their minds at ease finally.'

'I remember that. I joined in with a search team in some woods. Was that really 1998? I'm getting old, Fleur,' Lorraine said, the frown creasing her forehead. 'But you'll have to tell them he raped Janette, so it might not put their minds at ease at all.'

Fleur sighed. 'You're right, of course. And there's no way I can hide the fact. There'll be an inquest where everything comes out, so we're better telling them at the beginning, then it's not a total shock. And that means, of course, that our young victim has a half-brother and -sister.'

Lorraine stared. Problems seemed to suddenly be mounting, and she had no idea how she would explain the half-siblings to a girl who knew nothing of the world. She was a child; she might have thirteen years of life behind her, but her mind was only about five years old at the moment, and she was going to have to grow up very fast.

Picking up her coffee, Lorraine stared across at Fleur. 'How the hell do we work with this? You're going to break the hearts of that family, if it is Philip Hancock, and I'm going to have to explain the word rape to a child who has probably never heard the word in her life before. And who the devil is the second body?'

'I don't know, but I'll bet anything Janette Gregson knew nothing about it. David was quite firm that the body tied to a chair was much older than the one chucked down the cellar steps.'

Lorraine frowned. 'Janette's mother killed him?'

'Well, it seems there were only the two of them, Barbara and Janette. Could it have been history repeating itself? They were very attractive women from what I could see on the couple of photographs in the house.'

'No pictures of any men in their lives?'

'Nothing,' Fleur said. 'We have spoken to Janette's solicitor at Craigson and Marple, and it seems the house goes to Marta, along with whatever money is left. She didn't leave a will, so everything is going to probate as soon as we confirm Marta's parentage. She will inherit when she reaches eighteen.'

'Well, it's a beautiful house, but it might not be by the time Marta moves in. We're looking at a minimum five years, possibly longer if she goes to uni.'

Fleur shrugged. 'There's nothing I can do to help with that. It is what it is. Will you tell Marta?'

'I will, but I think it will go well over her head. She really doesn't understand the ways of this world or any other, I'm afraid.'

'You going to see her tomorrow?'

'I am, I'm going to be the one who takes her to the Needhams, introduces her to all three of them. And I'm not leaving her until I'm sure she's happy there. It's time she had lots of care and attention. I think the Needhams will be good for her. They took Ellie, their daughter, when she was tiny, and formally adopted her three years later. It's been a wonderful relationship. I had a lot of contact up to the point of the adoption, then they became like any other family, but we've always kept in touch. Christmas cards, birthday card for Ellie, that sort of thing. They've had about half a dozen short-term children needing care before going to their forever homes, and I think they'll bring Marta out of her shell, back up what I'm trying to teach her with what they can introduce into her life.'

'And the daughter is the same age?'

'Very close. They'll be in the same class at school when Marta eventually starts.'

'Then let's hope they become friends.' Fleur made a notation on the timeline sheet. 'Janette used a lot of violent punishments to keep Marta under her control. She drew pictures of the more violent ones.'

'I intend looking through them tonight,' Lorraine said, 'so I probably won't sleep much. I hate that side of my job, knowing that so many kids are physically abused. They can't fight back. And I know Marta was getting older, but she was so downtrodden by this bloody woman that she would never have gone against her.'

David Fenwick tapped on the office door and opened it. 'Thought you might want to know what I've found. We put a rush on everything, so here's my findings.'

He pointed to the buff folder in his hand. 'Briefly, Janette died from a heart attack. She'd suffered from angina for quite a long time, so she didn't trip over the bedding, it just happened to be in her arms when the pain became too much, and she catapulted down the stairs. Her head hit the newel post, but there was very little blood. Her heart had stopped before she reached that point.'

He handed the folder to Fleur. She took it with a grimace. 'And our two bodies?'

'Both male, as I suspected. The first one, the one on the cellar steps, is definitely the father of our young lady. And what's more, I can tell you who he is. His name is Philip Hancock.'

The two women sat perfectly still, trying to keep straight faces.

'Well, aren't you impressed?'

'Nope,' Fleur said. 'We'd worked that out for ourselves.'

'Bloody women,' David said. 'So have you worked out who the other one is?'

'No. Have you?'

'Not who he is, but I know what he is. He's the grandfather of our young lady. No relationship between the two men, but a strong relationship between them and Marta.'

'Good work, David. We've no chance of his DNA being on any systems, then?'

'I'm running it. Just occasionally we have something from an old case that matches up with a recent one, but he's definitely not recent. He is, however, definitely the father of Janette Gregson, and therefore the grandfather of Marta.'

Fleur made notes on a separate piece of paper, and smiled up at David. 'This is such a help. What did he die of, this grandfather?'

'Well, believe it or not, he had an indentation in his skull that perfectly matches the one in Hancock's skull, so I think we can safely say the same thing, i.e. a cobbler's last was used to kill both men, although that's not strictly true. Philip Hancock was dead before he was thrown down the cellar steps, but this other chap died strapped into that chair, with a rug thrown over him. There are blood stains on the rug, so he was most probably alive when he was locked up in that cellar. It would have been an awful death.'

20

Marta didn't look scared or worried. She stood by Lorraine's side, and as Lorraine lifted her hand to knock on the door, it was opened by a small woman, her blonde hair screwed into a messy bun on the top of her head. Her smile was genuine, and her blue eyes sparkled as she saw the new addition to her family.

'Marta... you couldn't be more welcome. My name is Wendy, and this is Stewart.' She indicated with a wave of her hand towards the man who had appeared behind her.

'Welcome, Marta,' he said, his smile huge on his face. 'I feel really outnumbered now with all you blonde ladies in my house. Maybe I'll have to go blonde,' he said, with a casual rub of his hand through the glossy black hair on his head.

Marta tried to smile, but it was obvious it was forced. Wendy held the door wide, and everyone went inside, leading them through to the large kitchen at the rear of the house. Marta stared around her, the shock apparent on her face.

'What is this?' she whispered to Lorraine. 'There's no bed.'

'No, Marta, there's no bed. This is a kitchen.'

A girl, about six inches taller than Marta, stood and came towards her.

'Hi, Marta. I'm Ellie. Love your name. I asked Mum if I could decide my own name now, because I liked what you had picked, but she said no.'

Marta looked at the other girl, then gave a brief nod. 'Hello.' She stood as close to Lorraine as she could get, watching as Wendy turned to switch on the kettle.

'Marta, we're having a hot drink, but I know Ellie won't want that. She prefers milk, but we have Coke, lemonade, orange juice, so just say what you'd like.'

Marta turned to Lorraine. 'Is it a milk day?'

'I'm sure that in this house, Marta, every day is a milk day. Is that what you would like?'

'Yes, please.'

Wendy opened the fridge and beckoned Marta towards here. 'If there is milk in here, you can always help yourself. We have fresh deliveries every day and are never short of milk.'

Marta had never seen a fridge. 'Is this a wardrobe?'

'No, it's a fridge. Its posh name is refrigerator, but in our home, it's a fridge. It's cold, it keeps our food cold. This one, however, is even colder.' Wendy moved a few steps to the right and opened a door that matched the fridge door. 'This is a freezer. Everything in here is frozen solid. We have a lot of frozen food because Stewart works odd hours, and I can prepare a meal for him quickly from in here.'

It was obvious her words meant nothing to Marta, and Ellie took her hand. 'Come on, Marta, come and meet Archibald. We'll have a milk when you've met him.'

* * *

Marta felt panic wash over her. Ellie's hand felt warm inside her cold one, and she looked back at Lorraine, hoping the older woman would say stop, but she didn't. A smile of encouragement flashed across her face, and Ellie led her towards the patio doors leading from the dining area to the back garden.

Ellie kept hold of her hand until they reached a small wooden house, with a wire fence surrounding it. A rabbit sat inside, delicately nibbling on a small piece of carrot.

'This is Archibald,' Ellie said. 'He's two years old now. I take care of him mostly, but now you're here, we can share him.'

'Is it a dog?' It was the only animal Marta knew. Even Marta Rose in the book had had a dog.

'No.' Ellie smiled. 'He's a rabbit.'

'Will he hurt me?'

'He's never hurt me, so I don't think he will. I'll show you how to hold him. You're lucky to see him outside, he stays in his house when it's cold.' She changed the subject. 'Mum says you've never been to school...'

'School? Lorraine says I will go. What is it?'

'It's a place where you go to learn stuff till you're sixteen, then you can decide what you want to do after that. We'll be together in school. Lots of kids go, there's about a thousand in our school.' Ellie watched as a blankness spread across Marta's face.

'What's thousand?'

'It's a number. A big number. Did your mum not teach you maths?'

'I need to go to Lorraine.' There was a note of desperation in Marta's voice.

Ellie took hold of her hand again and led her back inside. 'Come on, let's get that drink of milk. And this mum will teach you things, so don't worry.'

Archibald finished his carrot and watched the two girls leave him before scuttling back inside to his bed of straw.

* * *

Lorraine felt a strong sense of unease and was about to stand and follow the girls into the back garden when Ellie and Marta reappeared at the patio doors.

'Mum,' Ellie announced, 'we need to start teaching Marta about everything and we need to do it today.'

Lorraine flashed a quick look at Wendy, and Wendy laughed at her daughter.

'Ellie, my love, it's all in hand. We'll all help in getting Marta to the level she needs to be at, so don't worry. Lorraine will be starting tomorrow, when you're back at school, and there will be some peace here.'

'Back at school?' Ellie looked horrified. 'What do you mean? I thought I was having the rest of the week off to get to know Marta.'

'We said you could have today off to welcome Marta. It's back to school for you tomorrow.'

Disgruntled didn't even begin to describe Ellie. 'Come on, Marta, let's get our milk, and I'll show you your bedroom.'

* * *

Even though the sun had disappeared behind a grey-looking cloud, the room gave off a welcoming glow. The curtains and quilt cover were matching, with yellow sunflowers everywhere. A large vase of artificial sunflowers stood on the windowsill, and Marta walked straight across to the window and looked out. The bedroom overlooked the back garden and she couldn't see any sign of Archibald.

A white desk had been placed against one wall with a matching typist's chair tucked neatly under it. The laptop was closed, and Marta touched it. 'What is this?'

'It's a laptop... a computer. Have you never seen one?'

Marta shook her head, then repeated the word laptop.

'It will help you with your studies,' Ellie explained. 'I'm pretty good with technology, but Dad is superb. It's necessary for his job; got his own business making blinds, but a lot is done on the computer before they're made. Any major problems, just go to him.'

Ellie sat on Marta's bed and watched as Marta walked around the room, touching everything. She couldn't imagine never having seen anything of the world before, and yet that was what Mum and Dad had explained to her – that Marta had been locked in a bedroom all her life.

'I don't have a toilet.' The words were said in an absent-minded kind of way, almost as if it wasn't something important.

'You do. Let me show you.'

Ellie led her onto the landing. 'You and I will share this bathroom. Mum and Dad have an en suite, so at the moment, there's only the two of us for this one.'

A frown creased Marta's brow. 'What if I need to go during the night?'

'Then you go.'

'Who will unlock my door?'

Ellie felt sick. 'There are no locks on any of the doors inside our home, except the bathroom. The only locks are on outside doors. You can go wherever you want inside here.'

Marta walked to the door and opened it, looked carefully for a keyhole and closed it again.

'Oh.'

Ellie smiled at her. 'You'll get used to it. Mum's brilliant, and Dad is as well, but he's away a lot with his business. They'll fill your bookcase with books when they know what Lorraine recommends for you.'

'Books? I will have more books?'

'You can have as many books as you want. You haven't seen my room yet. And you know the biggest thing is you haven't yet read *Harry Potter* for the first time. I envy you that. I've read every one twice now, but nothing beats that first time of reading them.'

'Harry Potter?'

'He's a wizard. You'll love him.'

Marta walked towards the white bookcase. Every shelf was bare. She ran her hands over the top shelf. 'This is mine?'

'It is. I've got two because I've a huge collection of books, but I'm sure they'll get you a second one if you fill this one up. You lived in a house without books?'

'I did. I have one now. It is the book about Marta Rose in Poland. Lorraine gave me my own copy this morning because I couldn't take the one from the hospital.'

There was a brief knock on the door, and Lorraine opened it. 'I've brought your holdall, Marta. Maybe Ellie can hang up your clothes with you, and we'll get you some new stuff later this week.'

'Oh, thank you, Lorraine.' Marta unzipped the bag, fished around inside it and produced the book. 'See,' she said to Ellie, 'this is my first book for my bookcase. Would you like me to read it to you?'

Lorraine smiled. 'Give me chance to teach you first, young lady.'

Marta sat on the edge of the bed and Lorraine's heart froze for a second. She looked exactly as she had first seen the young child. Marta nestled the book on her knee and looked at the picture on the front. 'This is a story about Marta Rose who lives in Poland,' she began, then proceeded to tell the whole story word for word, exactly as written in the book. Lorraine and Ellie stared at Marta, who was still looking at the picture. She finished with the words 'the end', and lifted her head.

She waited, and Ellie clapped. 'Awesome. How do you do that?'

'It is in my head,' Marta said. 'Lorraine read it to me because I don't know...' She hesitated. 'I don't know letters yet,' she finished triumphantly.

'And it's all in your head?' Ellie looked bewildered.

'Yes.'

'Marta, have you heard of an alphabet?' Lorraine spoke quietly.

'No.'

'It begins with A B C.'

'No.'

'Listen to me, I'm going to say it two times. That is one, two. You understand?'

Marta nodded.

'A B C D...' Lorraine continued through to Z, then repeated the letters once more.

She waited as Marta seemed to be processing what she had just heard. Then Marta smiled. 'A B C D E F G H I J K L M N O Q P R S T U V W X Y Z.'

Both Lorraine and Ellie clapped and Ellie said, 'There was just one tiny mistake.'

'I know, Ellie,' Marta said. 'It wasn't a mistake, I was checking if you knew your alphabet. I said the P and Q the wrong way round.' She then repeated the whole twenty-six letters once more, this time letter-perfect, and dipped her head in acknowledgement of their laughter.

'You have a hidden cheekiness, Marta Rose Gregson,' Lorraine said. 'I can see interesting times in front of us, as you appear to have a brain and a half. Now get Teddy and your quilt unpacked, your clothes hung in the wardrobe, and head back downstairs. We have a timetable to sort out, and we must do it today.'

21

Fleur felt sick at the thought of going to the late Philip Hancock's house. There had been intermittent contact with Theresa Hancock over the years, but it had only been to report that there was nothing to report. Alex and Olivia, Hancock's children, flashed across her mind and she knew they would both now be in their early twenties, and possibly no longer at home with their mother. And it seemed that Theresa Hancock was now Theresa Palmer.

She thought it best not to warn in advance of her visit, so knocked on the door with no idea of anything beyond telling Theresa the bad news. The young man who opened the door had clearly fulfilled the promise of tallness he had shown as a ten-year-old.

She smiled. 'Alex? DS Lavers.' She indicated Alan, standing behind her. 'PC Jenkins. Is your mother at home?' She remembered, just a little too late, to wipe the smile from her face.

'She is. It's a long time since we've seen you,' he said, suspicion on his face.

'Your mother?' she asked again.

'Sorry, yeah, come in. She's not been up long. She's on the first cup of coffee, so she might not bite.'

He led them through to the kitchen, where Theresa Palmer was looking through the newspaper, and nursing a large mug of coffee. She glanced up, surprise on her face.

'Sorry,' she said. 'I thought it was the postman. It's Flora, isn't it?'

'Fleur. But near enough. Can I sit down?'

'Of course. Coffee?'

'That would be lovely, thank you. Alex still lives with you, then?'

'Not really, but he went to some local gig last night, so crashed in his old room rather than going to his flat. Olivia still lives at home; she's in her final year at uni, in Sheffield, so decided to stay where it wouldn't cost anything.' There was a brief pause. 'Why are you here?'

'Is Olivia at home now, or has she left for uni?'

'She's still in bed. Alex, you want to wake her?'

'If I have to. Best make her a coffee, you know what she's like when she wakes up,' he laughed.

'And your husband?' Fleur persisted.

'He's at work. Look what's going on? Alex, for goodness' sake, go and get your sister out of bed. Then these people can tell us all whatever it is they've come here for.'

Alex handed Fleur and Alan a mug of coffee, and headed upstairs. They could hear him trying to wake his sister, and her muffled comments as she tried to get rid of him. Eventually he came downstairs and re-joined them in the kitchen. 'Give her five minutes. She'd got as far as sitting on the edge of the bed, so that's a good sign.'

Olivia joined them without speaking, her short dressing gown wrapped around her, took the proffered mug from her brother and scowled at everyone. 'You do know it's only just after nine?'

'And good morning to you, darling,' her mother said. 'Now sit down. Fleur clearly wants to speak to all of us, so drink your coffee quietly and come round a bit.'

Fleur waited until everyone except Alan was seated. 'Okay, I have news for you. You have to be aware I am giving you facts, none of this is supposition. A body has been found, and has been formally identified as Philip Hancock.'

There was a choking sound from Olivia, and she put down the drink she had been cradling for comfort. 'Alex...' she wailed.

Alex pulled his chair closer to her, and put his arm around her shoulders. 'Hang in there, sis. We knew this might happen one day.' He turned to Fleur. 'Where? Where did you find him?'

Theresa carefully put down her own cup and stared at Fleur. 'Exactly what I'd like to know. Where did you find him?'

And with those few words, Fleur began the longest half-hour of her life thus far.

* * *

Alex accompanied Fleur and Alan as they walked down the path towards the Jaguar. He stared at the car appreciatively, then thanked them. 'I know it's horrific, what my father did, but he didn't deserve to die. Punished, yes. But death? It does seem murderers run in the family, doesn't it?'

'There will be an inquest when it is all revealed,' Fleur said. 'You and your stepfather will have to be very supportive of Theresa and Olivia when that time comes. Just warning you. It will bring the media here like hornets. The child conceived at the time will be identified as Child A, you won't know her name, but the details will come out at the inquest.'

He gave a thoughtful nod. 'He told Mum he was going out to pick up some cans of beer. I think there was a football match on that night. He must have planned it; you don't accidentally go to someone's house and rape them, do you?'

'We'll never know the full story, but we do know most of it thanks to the detailed drawings by Janette Gregson. Although I can't show them to you until this is all over and verdicts have been reached for both of the bodies we found, I think you will eventually come to understand that the drawings are even more powerful than words. She even detailed sealing up the cellar door, and because she dated each drawing, we can tell when every incident happened.'

Fleur climbed into the driving seat and lowered her window. 'Help your mum. This will be a difficult few months, but at least she now has closure on what happened to your father. And Olivia will need you. Is Brad Palmer a good stepfather?'

'He's ace. If I'm honest, he's done more for us than my real father ever did, but... Philip was my dad.'

Fleur reached into the side pocket and fished out her card, then handed it to Alex. 'If you need me, any questions, anything, that's my number.'

She drove away, keeping him in her driving mirror for as long as she could. He didn't move.

* * *

'We got a match.'

Fleur lifted her head from the report she was writing and stared at David Fenwick. 'What?' With her head still on the visit just completed and the report she had to write detailing it, it sent a small frisson of fear through her that David was only just confirming the match.

'The second body. I just let it run through the database, and we got a match with a crime committed in 1973. There was blood left at the scene, a newsagent robbery. The newsagent managed to injure the chap who attacked him, and it all fizzled out, really. The blood was placed on file, the feller was identified as Eric Yates but he disappeared off the face of the earth. Now we know why. And it matches his DNA. If we do some careful working out of dates, I think the shop attack was only days before he was killed, and I'm certain he was killed by Barbara Gregson. She lived alone in that house and like her daughter was a bit of a recluse. He was definitely, beyond any doubt, the father of Janette. And he was bashed on the head by that cobbler's last, but she tied him to that chair while he was still alive. She left him down there to die.'

Fleur stared at David. 'Well done! Two deaths cleared up, both old cases. You'll get an MBE for that, won't you?'

'Hope not, I haven't time to go to the Palace to collect it. I'll send you all the details, all the proof, in my report, but I just wanted to pop up and tell you myself. It's been quite a fascinating trio of cases this, all interlinking. I hope the little lass comes out of it okay. It'll be a heavy burden for her to carry for the rest of her life, I suppose.'

'She starts her official education today. She's gone to live with very experienced people who have a daughter the same age, and I had Lorraine Lowe on the phone last night telling me Marta has amazing memory powers. That at least is something good going for her, because she needs to be in mainstream education as soon as possible, to learn life skills as well as reading and writing and bloody numbers.'

'You're not good at numbers, then?' David laughed.

'My bank manager says I'm crap at numbers. Something about overdrafts and suchlike.'

'Good luck with that, then.' He closed the door and left Fleur to her thoughts.

She stared at the report, recognising that she'd completely lost the thread of what she intended to write next. She pushed her keyboard to one side and walked to the window. There was a glimmer of sunshine, reflecting in the rain-filled puddles of the car park, and she stared, mesmerised by the pretty flickers it created.

'Tea,' she said to herself. 'Fleur, you need a cup of tea.'

Alan had clearly read her thoughts because he knocked and opened her door. 'Am I just in time?'

'You are,' she said and reached for a second mug. She made tea for both of them and handed Alan his mug.

'I saw David,' he said. 'Interesting that we've got a name for the chair man as well as the steps man, as well as for the woman at the bottom of the stairs. Three bodies, sorted.'

Fleur laughed. 'All requiring reports. But you're right. Three suspicious deaths, cleared up speedily and tidily, but leaving us with a traumatised child who may never recover from the actions attributed to her parents and grandparents. And I don't doubt Alex and Olivia Hancock are both feeling pretty traumatised right now. All this crime, all these deaths, and we'll get the kudos and the congratulations for having cleared it up so quickly, but really we've done nothing; science has done most of it, and we're left with people who may never recover from this.'

She sipped at her drink, and sat down at her desk. 'Sit down, Alan. Let's take some time out. That was hard this morning. Although Theresa didn't look surprised, did she? The kids were completely shocked, but she wasn't. Maybe there's stuff we'll never know about, stuff she'll keep to herself, happy that it will never come to light now, never hurt her or the children.'

'You reckon? Maybe he didn't treat her too well. Let's hope they can put it all to one side now, and get on with life knowing he's dead, because even when you have somebody declared dead, there's always got to be that worry at the back of your mind that they might just turn up one day, completely out of the blue.'

She smiled. 'It must be awful to have somebody walk through the door after years away and say, "Hi, honey, I'm home," or words to that effect.'

'Theresa must have been expecting today for a long time. I think that's why she didn't really react. In fact, I think she knew we were there to confirm his death as soon as she saw us walk into her kitchen. And I don't think she was that surprised by news of the rape. The kids were horrified, but she wasn't.'

'You're right. They're going to have this on their minds for ever, but Theresa isn't. For her, it will be relief.'

Fleur's computer told her she had an email, and she saw it was from David. 'Guess this is the full report from our wizard in pathology. He's the one who sorted this for us, no doubt at all.'

'I like David. No airs about him, but he did ask me if we could step back a bit on the body count because he's going out tomorrow night whether he's got dead bodies or not.'

Fleur grinned. 'We'll try. Can't guarantee anything, though. Drink up, we'll go and tell the DCI what's happening; that'll cheer him up a bit.'

22

The girls reached their fourteenth birthdays within a month of each other – January 2013 saw Marta get there first, followed in February by celebrations for Ellie.

But it had been the Christmas festivities that had dumbfounded Marta. She had no idea of the concept of Christmas, and queried everything she was told about the events in the Bible.

'They rode a donkey, she had a baby in a stable of all places, and we ended up with a tree the size of a house to celebrate it all. Have I got that right?'

Ellie lifted her head from her notebook and looked at the girl she now considered her sister. 'Kind of. We celebrate Christmas because Jesus was born, but lots of people don't actually believe that. I'm struggling to believe you've never had a Christmas present, or a mince pie or anything else that goes with Christmas, like turkey and Christmas pud.'

'I'd never even heard the word until Lorraine told me about it. We've done a lot of work on it since then, but I feel a little scared by it.'

And Christmas morning was something that almost blew

Marta's mind. Ellie had insisted they go to bed early so they could get up at dawn to open gifts, but Marta couldn't comprehend what exactly was to happen so in the end had a night of only intermittent sleep, her brain refusing to shut down.

Her first Christmas Day was something she knew she would remember for ever. She had so many gifts, both girls benefiting from an assortment of goodies sent them by the police personnel they had grown to know, and Lorraine had bought them new winter coats after taking the advice of Wendy. A gift that both of them loved had come from Wendy – she had knitted them a scarf each, Gryffindor colours for Marta, Slytherin colours for Ellie, and they kept them on all that joyous day. Marta had finally embraced *Harry Potter.*

* * *

Two weeks later, and a day after Marta's fourteenth birthday, Lorraine restarted the lessons that she knew would soon be at an end. Marta's retention of everything she was told and shown was truly remarkable, and Lorraine had been to see the head of the school to discuss Marta's case, and the likelihood of her starting school after Easter.

Jack Kenning confirmed it wouldn't be an issue and she would be in the same class for all lessons as Ellie; they were keen for her confidence to grow and not be knocked by feeling alone in a strange new world of education as the government decreed it should be.

'Her mother taught her nothing?'

Lorraine shook her head. 'Nothing at all. She was abused physically, and quite regularly. It didn't take much to upset the mother. She does have talents that will benefit from being with a tutor who will work closely with her – she is an excellent artist. When I first met Marta, she hadn't even seen a pencil before, but now she has filled several sketch pads as she works to perfect her drawing skills.'

The headmaster stood. 'Don't worry about her, Ms Lowe. I'm sure Marta will settle in very well, and I'll call a staff meeting to explain Marta's issues before she starts. You say she has a photographic memory?'

'It's not just photographic. If she hears something, if she sees something, she remembers it. It's truly phenomenal to witness. If she'd had a normal childhood...' Lorraine sighed.

'I'm sure she'll prove to be a valued member of our school, just as Ellie Needham is. Ellie is well liked and well respected, and Marta will learn from that. Now, let's set a date for you to bring her in. I suggest you leave her with us for the day; I promise we'll take good care of her, and she'll learn where the communal areas are around the school. I'll make sure she sees a fair bit of Ellie, and she can begin a more normal life after Easter. Does that sound good?'

'Mr Kenning, it sounds excellent. I shall miss her like crazy, but we're rapidly reaching the stage where she needs the next level, something I can't take her to. She needs to prepare for future exams, and I was a primary-age teacher before joining social services, not a senior-age teacher. I can't take her beyond where we've reached now, and if she hadn't had this memory gift, she would have really struggled to ever get into mainstream education, I'm sure. As it is, it's me who's now struggling, and not her,' she finished with a laugh.

They shook hands and Lorraine left his office feeling much more settled in her mind.

* * *

'This is you,' Marta said, and pushed a piece of paper towards Lorraine.

'Me?' She picked it up and stared at it. 'May I keep it?'

'Of course.' Marta's maturing voice had retained the sing-song quality that Lorraine had heard the first time she had seen the little girl sitting on the edge of her bed, unmoving.

'You haven't signed it.'

'I didn't know what to put. Maybe I should still be Marta Gregson because I won't be Marta Needham for another two weeks. But then I'm Marta Needham forever, so maybe I should just sign everything Marta without a surname, and you're going to say shut up in a minute, aren't you, stop waffling, Marta.'

Lorraine roared with laughter. 'I only tell you to stop waffling when you're trying to get out of studying something that you don't like. And are you truly happy to be Marta Needham? You don't speak much about it.'

Marta shrugged. 'It makes sense. Ellie and I will be proper sisters then, with the same surname, and the same parents, and when Wendy and Stewart die, we'll inherit this house and all their money equally.'

A shiver ran through Lorraine's body. 'I don't actually think that should be a consideration...'

It was Marta's turn to roar with laughter. 'I knew that would wind you up. I've agreed to being adopted because I love these people you've found for me, and it would make no difference if they had no money at all, they love me. Don't you understand? I never had love, didn't even know it was a word until you and Fleur rescued me. Of course I'm happy to be a Needham, I just didn't want to jinx things by signing your picture Marta Needham.' She took the picture out of Lorraine's hands, picked up her pencil and wrote *Marta Needham, February 2013* in the bottom corner. She handed it back to the woman who also loved her.

Lorraine slid the picture into her briefcase, inside a folder to keep it from being creased. She knew it would be in a frame and on her wall before the end of the day.

* * *

Two hours later, Wendy knocked on Marta's bedroom door and opened it. She was carefully balancing a tray with drinks and biscuits on it, and Lorraine and Marta looked up with a smile.

'Yeah!' Marta said. 'Chocolate digestives.'

Lorraine sat back, pushing some paperwork to one side. 'That's a very welcome sight, Wendy. This little genius in front of us is testing me sorely today, and I need coffee.'

Wendy smiled. 'What's she done now?'

'She's using words in her essays that I'm having to look up.'

Wendy placed the tray on the table, and swept her arm around the room. 'We've asked a builder to come and give us a quote for building proper bookshelves into this room. As you can see, she's already filled two IKEA units in what's turned into a library rather than a bedroom, and ask her what her favourite book is.'

Marta blushed. She had taken some stick for it the previous night with comments about a crap storyline, and everything else her family could throw at her.

'Marta?' Lorraine almost felt afraid to hear the answer.

'The dictionary,' Marta mumbled.

'In case you didn't catch that, Lorraine, she said the dictionary.'

Lorraine picked up her coffee and sipped at it. 'So that's why I don't understand some of the words?'

Marta nodded. 'Trying them out. Correlation. Complexity. Conversant. Criminality. Words I hadn't heard before – I read the Cs last night,' she finished with a grin.

'And it's the Ds tonight? Marta Rose, you're an awesome child. I can't wait to see how this school handles you when you walk in and take over the head teacher's office.'

There was a sudden shudder from her. 'I'm scared of going to school.'

'I know,' Wendy said. 'We're all a little scared for you because it will be such a big change in your life, but think of all you have been taught over the past year, and know that it is just the beginning of two years of concentrated learning to get to your GCSEs. Then there will be a further two years to get to your A levels. With your learning capabilities, Marta, you will do it. None of us doubt that, and then the world is yours to do with as you wish. You can choose what happens next, whether it be university or some other direction you wish to take.'

Lorraine kept quiet, recognising this as important mother and daughter time. She picked up a biscuit and listened to the gentle way Wendy spoke to Marta, passing on her own confidence as she built it in Marta.

'And I will be with Ellie?'

'Every step of the way. And don't forget Ellie has many friends at school, both boys and girls, who are all going to be looking out for you. You won't be alone. Although the children know that your mother died and you became a ward of the state, they don't know anything beyond that. You're simply an orphan who has found a new family who all love you very much.'

'And nobody will hurt me?'

'With Ellie by your side? No, nobody will hurt you, precious Marta.' Wendy clasped her hand. 'Why would anybody hurt you? You cause no trouble, you're polite, and at a letter a day in the dictionary, you'll soon know every word in the English language.'

She stood and walked round to Marta, hugged her and planted a resounding kiss on the top of her head. 'I'll leave you two to carry on, sorry for disturbing you. Lorraine, can I have a quick word when you've finished lessons for the day? I'll probably be in the garage; I'm throwing stuff out and trying to get it so we can actually put a car in it.'

Lorraine glanced at her watch. 'I've a meeting at three so we're finishing a little early anyway. I'll be about an hour?'

'That's fine. I'll definitely still be in the garage in an hour. In fact, could be in it for a week,' she said with a laugh as she left Marta's room, closing the door gently behind her. She would miss seeing Lorraine every day, but what a change that absence would bring to her family.

* * *

Lorraine and Marta finished off the work started earlier, and then both sat back with relief.

'Intense,' Marta said. 'You've worked me hard this morning.'

'It's what it will be like as you approach your GCSEs, especially for you because I've had to try to give you eight years of our education system in one year. When I started this journey with you, I had no idea what to expect, but you've made it so easy and so wonderful, Marta. Have you had any thoughts about a future career?'

'I have, but I'm not sure it's practical. Although I love learning, I also love my art. I've watched television shows and people who are like me have studios where they don't have to pack everything away, they can get up in the morning and simply paint, or draw, or just create. Is it wrong of me to want that?'

'Oh, Marta,' Lorraine said. 'Although it will be nothing to do with me by then, I will move heaven and earth to help you with that. Hold on to your dreams, my Marta. Who knows what your future holds?'

23

Marta sat between Wendy and Stewart, clasping their hands tightly. She couldn't for the life of her remember what the man had said his name was, but she knew it didn't matter. Whatever it was, her future was being held in his hands at the moment.

Ellie reached across her father and squeezed Marta's hand. No words were needed; this was Marta's family and they were there for her on this special day.

The man removed his glasses, closed the file that was open in front of him and smiled at the small family.

'Marta Gregson, I am delighted to tell you that I have approved the application for adoption, and you are now Marta Needham. I wish all of you the very best for the future, and I'll leave you to the celebrations that I'm sure are now planned for this wonderful day.'

He stood and left the room, but the Needham family didn't see him go through the door. They were all on their feet, hugging each other, crying.

* * *

Lorraine and Fleur were waiting for them at the restaurant, and even more tears flowed. They were shown to their table, where champagne was waiting in an ice bucket.

It was a noisy lunch with much laughter, especially when they made Marta confess to being on the letter N in the dictionary. 'I wasn't going to go past the letter N if the judge said no,' she said with a wicked grin. 'N is for Needham.'

'Judges don't take kindly to blackmail,' Fleur answered with a smile, 'so it's a good job you didn't mention it to him.'

It was just before they were thinking about heading home that Marta reached into her bag and produced a beautifully wrapped package. 'This is for you.' She handed it to Stewart and Wendy.

Wendy opened it carefully. Inside was a framed picture of all of them, Wendy and Stewart standing behind their daughters, a pen and ink drawing, and signed *Marta Needham, 15 March 2013*. It was exquisite.

'Oh, Marta,' Wendy breathed. 'Oh, my love. Welcome to our life, our world.'

* * *

Marta headed up to her room to change into something more comfortable than the formal clothes she had worn for court, and paused at the mirror on the front of the wardrobe. She touched her finger to the finger that reached back to her.

'Hi, Child Two,' she whispered, 'we did it.'

She nodded, and Child Two nodded. Together, they'd done it.

* * *

Ellie handed Marta her new backpack, and grinned at her sister. 'You look great. I'll show you how we shorten our skirts when we get to school, but make sure you lengthen it before we get back home.'

The navy-blue uniform with a white shirt was compulsory, and Marta did a twirl for her mother and father as they came into the hallway.

'Fantastic,' Wendy said. 'Now come on, we don't want to be late today.' She ushered them out the door and to her own car, newly acquired the day after they had acquired their second daughter.

It seemed that with after-school clubs for two daughters, life would probably become more complicated very quickly, so a second car was felt to be necessary.

The journey to school was short, the girls almost silent. Wendy parked in the school car park, and walked with Ellie and Marta to the main entrance, where she was directed to the headmaster's office.

Jack Kenning greeted them with a smile. He had been impressed by the young Marta when he had first met her, and he was looking forward to monitoring her progress as she went through the next two years under his care.

'Good morning, girls, Mrs Needham. Mrs Needham, before you head back home after delivering these two precious charges, do you have any questions?'

Wendy knew when she was dismissed. She smiled. 'No, I don't think so, Mr Kenning. I just wanted to make sure they were safely with you.' She turned to them. 'I'll pick you up tonight, but after that, you're on your own when it's a normal finish time. Okay?' She wiggled her fingers in a goodbye gesture, and left them to their first day together in education.

They watched her go, Ellie feeling a little overawed by being in the head's office first thing in the morning, Marta simply scared to death.

He led them out. 'First lesson is English, and for this final term of the school year, Marta, you'll be shadowing Ellie in everything. We will work out individual timetables in the run-up to GCSEs when we know your choices. September will be a very busy period for both of you. Now let's get Marta introduced.' He opened the door that said 'Niamh Chambers' on it, and immediately there was silence.

'Good morning, everybody.'

There was a muted chorus of good mornings back at him, and he pulled Marta and Ellie in front of him. 'As some of you already know, we have a new starter this morning. This is Ellie's sister, Marta. Marta has never been in mainstream education before, so I hope you will all treat her with consideration, but most of all friendship. She will accompany Ellie at all times, as she needs to learn her way around the school, and discover our systems.'

He took a look around, as if impressing every child in that class into his brain. 'If I hear of anything, anything at all, that causes any problems for these two girls, either one or the other, you will be suspended while I investigate the issue. I will leave it to you to explain to your parents why you can't go into school. Is that understood?'

Every child either nodded or said, 'Yes, sir,' in response. He had no doubt his words would be dismissed as soon as he was out of their sight, but what they didn't know was that it wasn't just a threat of punishment, it would actually happen. It was his job to get this poor lassie through her school years. He had received the social services report on her background, and had been horrified by it. A hidden child. How could that happen in this day and age?

He'd make damn sure she wasn't hidden now.

* * *

And Marta wasn't hidden. For the first week, she was in several different classes with Ellie, finding her feet, learning her way around the school, meeting some of Ellie's friends that she had already met at the Needhams' home, and meeting new ones she hadn't seen before.

She remained in the background, watching how Ellie mixed with everyone, and especially noticing how her sister didn't only chat with the girls, she was equally friendly with the boys. Marta's experience of boys was virtually zero.

When Harry Banton approached Marta on a sunny May afternoon, she was sitting on the grass, reading *The Tempest*. He sat down beside her, and she jumped.

'Sorry,' Harry said, a slow smile spreading across his face. 'I didn't intend making you jump, I just wanted to say hello.'

'Hello,' she responded, not having a clue what else to say.

'You like Shakespeare?'

'Yes. He was very clever with words. Not just with storylines.'

'Couldn't agree more. We did *Macbeth* in the first half of the year, before you started here, and I thought it was brilliant. You're settling in okay?'

Marta gave a brief nod, looking surreptitiously around for Ellie. She needed rescuing. She didn't do talking to other people.

Ellie was talking to a couple of girls, unaware of the panic building in her sister.

'You always look scared.' Harry smiled at her. 'You don't need to; we're all looking out for you. We know you never went to school, so if you've any problems, just ask any of us.'

Marta stood and brushed the grass from her skirt. 'You know nothing about me. And if I need to know anything, I ask Ellie.' She turned her face towards him. 'And don't ever underestimate me.' Her stare was cold, hard and angry, and Harry involuntarily flinched.

Marta's sudden act of standing up had drawn Ellie's attention towards her, and Ellie whispered something to the girls before running towards Marta.

'Piss off, Banton. Keep your drugs for the kids who want them, and don't come bothering Marta.'

'You're a gobby cow, Ellie Needham. One day, it'll get you into such a lot of trouble...'

Ellie stepped in front of Marta. 'I said piss off, Banton. Even your mates are talking about you upping your game, so it's only a matter of time before Kenning hears about it, and then you'll be gone. Now leave Marta alone, because I swear if I see you near her again, it'll be me who's telling Mr Kenning.'

Harry bent and retrieved his bottle of water from the grass. 'Fuck off, Needham. One word from me about how good it was shagging you behind the canteen and your little miss goody-two-shoes rep will be shot to hell.'

Ellie felt the rage build inside her. 'Nobody would ever shag you behind the canteen or anywhere else, Harry Banton. Now fuck off, and if I see you near Marta again, or any of my mates, you're done for.'

He spat on the grass, and headed up the slight incline with a swagger.

Marta felt herself wrapped in someone's arms, and saw it was Rosie Shaw, one of the girls Ellie had been talking with. She froze, then slumped against Rosie. This was not the time to show she didn't like any form of support; that would come in the future when she knew she would be stronger.

'We've got your back,' Rosie said, 'but maybe it's time we told you who it's best to avoid and who is okay. Harry Banton's dad deals drugs. You understand about drugs?'

Marta gave a little nod. 'I was home-schooled for a year, and we touched on it. Lorraine, my teacher, explained they take away control if you use them, so to always say no. I didn't think they'd be available in school, though.'

'They're not. Harry's dad won't risk Harry being caught with them on him, but if anybody wants anything, they tell Harry and he organises it with his dad, who turns up at the school gates two or three times a week. The police have been several times, but funnily enough, not at the times when Banton senior is there.'

Ellie's eyes had remained on Harry until he was out of sight, then she turned back to Marta. 'You okay? How can anybody get into trouble while they're sitting on the grass reading Shake-speare?' She smiled at Marta. 'Did he mention drugs?'

'Not sure I would have known what he was talking about, but no, I don't think he did. We actually talked about Shakespeare.'

'Just avoid him. He's bad news, but one day, it'll all come crashing down.'

The small group of girls headed back to the school building, with Ellie seething inside. She had kept everything quiet, knowing it would be a stupid move to set Harry against Marta, but she had felt it was necessary to send him away from her sister. Marta was still vulnerable; a few days in school weren't enough to give her any sort of savviness about school life. She needed protecting from the Harry Bantons of this world, and she would get Ellie's whole-hearted support.

* * *

Geography wasn't the best subject to finish the school day, but at least they didn't feel too stressed by the time they headed out of the doors.

'Bus or walk?' Ellie asked.

'Let's walk. It's a lovely day.'

'Okay, I'll let Mum know.' Ellie texted Wendy, and they set off for a comfortable half-hour stroll.

'You feeling okay about school?'

Marta smiled. 'I'm learning lots. Still a bit jittery around the others, though.'

Ellie slipped her arm through Marta's. 'That'll get better the more you get to know them. It's because you didn't see anybody but your mother for all those years.'

Marta nodded. 'I know. Puzzled about one thing, though.'

'What's that?'

'What's shagging?'

24

Marta finished her essay on the political changes in Tanganyika since 1950 and its subsequent inclusion in Tanzania, and sat back with a sigh. It had been difficult because she hadn't even heard the word Tanganyika prior to that afternoon, but a quick flick of the switch leading to her brain meant she only really needed to see the information once and it was locked inside her for ever.

She read through all 1,500 words once more, smiled and nodded, and sent it to her printer. Just maths homework now, and she could get back to her book. The printer stopped and she gathered up the papers, happy to read it through one more time to make sure everything was okay. The first page was fine, but then it was very clear that subsequent pages had suffered from a lack of ink.

She rifled through her desk drawer to get a black ink cartridge, but the drawer revealed a lack of any cartridges.

She opened her bedroom door and listened for any sounds telling her that Ellie was upstairs. She heard a giggle, and guessed her sister was chatting on her phone, so she tapped on her door and opened it. She smiled at the anger she knew Ellie felt when

Marta interrupted her lengthy phone chats with her friends, and began talking as she went through the door.

Ellie smiled at her and waved her in. 'I have to go, Abbie, see you tomorrow. Bye.' She disconnected and looked at Marta. The smile had disappeared. 'You okay?'

'Not really. Have you taken a black ink cartridge from my room?'

'Oh... yeah, I did. Sorry, I meant to tell you, but I forgot.'

'I can't print off my essay. If I email it, will you print it on your printer, please?' Anger was evident in Marta's tone, but Ellie didn't respond in kind.

'Course I will. I'll probably do it tomorrow morning before school, don't panic. The new ink should be here tomorrow, anyway, I did remember to tell Mum we needed some.' She grinned. 'I can't do it yet, though, I've to go and clean out Archibald's hutch, and feed him. You want to help?'

'No, I've other homework to do.' Marta's tone had changed; sullenness had crept in.

Ellie stared at her sister. A couple of times lately, she had seen a different side to Marta, and yet she had no idea what was causing it.

'I'll print it as soon as I've finished our rabbit, if I've time. If not, I'll make sure you have it before we leave for school.'

'He's your rabbit,' Marta said, and headed back to her own room.

* * *

The moonlight lit up the back garden, and it was close to midnight when Marta quietly opened the back door and slipped outside. Ellie had been asleep for quite some time, but Marta had hung on to make sure that Ellie wouldn't spot her outside. The two girls' bedrooms both overlooked the back garden, but all other rooms overlooked the front of the house. Tonight, Ellie would find out it was wrong to steal ink cartridges – even to enter Marta's room without her knowledge – and it was certainly the wrong action to delay printing off the homework when she was the one who had caused the problem.

She crept stealthily towards the rabbit's home, inserted the tiny key always kept hanging by the back door into the padlock, and opened it. She removed the lock, and laid it on the grass, then opened the hutch door that would normally give Archibald access to his run. This time, the run, standing by the side of the hutch, hadn't been carefully fastened into place; this time, Archibald could make his own decisions.

Marta moved stealthily back to the kitchen door, re-hung the padlock key, and locked the house up securely once more. Lesson one, Ellie Needham. Don't fuck around with Marta Needham. She ran the tap, got herself a glass of water and headed back upstairs. It always paid to have a reason for being somewhere she wouldn't normally have been, she figured. *Sorry, Mum, I didn't mean to wake you. I was thirsty so got up for a drink.*

* * *

Archibald, ever curious, pushed his nose through his open door and shuffled out onto the grass. By the time Marta had snuggled down in bed, ready at last to go to sleep, the rabbit had ventured under the hedge and into the garden next door. Within the hour, he had left the Needhams' cosy quarters, and was on the playing fields, running scared and with no homing instincts at all.

* * *

Ellie took out a fresh bottle of water for Archibald before leaving for school, and Wendy ran out of the kitchen at some speed as she heard her daughter's screams.

'What's wrong?' she yelled as she ran towards Ellie.

'He's gone. I found the padlock on the grass, so I must have forgotten to lock him in after I cleaned it all last night.' Ellie was sobbing, and Marta put her arms around her.

'Come on, El, let's go look for him. He's probably still in the garden,' she said, turning a troubled face to her sister.

They split up and began to search the garden, Ellie growing more desperate by the minute, Marta trying to stop the smile from showing. Wendy had disappeared round to the neighbours to ask if she could search their back garden, and they could hear her telling the tale of the disappearing rabbit to all the neighbours, until Marta began to grow concerned that somebody might find the animal.

But it didn't happen, and when Marta tentatively suggested to Ellie that she could maybe get another one, it caused even more grief. Ellie was distraught and trying to hide it. She knew the padlock had been locked, because as she had pressed the arched top into place, she had trapped her skin, extremely painfully, bad enough to leave a blood blister on her right index finger. Only one person would have opened that padlock, only one person.

Round one to Marta, or so Marta thought.

* * *

Lorraine visited the Needhams every six weeks or so, not as a social worker but as a friend. A couple of times she had collected the girls from school, and loved to hear them chatter about the day they had had, whether it be good or bad, and she simply waited for Marta to grow up.

Following a lengthy meeting with Janette Gregson's solicitors, it had been agreed that Lorraine would keep an eye on the property to make sure it didn't fall into disrepair before Marta would inherit at the age of eighteen.

As a result, she called in every three months or so, checked there were no leaks, and forwarded all mail to the solicitors. She opened doors to let in the fresh air, dusted the furniture and let her thoughts dwell on Marta, and how she would be when she had to eventually make decisions about this property, and about the money that was increasing, sitting in a bank waiting for her.

She had recognised a very bright, inquisitive mind in Marta, and wondered if she would go on to university, or do what she had always wanted, to become an artist. Would she want to do both?

That sunny afternoon, sitting in the lounge of Marta's eventual home, Lorraine looked around her. She knew that if Marta decided she would live here instead of selling it, it would very quickly become a different place. Janette had lived in a brown home. Everywhere felt brown, and she could only imagine how depressing it must have felt to the little girl growing up and spending all her impressionable years in the one brown room upstairs.

Now she had colour, and she knew that would continue into her adult life, a life possibly spent in this house.

* * *

Lorraine went around closing all the windows and doors, safe in the knowledge that the house felt so much fresher than when she had arrived. She walked past the cellar door, and cautiously opened it. Fleur had organised for the cleaning company the police used for cleaning up crime scenes to come in and clean the downstairs room, but Lorraine went no further than the cellar head. She wondered what Marta would want to do with it – leave it as it is, or block it up and pretend nothing had ever happened down those steps, her mind closing down to the two bodies, her father and her grandfather, both finishing their lives underneath her house.

She had four years to get her thoughts in order, to care for this house and keep it in good repair for a possible new incumbent, to talk to Marta and discuss her options. It would be so hard not to influence her, but she had to guide her, not push her.

Lorraine locked the door behind her, and walked to her car. Time to head back to work, to a job she was finding increasingly frustrating, but at least it kept her in contact with the young child she had grown to love. She picked up the large envelope addressed to Dominic Craigson at the solicitors keeping an eye on Marta's affairs, and placed all the mail inside it. There had only been half a dozen items; as the months passed, the mail got less. A two-minute stop-off at the post office saw the envelope on its way, and she arrived home feeling lonely and out of sorts.

* * *

Ellie opened up the attached document in Marta's email, and felt an overwhelming sense of anger. She picked out three words in the perfect essay and changed the spelling, then printed it out for her sister. She'd make damn sure smart-arse Marta didn't get an A for this essay, and she would simply plead ignorance of any misspellings in her sister's homework.

But Marta would know, and Marta would know that she knew what Marta had done; she giggled at her convoluted thoughts. Marta might think she could put one over on her sister, but she was about to find out she couldn't.

* * *

Marta received a B+ for her essay, marked down because of three spelling errors. The note at the bottom said it would have been an A if the errors hadn't been there, and Marta needed to take more time proofreading her work in order to get the higher grades she usually enjoyed.

At lunchtime, Marta left the group she normally spent the hour with, and went to sit on her own. She had broadened her own horizons by not spending every minute of every day with her sister, and she had been welcomed by others keen to get to know the girl who had gained notoriety by dint of her early life. She needed time to think, had immediately understood the situation when she saw the comments on her work, and knew when she checked the original document saved on her own laptop that it would show correct spellings.

Her head was thumping, her headache spiralling out of control, and she realised things could never return to how they were between her and Ellie. They were two like minds, intent on being top dog in their sisterly relationship.

She watched, her eyes almost closed against the glare of the sun, as Harry Banton walked towards her. He sat down by her side, and looked around.

'No Ellie?'

She shrugged.

'Watches you like a hawk, doesn't she? Time you told her you've got a life of your own. Fancy a smoke?'

She looked at him with disgust written across her face. 'Piss off, Harry. Nobody in their right mind smokes. And that says it all, really.'

'Oooh, miss high-and-mighty, get you. I meant an ordinary fag, you know, not a spliff. You fancy going out one night? Movies or something?'

'No, thanks.'

'You sure? My treat.'

'No, thanks.'

She stood and looked down at him still sitting on the grass. 'You're a born loser, Harry. Keep away from me, I'm not interested in having anything to do with you, not now and not in the future.'

'Well, if you don't fancy a quick snog, I'll ask Ellie. Then we'll see how you feel.'

She laughed. 'Yeah, go on, ask Ellie. You carry on pretending you don't know what she's likely to say. She'll spread it all around the school that both of us turned you down, so go on, Harry, ask her.'

25

Lorraine was surprised to get an early-morning call from Craigson and Marple, asking if she could find a ten-minute slot to pop in and speak with Dominic Craigson.

'Of course I can,' she said to the throaty-voiced secretary. 'You okay, Hannah?'

'Streaming cold, but I'll live,' was the rejoinder. 'Mr Craigson is free between ten and eleven today, so shall I book you in for half past ten?'

'That will be fine. Do I need to bring anything?'

'No, it's something to do with the mail you posted yesterday to us. He opened it and immediately asked me to ring you, specifying this morning if you could do it. He also asked that if Mrs Needham was free, could she accompany you.'

'Good lord, what on earth did I send him? I thought it was mainly junk mail. And of course I'll see if Wendy is available.'

Hannah laughed. 'Judging by his reaction, I'm guessing something wasn't junk. I don't open any mail that's personally addressed to either of the partners, so I can't begin to even guess what has thrown him off balance, but he'll explain later, I'm sure. Coffee and biscuits at 10.30, Lorraine. You're in the diary.'

The two women disconnected, and Lorraine stared out of her window, deep in thought. They had set up annual meetings to discuss Marta's finances, and go through Lorraine's report not only on Marta but on the property she would inherit. Expenditure would be approved if anything needed repairing at the house, but that first meeting had thrown up no problems back in January. It now seemed something had cropped up. She picked up her phone and rang Wendy, who confirmed she would meet her at the solicitors.

Lorraine quickly typed up her report of the previous day's visit, noting that she had dusted throughout the house, checked all the taps were working efficiently, and checked there had been no attempts at unlawful entry at any point. She printed it off and popped it into her briefcase, ready for it to be added to Marta's file. Everything in that file would be handed over to her on her eighteenth birthday.

Logging onto the online diary, Lorraine added her appointment time at the solicitors, and left the office. She was a little early so sat back in her car and looked around her. This job suited her so well, and she thought back to her early career in teaching. Without that time on her CV, she would never have been allocated to Marta's case, and she blessed her decision to work those early years with five- to eleven-year-olds. She had watched the blossoming of Marta as if she was a flower; Marta Rose was indeed a perfect name for her.

She hoped the meeting requested for this morning wasn't about anything that would cause issues for the young girl; Marta had suffered enough.

She parked in the Craigson and Marple car park, gathered up

her bag and briefcase and walked through the automatic doors. Wendy was already there waiting for her.

The receptionist informed Hannah of their arrival, and the two women walked down the corridor leading to Hannah's room, which in turn opened into Dominic Craigson's office.

Dominic stood to shake their hands. 'Lorraine, Wendy, glad you could fit me in this morning. Hannah's getting us some coffee, so we'll wait until that arrives.'

They filled in the five minutes or so with chit-chat about Marta, and settled back once Hannah had left the room.

'Hannah will hear about this eventually,' Dominic said, 'because obviously she types my letters and I am going to have to respond to one, but I wanted both your thoughts before deciding what to do. In those few letters you sent me yesterday, Lorraine, was this one. The envelope was addressed just to the address, not to any one person, and, like you, I thought it was probably junk mail. It wasn't.'

She took the paper from him, and spread it out in front of her. At the top was a mobile phone number and an address.

Hello to the girl who lived here,
My name is Alex Hancock, and I am your half-brother.

Lorraine looked up and met Dominic's eyes, firmly fixed on her, assessing her reaction.

Our life paths briefly crossed when my father's body was discovered in the cellar of the house where you had been hidden away by your mother. She, apparently, killed my father after he raped and impregnated her with you.
I hope and pray you already know these facts, as I don't want to surprise you with them.

I would like to meet you. I have a sister, Olivia, who has tried to talk me out of doing this, but I feel it is important. I don't know where you are now, but I do know the house is still in your mother's name so I'm assuming you still have a connection with it.

I would love to hear from you, even if it is just to find out your name initially, then hopefully we can meet one day soon.

I look forward to our new relationship.

Alex

Lorraine read it through twice before passing it to Wendy, then lifted her head to look at Dominic. 'This has been an ever-present fear as far as I'm concerned. We knew as soon as the facts became known publicly at the inquest that there might be repercussions. We've managed to always keep Marta's name and whereabouts out of it, but she was thirteen when it all blew up, not a young child whose memory would eventually fade.'

'What do you want me to do?' Dominic watched as she picked up her cup and took a sip to calm herself down.

'Is going to his house and shooting him out of the question?'

'It's frowned upon.'

'Then I don't know. My first instinct is to ask you to write to him in your official capacity as her solicitor without revealing anything about her, but somehow I don't think even that will make it go away. If he's determined to find her, he will. I wonder if I went to his home and spoke to him...'

'Not advisable, Lorraine. You don't know anything about him, he could be a psychopath, he could have mental issues... we really don't know, and I would strongly advise against you going, especially on your own.'

Wendy was reading the letter for a third time, and eventually she handed it back to Dominic. 'So what are your thoughts?' she asked the solicitor.

'I suggest I write to him today, very politely, and explain we'll keep his address on file until such time as the file goes to his half-sister on her eighteenth birthday.'

Lorraine sighed. 'Marta is quite strong-willed. I hope we're making the right decision on this, because I'd hate for her to decide when she sees this letter that we should have consulted her when it arrived.'

'You want to consult her? You could do it without her actually seeing the letter, I suppose, then she won't know where he lives.'

'No,' Wendy interrupted with some force. 'I'm so afraid she'd want to see him. As an adult, I can see the potential problems in them meeting up, but she is still a child and won't see issues that could go wrong. This is a nightmare situation, and I honestly never saw it coming.'

Dominic sat back in his chair and sipped at his coffee. 'We have to make a decision. I have to respond to him, that's a given, but it's how I respond that's the issue in front of us.'

Lorraine straightened her spine and sat up. 'Okay,' she said. 'I'll put on my big girl's pants and tell you what I'd like to happen. Tell him no, not at this time, but when his half-sister is old enough to make her own decision, she will have sight of his letter, and subsequently will either contact him or not, but it will be her choice.'

Wendy nodded. 'And I agree with that. This is a massive thing, and she's simply not mature enough to make any plans for something so huge and that could impact the rest of her life.'

'I think that's sensible, ladies. It's the avenue I would have taken, but I needed you to tell me. I'll dictate the letter, Hannah will type it and she'll email it to both of you for your approval before we send it. I also suggest you tell Marta's dad about it, so he is aware, Wendy.' He hesitated. 'You know, if the letter had been... warmer, I might have reached a different thought. It just felt so stilted and formal, and it worries me that he's blaming our Marta in some way for the death of his father.'

'My thoughts exactly,' Lorraine responded. 'Let's hope he puts it out of his mind for the next four years or so, and maybe by then Marta will be on her way to university and out of his life without ever being in it.'

She stood, carried both hers and Wendy's cups to the tray, and shook Dominic's hand. 'Thank you for caring, Dominic.' Wendy repeated the handshake, and followed Lorraine to the door.

'No problem.' Dominic smiled. 'I've seen the reports of what Marta went through before Janette Gregson died. I will always do everything in my power to protect her, and I'm sure you both feel the same.'

* * *

The subject of their discussion had been called into Jack Kenning's office for a general chat about how she was feeling.

When she asked for extra homework in maths, he was almost reduced to speechlessness. 'Extra homework?'

'Yes. I'm aware I'm not at the same level as the others, and the tutors make allowances for me, but that needs to stop. If I did extra, I would soon be at the same stage, or even beyond them, because I've only just over a year before GCSEs start.'

'You can handle extra homework?'

She nodded. 'Yes, it gets me out of doing things like helping with meals, doing dishes, that sort of boring stuff.'

Kenning laughed out loud. 'You'll not be going into the hospitality business when you graduate, then?'

She smiled. Marta liked this man. 'Not likely. My ambition is to be an artist, with my own gallery. But first it will be a degree in art history, I think. I may change my mind, but that's my aim at the moment. Yes, I like English and maths and I certainly enjoy all the sciences, but if I could earn a living making beautiful things, painting beautiful pictures, being generally creative, I would be happy.'

'Then that will be our goal. Making Marta happy. I will play a small part in that and ensure you have adequate art time on your timetable over the next two years, and we'll speak again when we need to start making decisions about your future. You're still a child...'

Kenning watched as her cheeks visibly flushed. She stood. 'My name is Marta, not Child.'

If Jack Kenning could have cut out his tongue, he would have done. Child. She had been called Child for the first thirteen years of her life, and he had just used the word, although not in the same context.

'I'm so sorry, Marta. Forgive me, I was thoughtless. It won't happen again. Please sit down.'

'I'd like to go back to class now.' Her tone was icy.

He nodded and escorted her to his door. 'Of course. And I am sorry, I wasn't using the word as your name, merely referring to your age.'

She dipped her head quickly, and left his office. Kenning hoped she was indicating that she understood and he watched her walk away, her shoulders held rigidly. He felt sick. Of all the kids under his care, this one was the most fragile, and he had clumsily put both feet firmly in whatever was still wrong in Marta's life.

26

Alex Hancock was lying on his single bed, his hands behind his head, staring upwards. There was a damp patch on the ceiling that a previous tenant had, with a degree of skill, turned into a portrait of Winston Churchill, complete with cigar. When Alex had put a coat of white paint on every wall immediately after moving in, he had chosen to leave Churchill where he was; today his eyes were firmly fixed on it, for no reason other than in concentration.

It had been a week since he had pushed the letter through the letterbox of his half-sister's home, the house she had shared with her killer mother. He knew she couldn't be there, she was too young, but at some point, he guessed somebody would check out the property, and check out the mail.

It was almost an ache inside him that he knew could only be helped by talking to her, by finding out exactly what had happened in that house, because somebody must have worked it out by now. It seemed she had been the result of the rape, so obviously knew nothing unless her dead mother had told her. Though the police-woman had said quite clearly that the girl knew nothing, he hoped it was otherwise. He didn't even know her name, although the inquest had revealed the mother's name.

He recognised an obsession when he saw one, and he knew he was obsessed with seeing her, with speaking to her. Did she resemble him? Did she share his interests? He no longer felt as close to Olivia as he had once. Olivia had been disgusted by what they had discovered about their father, and a blazing row between the siblings had resulted in very little interaction since, but maybe this third half-sibling could heal them. Or not.

He checked his watch and rolled off the bed. A five-minute walk would see him outside the betting office where he worked, time enough to put him in a better mood for dealing with the customers. Thoughts of her could be shelved for the rest of the day.

* * *

Marta and Ellie set off for school together, both pleased that it was the last week of term. Ellie's feelings towards Marta had changed; she knew Marta had released the padlock on Archibald's hutch, but had wisely kept it to herself. Nobody would have believed her anyway. The golden girl came across as a well-behaved, quiet member of school and society in general, but Ellie knew. Oh, Ellie knew. One day, her time would come, and Marta would pay in triplicate.

They walked along in silence, eventually meeting up with Rosie, who waited for them every morning. Marta began to chat to Rosie immediately, leaving Ellie to feel more and more left out of things.

It was during the last lesson of the day that Ellie's unhappiness, instigated by her sister, erupted into anger. The class was having a group discussion about *The Tempest*, and about the final speech that was believed to be Shakespeare's own final withdrawal from his writing. The class had been pre-warned that they would be having the exercise, and Ellie had spent a considerable amount of time on it.

The discussion was opened by the teacher who then threw it out for feedback from the class. Several hands were raised, including Ellie's, but Marta was chosen to speak.

Ellie's mouth fell open as she heard words coming from Marta's mouth that were her own words on the document that she thought was password-protected in her computer. Marta spoke in her gentle, sing-song way, glancing down every so often to check if she had missed anything on the paper in front of her.

She eventually sat down and Ellie stood. 'That was my work.'

There was silence as everyone looked at her. Rosie leaned across and touched her arm. 'Sit down. You'll end up in bother.'

But Ellie didn't sit down. She looked around at everyone. 'You all know me. I don't cheat with homework or classwork, I just do it. That was my work.' She stormed out of the classroom and ran down the corridor, heading for the toilets.

The tears came quickly, and she locked herself into a cubicle. She tried to stifle the sound of her tears when she heard the door open and Niamh Chambers call her name.

There was a gentle tap on the cubicle door, and again Ellie heard her name. She slowly slid back the bolt, and stared at the teacher.

'Look, it's almost home time. Go to the secretary's office, tell her I've asked you to wait for me there, and as soon as I've dismissed the class, I'll come along to talk to you. That okay?'

Ellie nodded, misery written all over her face.

* * *

'So you're saying Marta must have accessed your files?'

Ellie nodded. 'I put the password on my computer before Marta came to live with us, and it's never occurred to me to change it. It's only schoolwork that's on it, anyway.'

'Okay.' Niamh looked at her watch. 'Is Marta waiting for you to go home?'

'No, she goes to the after-school art group tonight. I walk home alone.'

'And what time will you be home?'

'Four.'

'I want you to immediately email me that file from your computer. Here's my personal email.' She scribbled it down quickly and passed the small piece of paper to Ellie. 'Immediately, Ellie, so I know it's already on your computer. Marta would have got an A for that presentation this afternoon, the arguments she used, the conclusion she drew. If it's not her work, she doesn't get it. It's as simple as that.'

Ellie stood. 'I'll go now. I'm okay, I'm over it, and I apologise for running out. I've just had a rotten time recently, and it was the killer punch.'

Niamh nodded. 'I really do understand. Now go and send me that document.'

Ellie walked away, hating what she was becoming. Prior to Marta's arrival, school had been the place she loved. Now it wasn't. Now Marta had infiltrated everything, and caused damage not only to Ellie and her friendships, but it had also seemingly spread to her work. Thank god for Niamh Chambers, who had believed in her.

* * *

The email arrived five minutes before four o'clock, and Niamh read it with a sinking feeling. It was very clear who had done the work and who had stolen it. She could have done without the complications this near to the end of term, but she knew she had to speak to both girls, and she had to make it very clear to Marta that it was unacceptable to copy homework done by someone else. Ellie had put at the end of her email that she was about to change her password, and nobody would know it.

As Marta had left the classroom at the end of the day, she had screwed up the piece of paper she had used to help her give the presentation, aware that even a photographic memory couldn't take in almost 2,000 words, and casually tossed it into the wastepaper bin as she passed it. As soon as the classroom was empty, Niamh had rescued the A4 sheet of paper and smoothed it out. With the arrival of Ellie's email, she was able to compare the two documents, hoping and praying they would be different enough for nothing to be proven. They were identical. Clearly Marta had simply accessed her sister's file and sent it to the printer.

All she had to do now was decide how to tackle this, given they all tended to walk on eggshells around Marta Needham.

* * *

Jack Kenning listened quietly to what Niamh Chambers was telling him, then held out his hands for the two pieces of paper, one directly from the printer, the other crumpled from being in the bin.

He scanned them quickly, then rubbed his eyes. 'You have to speak to them both, but I suggest separately.'

'I know. And if it had been any other pupil but Marta, I wouldn't even have troubled you with it, I'd just have made a note on their record, and dealt with it, but Marta is... different. I never have to tell her anything twice, she has a phenomenal memory that absorbs facts and retains them, so why she felt it was necessary to do this, I don't know. I should have known something was wrong, because nobody else had anything written down, they simply spoke about what was in their head with regard to Shakespeare's words, but Marta had this printed piece of paper, and she kept glancing down at it all the time she was speaking, as if checking she wasn't missing anything out. She has this phenomenal memory, but even she can't remember something of this magnitude. And if she'd only seen it the night before, she couldn't remember all of it. I believe she hadn't done the work, and thought she'd hijack Ellie's presentation. Totally unlike her. Then it all exploded when Ellie shouted out it was her work, and ran from the room. We had an initial chat after I found her in the toilets, then a longer one after school. Look, Jack, I know Marta is a special case, but she's smarter than 90 per cent of the kids in this school. She surely knows right from wrong.'

Jack gave a small shake of his head. 'She's fourteen now. For her first thirteen years, she was locked in a room, and I don't believe she even knew there was a right and a wrong when it comes to normal behaviour because she never had to display any normal behaviour. And she's only had to learn in a class of her peers for what? Three months? You have to treat this with velvet gloves, Niamh. With both girls.'

'I know. I am constantly aware that they're sisters, and that makes everything more difficult.'

'Well, they may be sisters, but they've only known each other for eighteen months, and they've not had much chance to bond, with Ellie having been in mainstream schooling and therefore away from home during the day, and Marta with adults learning her ABCs. They're certainly not sisters in the way the Mayberry twins are sisters; you couldn't prise those two apart with a crowbar.'

* * *

Marta listened to her English teacher with her blue eyes swimming with tears. She was starting to learn the value of crying; during her early years, it had brought harsher punishment, but she was beginning to realise it had definite benefits in getting whatever she wanted.

'I'm sorry,' she said, in between gulps. 'I only put my hand up because I thought I was safe to do that. I never get chosen to speak. All the other teachers leave me to sit and listen, but this time you called out my name. I'd printed Ellie's work off to sit and read through it because I knew she'd put a lot of effort into it.' The tears now flowed down her cheeks, and she let them run. 'Then Ellie ran out the room and I knew I was in trouble.'

'Not trouble, Marta. I just needed to explain to you that one of the biggest lessons we try to instil into our pupils is you do your own work. You don't steal from other people, or ask anyone else to do it for you.'

Marta kept the tears running, and she sniffed. 'I'll apologise to Ellie. I didn't see her last night, she stayed up in her room, or else I would have said something then. And this morning we were dropped off by Mum, so again I couldn't talk.'

'Okay, Marta. You must realise you have the most difficult two years of learning ahead of you when you return in September, so please remember what's happened here. Remember it always. I don't doubt you will go on to uni, and there you're not given second chances. Apart from all of that, you don't need to cheat. You're one of the brightest kids I know, and I don't doubt you'll go on to achieve great things. But let it be by your own efforts.' She pushed the box of tissues across to Marta, who took one and stood.

'Thank you, Miss Chambers. And I am sorry.'

* * *

Ellie listened to Niamh without tears, then quietly walked away from the pastoral room. She knew that once again the golden girl had pulled the wool over someone's eyes, and she vowed that one day she would get even – maybe not this year, maybe not next year, but one day, Marta Needham would pay for perfecting the little girl lost persona. She would pay a lot.

27

Alex Hancock watched the clock slowly creep towards three o'clock, then downed tools. 'I'm off,' he said to his cashier, who was acting manager for the next hour until the evening manager arrived to start his shift.

'Okay, Alex. Have one for me.' Alex grinned and lifted a hand in acknowledgement.

The Hogshead wasn't very busy, and he ordered a pint and a cheese and pickle sandwich, before sitting in a booth where he wouldn't have to chat with others. He had been an outgoing type of person until the news had broken about his father, but now he had taken to hiding himself away from the world, limiting conversations, even with his punters in the shop, to the bare minimum. Alex knew he had turned into a recluse, and he didn't know what to do about it.

He finished his drink and sandwich and stood to leave, again without speaking to anyone in the pub. He walked quickly home, letting himself into the entry door and picking up his mail from the table before climbing the stairs to his own bedsit.

He put the letters on the small dining table and moved towards the fridge. The water was cooling, and he drank deeply before screwing the top back on the bottle. He stepped into his minuscule shower before changing into shorts and T-shirt, thinking he might head out for a run later.

He picked up his mail, discarded two junk envelopes and stared at the third one. The back flap of the envelope said the name of a solicitor, and he sensed immediately it concerned his half-sister. The solicitor had been quick to reply; his own letter had been pushed through the door of the late Janette's house only a week earlier. He had expected to wait some considerable time for a response.

He picked up the bottle of water and again drank deeply before investigating the contents of the envelope. He opened it carefully, and eased out the letter.

Dear Mr Hancock,

It is with regret that I have to tell you that we will not be forwarding your letter at this time to your half-sister.

As you know, in three and a half years she will be eighteen, and at that time, we will be handing over a file to her. In that file will be your letter to her, and a copy of this letter we are obliged to send to you. She will then be able to decide whether she wants to meet with you or not. Whichever way that decision goes, it will be hers, and hers alone.

Thank you for your query, and I hope this answers it fully.

Regards,

Dominic Craigson

Alex felt sick initially, then he felt angry. And finally he felt defeated. January 2017 seemed an age away.

He put the letter back in the envelope, and stood, feeling the chair tip and fall backwards onto the small bedside table. He picked it up and slid it back under the table before looking around the tiny room. How could he have thought he could bring his half-sister here?

Time to take stock, step back and bring the plans to fruition that had been part of his future before the truth about his father had been revealed. He needed a proper home, he needed a car, and he needed a personality. He would prepare, and ultimately convince her that he was a brother she would want to meet, and he would mend bridges with Olivia, bring her on board with the idea of meeting their sister. It was time to forget the pain of the Philip Hancock debacle; he was dead, and it was burial time. They would be a family of siblings.

* * *

The last day of the school year was sunny, and all the pupils had been told they were finishing at lunchtime. The Year Elevens had left in May, and Marta and Ellie's Year Nine colleagues were shown where they would be on the first day of the new school year as they returned as Year Ten pupils. The Year Ten pupils, soon to be Year Elevens, walked around trailing backpacks, investigating their new rooms and feeling worried about the prospect of exams starting pretty soon after their return in September.

Jack Kenning watched as pupils crossed the yard, chatting and laughing, and spotted Ellie Needham with a couple of her friends. Marta was with other friends some distance away and he sighed. Could they have handled it differently? Maybe if Niamh had spoken to them together instead of individually?

He left his room and clattered down the stairs, heading towards Marta.

'Marta! Where's your sister?' he called.

She turned and pointed. 'There.'

'Okay, come with me.' Marta looked at the two girls she had been talking to, and shrugged. She followed the headmaster across to where Ellie was, and he led both off to one side.

'You've fallen out?'

The girls dropped their heads and stared at the floor.

'Then listen to me. Ellie, you have been the absolute star of Year Nine, and I don't doubt that you will be exactly the same in Year Ten. Marta, you've only been here for one term and you have shown where your future is leading. You are sisters, and shouldn't allow something so trivial to come between you. I do realise you have learnt your lesson, Marta, and I really do understand what happened, that you never expected to be called upon to speak in class.'

Ellie looked up at him. 'What are you saying? That what she did was okay?'

He shook his head. 'No, but I am saying it's not a big enough issue to fall out over.'

Marta turned to Ellie. 'He's right, Ellie. And I am sorry. I thought I was just picking your brains, not taking any credit for anything. Nobody ever asks me to speak in class, not yet, anyway. I promise next term will be all my own work, not yours.' She smiled at her sister, allowing a glimmer of tears to infiltrate her eyes.

Ellie paused, then smiled back at her. 'Okay, big sis. We'll forget it. You can't get into my computer anyway now.'

* * *

They left school at twelve o'clock and walked home together. The conversation was a little strained, but they steered clear of talk of stealing homework, and Wendy was waiting for them as they walked up the path.

'Chicken salad for lunch, girls, then tonight we're having McDonalds and the cinema.'

'Yeah!' Marta squealed in delight. She had only been three times, and loved the experience each time. Especially the popcorn. 'What are we going to see? Please say *Monsters University*.'

'Rosie's been. She says it's brilliant,' Ellie chimed in.

'Oh, good grief. How do I tell your father we're going to see *Monsters University*?'

The girls laughed. 'Not our problem.' They headed to their rooms to change out of the uniform and into shorts.

Wendy shook her head, a smile on her face. The girls appeared to be okay today; it had been a stressful couple of weeks. They seemed to have stopped talking, but hopefully they'd sorted out whatever was wrong. One term, Easter to July, and her girls had changed. She hoped they could look forward to six weeks of peace, before they restarted in Year Ten.

* * *

The girls and Wendy loved the film. Stewart loved Wendy and his girls, so he tolerated the film. They arrived back home still talking about various scenes that he felt he must have missed, and wondered how much of the film he had snoozed through.

He poured himself a small whisky, and switched on the television, but after scrolling through decided there was nothing he wanted to watch. How could anything compare with *Monsters University*? All was quiet upstairs, his wife was making some cheese and biscuits in the kitchen, and he allowed his thoughts to roam. They had never hesitated about adopting Marta; she had been a wonderful addition to their family from the very beginning, bright, and an absolute glutton for learning. Lorraine had never had to nag her to do anything, she wanted and needed to learn, and the wonderful skill of photographic memory was something he so wished he had.

He hoped she was as happy with them as they were having her to permanently live with them. They saw very little of Lorraine since Marta had started school, and for that he was sorry. He knew Lorraine must miss the delightful girl. Although he had never seen the scars on his newest daughter, Lorraine had spoken of them, and he wondered just what the child had done to merit such actions from her mother. Beaten with the buckle end of a leather belt? He couldn't begin to imagine how life would have turned out if Janette Gregson hadn't had the heart attack that killed her.

Marta had already been thirteen, and Janette couldn't have held her prisoner for ever. Or could she?

He looked up as Wendy carried in a tray bearing cheese – several different sorts, he noticed with delight – and some biscuits, plus two large mugs of hot chocolate. There was a small dish of pickled silverskin onions, and he felt his salivary glands begin to work overtime.

'The girls joining us?' he asked, reaching across to help himself to a plate.

'They've taken crisps and chocolate biscuits up to their rooms.'

'They're not on a diet then?' He grinned, helping himself to the food on offer. 'This looks delicious, slave wife.'

She picked up a pickled onion and threw it at him. For a second, he looked shocked, then picked up the onion from the floor and threw it back at Wendy. She launched herself at him, pinning him to the sofa and began to smother him with kisses, shrieking with laughter while he yelled, 'Get off me, woman! This is physical assault!'

The door opened and Ellie looked in. 'For goodness' sake, can you wait until we've gone to bed before you start your sex games?'

'They're not sex games,' Stewart protested, trying to extricate himself from under his wife. 'She threw a pickled onion at me.'

'You probably deserved it. Mum, can I have a quick word?'

'Is it women talk?' Stewart asked, continuing to load his plate with cheese and biscuits.

'It is,' Ellie said, blowing him a kiss from the doorway.

He blew one back to her, and Wendy followed her daughter through to the kitchen. 'You okay, sweetheart?'

Ellie nodded. 'Just something that's on my mind. Mum, do you ever have stuff on your computer that's about either me or Marta? Private stuff we shouldn't know about yet? About our adoptions, I mean.'

Wendy hesitated, remembering the email that had arrived the day before from Dominic. It had contained an attachment of the copy of the original letter from Alex Hancock, plus the letter that would by now probably be with the young man. 'Erm, yes, I suppose so. Why?'

'And is your password still *meandstew*?'

'It is. How did you know that?'

'It doesn't matter how I knew it, the point is I did. And I'm guessing Marta knows it as well. Will you change it, Mum? Please? And I mean before you go to bed. And don't tell anybody, except perhaps Dad, what it is.'

'This sounds so serious, Ellie. What's wrong?'

'Let's just say I've been made aware at school about the importance of nobody knowing your password. And don't change it to *stewandme*. Make it something completely different, something nobody could guess. Okay?'

Wendy felt taken aback by the seriousness in Ellie's voice and she frowned. 'Of course I will. I'll do it now, before Dad eats all the cheese, then I can forget about it. Now go to bed and stop worrying.'

Finally Ellie smiled. She'd been worrying all day about how to get her mum to change the password, and in the end, it had been fairly simple. She kissed her mum's cheek, and headed back upstairs, calling goodnight to Marta as she went past her bedroom door.

It had been an excellent evening, they'd all enjoyed the film, even Dad had watched most of it, and she and Marta had made up. But the hurt went too deep for them to ever be as close as they once had been. She had one word for sister Marta – Archibald.

28

Stewart stood at the landing window, watching the activity in the back garden. When Wendy had called him at work and asked if it was okay if she took the girls to get a pool for the back garden, he had laughed aloud and made some comment about how she'd never asked before about reducing their bank account, why would she start now?

He, of course, hadn't considered she might mean a pool big enough to swim lengths in, which was what now graced the back lawn. He laughed as Ellie dunked Marta under the water, watching the splutters as Marta rose to the surface and set off after her sister. Ellie escaped the pool, and ran to the chairs, where she picked up her juice to have a drink. Marta scooped a glass full of pool water and threw it at Ellie, then scampered indoors before further retribution followed. Stewart felt relieved that the tension between them had eased, and the price of the pool was a small amount to pay for peace and happiness, he felt.

Ellie stood, not only dripping with pool water but also with the orange juice that she had tipped while trying to avoid the water.

'I'll drown you, Marta Needham,' were the words that fell from her lips, and she looked around the garden before unhooking the back strap of her bikini top and taking it to the pool to rinse it. She clambered in and swam a few strokes to rinse the orange juice from her breasts, then returned to her seat, wringing the water from the bra top before replacing it on her body.

Stewart stood mesmerised, wishing he wasn't there, yet feeling unable to move.

'Like the view, Daddy dear?'

He spun around. Marta was behind him, looking at what he had looked at.

'You're a pair of monkeys.' He tried to bluff his way through it. 'I saw what you did to Ellie, and now she's covered in orange juice. You might want to apologise.'

Marta grinned. 'Oh, don't worry. I'm going down to talk to her right now. Shall I apologise on your behalf as well?'

'Nothing to apologise for, as far as I'm concerned. Just be aware there are other houses around here that have a view of our back garden.'

Marta looked at him, then turned and walked away, her hips swaying.

* * *

Stewart watched as Marta approached Ellie, saw her speak and then saw Ellie turn her head to look up towards the landing window and wave.

He felt sick, wondering what Marta had said to her sister, and he decided a bit of damage limitation might be called for. He headed down to the garden, and to where the two girls sat enjoying the warmth on their bodies.

'Ellie,' he said, 'has Marta warned you about stripping off in the back garden? Be careful, love, these fences don't screen you from eyes in the upstairs of other houses.'

Ellie didn't open her eyes, simply smiled. 'I got the message from Marta, Dad, thanks.'

He stood awkwardly for a moment, then went back indoors. He didn't hear the laughter that came from his two daughters. 'Pervert,' Marta said, and closed her eyes to enjoy the afternoon sun on her face.

* * *

Wendy could sense some discomfort in her husband, and knew it would be something to do with the girls. Stewart loved his daughters, of that there was never any doubt, but since their meteoric push towards womanhood, he had become increasingly ill at ease. It was almost as though he had nothing in common with them; the acquisition of breasts and a curvy waistline had taken his girls away from him.

When she asked him what was wrong, he said he'd had to tell them about stripping off in the back garden, and he had been uncomfortable having to do it.

'Did you watch?'

'I did, quite by chance. I was watching both of them in the pool, until the rough play crept in, and Ellie ended up with orange juice down her. She simply stripped off her top and jumped back in the pool. I didn't want her to know I was there, I thought it would embarrass her, so I stayed still until her back was to me, but then Marta was behind me, making me feel like a proper pervert. I'm not handling our girls growing up, am I?'

'Not many dads do,' Wendy said. 'You'll get over it. It'll get a lot worse than that before they head off to uni.'

'Don't tell me that,' Stewart groaned. 'I don't think I'll ever recover from this afternoon. Don't leave me in this house alone again.'

'You do know they'll torment you now, don't you?' Wendy grinned at her husband. She leaned across to kiss him. 'I'll talk to them both – not about you seeing them, but about the neighbours. I don't suppose they thought for one minute that others could see into our garden, but they need to be more aware of stuff like that. Leave it with me, I'll smooth it over.'

* * *

Sleep didn't come easily that night to Stewart. It hadn't been the sight of Ellie's almost naked body that had caused his brain to go into overdrive, it had been his reaction to it. His erection had been sudden, and strong. But it had been the proximity of Marta in her bikini that had overwhelmed him.

Finally he gave in and headed downstairs, leaving Wendy to her dreams. He poured himself a whisky, picked up his book and read for an hour before heading back upstairs. He hoped a book on aeroplanes of the Second World War was sufficient to send him off to sleep, and take his mind off the daughters who had turned into sirens, seemingly overnight.

* * *

The fact that her father had sported a huge erection hadn't passed unnoticed by Marta, and a mental note was made, ready for use one day when it might be needed. She went to bed, stopping at the mirror to press her fingers on it. 'Hi, Child Two,' she said. 'It seems we're growing up.' She stepped forward and pressed her naked body against the naked body in the mirror. 'He'd like to do this to us.' Then she laughed.

She slept through the night with no anxiety, not worried that the only thing that she had said to Ellie was *Dad's a bit concerned you took off your top*, when she had knowingly left him with the impression that she was going to tell Ellie he had been deliberately spying on his girls, enjoying their semi-nakedness in a way he couldn't disguise.

Things were changing; Ellie, still a little naïve, but available for moulding into the person Marta wanted her to be, and Stewart, ripe for whatever Marta could bring down on his head in the future.

* * *

A barbecue was planned for the Saturday night, and Lorraine slipped on a short pale blue dress, taking a white cardigan with her in case it turned cool later in the evening. Marta had told her to bring a bikini, so she slipped one into her bag, not convinced she would be brave enough to wear it, with or without alcohol inside her.

The August evening was warm, and there were several people already there by the time Lorraine arrived, and she immediately moved over to greet Fleur. Both women had remained in close contact with Wendy; Fleur in particular had kept Wendy and Stewart fully apprised of the verdicts that were produced by the Coroner's Court regarding the two men found in the cellar and the death by heart attack of Janette Gregson.

Marta ran across and hugged Lorraine. 'I miss you,' she said.

'You do? That's good to know, lovely Marta Rose Needham.'

'I've still got the book, you know,' Marta said, a smile on her face. 'I'll keep it forever.'

'Good. Know your roots.'

'I intend discovering everything when I'm eighteen,' Marta replied, the smile disappearing. 'My life didn't start when I was thirteen, it started back in 1999.'

Lorraine felt a shiver travel down her spine and she looked at Fleur, who made no response at all.

'Everything is with your solicitor,' Lorraine said gently, 'who isn't allowed to reveal anything until your eighteenth birthday, but rest assured, Fleur and I will always be there to steer you, as will Wendy and Stewart. You make us very proud, you know; Wendy sent us a copy of your school report, and what you have achieved in such a short time is nothing short of a miracle. But learning doesn't stop at eighteen, because then you'll really start to mature and make decisions about what you want in the future.'

'I know what I want.' Marta gave a brief nod of her head as if to emphasise the point. 'I want a gallery where I can display my work, a studio where I can work...'

'You have a house, as you know,' Fleur interrupted. 'It's a large house, and it has enough rooms that you can convert one into a studio. I'm sure when you've finished at uni—'

'I'm not necessarily going to uni.'

Fleur and Lorraine looked at each other but were prevented from saying anything further by the arrival of Stewart, bearing glasses of wine. He handed them to the two women, and he pointed in the general area of the barbecue. 'All sorts of stuff already done, so go help yourself. Salad table is inside the summer house to try and keep it a bit cooler, and just help yourself to drinks from there whenever you need a top-up.'

Marta had slipped away, so Fleur and Lorraine headed over to grab themselves a beefburger before finding a small table with just two chairs in a more secluded part of the garden.

'Well,' Fleur began, 'our little girl is growing up. Clearly that artist in her is desperate to come out, but I'd feel so much happier if we could persuade her to allow that to take her through uni, maybe with a degree in art history or something.'

'It's not our concern,' Lorraine said. 'She's adopted now, and it's the worry of Stewart and Wendy, but knowing them as I do, I don't think it will be a worry. I think they'll encourage her to follow her heart, and that is to exhibit her own work. She's not going to be poor, you know. There's a fair bit of money as well as that house, and I'm sure the house can be altered to give her the studio she needs. If it can't, there's space enough in that massive back garden for an office studio. She knows nothing of this, because all she saw was her room. It bothers me that she will receive her mother's drawings when she gets that file from Dom Craigson, but we can't keep her history from her just because we think it's upsetting.'

Fleur gave a small laugh as she lifted her glass to her lips. 'And we thought that with her adoption the worst was over and she could look forward to a happy and settled life. Boy, did we get it wrong.'

Lorraine's eyes clouded over. 'Nothing in my life has ever given me such concern as this young lady, and have you really looked at her? She's definitely a young lady now. Both her and Ellie. God knows how Stewart will cope with a stream of young lads knocking at the door for these two.'

'He won't. He'll pass it all on to Wendy. She's an amazing mum. They never had kids of their own?'

'No, Wendy had to have a hysterectomy when she was in her early twenties, cancer, I believe. They hadn't been married long when that happened, so when Ellie landed in their laps as a foster child, it was a natural progression to adopting her as soon as they could. They had to wait three years because Ellie's birth mother couldn't make her mind up, but eventually the adoption went through. And then along came Marta for fostering, but that adoption was much smoother because there was nobody except Marta herself to say no.'

'She's a lovely girl. I'm sure she's really settled in, and is so happy here.'

29

Lorraine remembered that night as a kind of turning point in her relationship with Marta and her adoptive family. It seemed to her that things began to change almost overnight following the barbecue, and when she began to analyse everything, she realised Marta was at the heart of the changes. She had become the dominant one in the girls' affiliation, although an observer would notice the sadness flash across Ellie's face at odd moments. She felt that she could no longer be their support – that role had passed to Wendy and Stewart, and she could only watch from a distance.

It seemed to her that although both Marta and Ellie were maturing physically, they were very family oriented, and not part of the wider world. It was only when they both passed their driving tests in the last couple of months of their lower sixth year that their minds opened up. Her professional observations showed her a happy family, a cohesive unit, and she knew she had to accept that her role in their lives was over, unless they specifically asked for help.

Their seventeenth birthdays in January and February 2016 were expensive times for their parents, as cars were bought for the girls.

The Minis, one blue, one red, arrived gift-wrapped with a huge matching bow around them, and by early May, Marta had acquired her driving licence. By mid-May, Ellie followed.

Marta had been given the privilege of choice as the first one to reach seventeen, and she chose the blue one. Stewart found himself frequently having to park his own car on the road because he couldn't get a spot on the paved area that had originally been their front garden.

The day Marta passed her test was the day after her final exam for that penultimate school year. Her mother had given her the sloppiest kiss ever when she heard the news, plus a new credit card for Marta to use for petrol until she was earning her own money. Marta drove the blue car to school to collect Ellie, who had completed her exams a day later than her sister.

'That yours?' Harry Banton strolled up to the car and leaned through the open window.

'It is.'

He glanced into the back seat. 'Not much room in there for sex, but I'm willing to give it a go if you are.'

'In your dreams, pal,' Marta said. 'Get on with your drug dealing, and keep away from me.' She paused for a moment. 'And Ellie. School's a much better place now you're not in it.'

Harry leered at her. 'You don't know what you're missing. Ask your sister.' He strolled away, and her stare followed him. He was winding her up... wasn't he?

She sat quietly, waiting for Ellie to leave the school gates, then got out of the car as she spotted her sister's blonde hair. She waved and Ellie ran to join her.

'You passed?' It came out as a squeak of excitement.

'Did you ever doubt it?' Marta grinned at Ellie. 'Jump in, let's go and see if we can bump off Harry Banton on the zebra crossing.'

'With pleasure,' Ellie said, and put her bag on the back seat before climbing in beside Marta. 'Does it feel good?'

'Driving? It feels awesome. Mum will be sat at home chewing her fingernails off, but it felt so good to get in a car and just drive, without having somebody instructing me. I've got to think for myself now.'

Ellie laughed and turned towards Marta. 'So what's new? You always think for yourself. I've never come across anybody as smart as you for thinking things through carefully while hiding the fact that you're doing it. Was it hard? The test, I mean.'

Marta hesitated for a moment before answering, then pulled out onto the main road leading back to their home. 'I'm not going to lie and say it was easy because it wasn't, but also I'm not going to say it was hard. I think really I switched off, just listened to the instructor's words but didn't dwell on them. I drove as I'd been taught, and it worked. Tell you what, though, it's a brilliant feeling when he hands you that pass certificate.'

'So this is your first journey on your own? Should I be worried?'

'No, but Harry Banton should.'

* * *

Wendy breathed a sigh of relief as she saw the blue car pull onto the driveway. Would it always be like this? She smiled as she saw her girls get out, talking and laughing. School was now officially finished until September, when they would be moving into the upper sixth to complete courses in preparation for university life, and she knew the house would be like a mausoleum once they had gone; both girls were favouring Durham, although she knew that might change once Marta was handed her file on her eighteenth birthday. That file could change everything. Wendy wondered how easy it would be to set fire to Dominic Craigson's office, then smiled to herself. She was a bit old to be starting a life in prison, she reckoned.

'We're home,' they called as they headed upstairs to get changed. Although no longer required to wear uniform, it still felt good to get out of the clothes worn during the day, and into shorts to take advantage of the warmth of the sun.

'I can hear you're home,' Wendy raised her voice in response. 'Dad will be home shortly; we've booked a table for six o'clock to celebrate.'

Ellie and Marta high-fived as they separated to go into their own rooms, and Marta walked across to her mirror before doing anything. She pointed her finger onto the glass. 'We did it, Child Two. Nod if you're pleased for me.'

Child Two nodded, as did Marta.

* * *

Stewart and Wendy tried to look completely at ease as they listened to Marta and Ellie make plans to drive out into Derbyshire. Stewart was now regretting filling up the tanks of the Minis before having them delivered – with no petrol, they couldn't have gone anywhere. He groaned and everyone looked at him.

'My girls are growing up fast, and to hear you both talking of taking off in the car is more than scary. Marta, you'll drive carefully, won't you? And don't teach your sister any bad habits, she's not passed her test yet.'

Marta smiled at him, staring into his eyes. 'I've got a satnav,' she said. 'And if I really do get lost, I'll ring you.'

He knew he had no answer. His girls were no different to how he had been after passing his test, and he now understood how his mother had felt when she did everything to persuade him to still carry on catching buses.

* * *

They erected the pool later that night, although the water going into it was a separate job for the following day. Stewart moaned all the time, saying it all but killed off his grass, but Wendy, backed by Ellie and Marta, said it was worth losing some grass to have a pool for the summer evenings.

After the completion of the pool and the steps to get in it, Stewart lay back on his deck chair and closed his eyes. He knew the pool would be full of water when he arrived home from work the following day, and he breathed a sigh of relief that he didn't have to supervise that job. It was a beautiful evening and he allowed himself to relax.

He felt a gentle kiss on his forehead, and grabbed at Wendy without opening his eyes. 'It's a good job there's no water in that pool; you'd be a very wet wife.'

'Or a very wet daughter,' Marta said throatily, before removing his hand from her breast. 'Naughty Daddy.'

His eyes widened, and he almost threw her off him. 'What the...?'

Marta smiled. 'You looked so peaceful, I thought I'd give you a little kiss to say thank you for helping me pass my test.'

Stewart eased himself out of the deck chair with some difficulty, and gazed at her. 'I have no words for you, Marta.'

'Oh, I'm sure you could think of some. Bitch? Would that cover it?'

'It's a start.' He knew he was snarling at her. 'It'll be a word I use when I tell your mother about this constant torment. I did not deliberately watch you and Ellie when you thought I was perving. I'm not that sort of bloke.'

She shrugged. 'Okay, tell her. I'll tell her about you always coming into my room, especially after I've been in the shower and only wearing a towel...'

'She wouldn't believe you.'

Marta laughed and turned to walk away from him. 'Shall we see?'

* * *

He realised Marta couldn't possibly have told her lies when Wendy came outside to sit with him. They chatted for an hour, and eventually called it a night, before heading upstairs to bed.

Wendy went first, and he went around the house checking everything was secure. He glanced out of the bay window and saw the assortment of cars parked outside; he shook his head, wondering if maybe they should consider moving, finding a house with more room for vehicles.

He hoped Ellie would pass at the first attempt; he sometimes thought his younger daughter came in a poor second to Marta, and he didn't like that situation one little bit. He was now seeing a side to Marta that truly sickened him, while tormenting him. Everybody explained her manipulative side away by saying it was down to her early life, but he actually thought genetics had a lot to do with it. Her mother and grandmother had both murdered, her mother had abused her child, imprisoned that child for thirteen years, and the life he and Wendy had given Marta seemed to be counting for nothing. Her true colours were becoming more and more visible as she grew older. As she discovered sex.

He closed the curtains, gave a deep sigh and headed towards the stairs. As he reached the top, he heard the bathroom door open and Marta stepped out.

'Just had a shower.'

He nodded. 'Goodnight, Marta. See you in the morning.'

She dropped half her towel, and fumbled with it to catch it, as if it was accidental. He couldn't take his eyes from her breasts, and she ran her hand carefully down them, before refastening the towel.

The disgust was evident on his face, he knew it was. 'Cover yourself up, Marta. Stop playing silly games before you cause trouble you can't handle. You are still only a little girl, you know.'

He saw Marta's face redden, and he turned his back on her to enter the bedroom he shared with Wendy. 'My god,' he said, 'it's like living in a bloody harem, with all these women about the place.'

She laughed. 'I know. Remember when we used to talk about adopting one of each? Where's our boy when you need him?'

'Two girls wouldn't be so bad, if only they'd been different ages, and we didn't get all these hormones and stuff floating around the place in duplicate.' He shook his head. 'I'm sick of seeing semi-naked teenage girls.'

Again, Wendy laughed. 'I never thought I'd hear a man say that. Now come on to bed, and put up with this middle-aged old dodderer. Forget the nubile kids for tonight, they're going to be on full display from tomorrow onwards when that water fills the pool again. It'll be bikinis at dawn, and you'll spend the whole summer once again not knowing where to look.'

He switched off the bedside lamp. The only illumination remaining was the strip of light under the door from the landing light that was always left on all night. Ellie had always been afraid of total darkness and, it seemed, had been locked away in a cupboard many times until social services removed her from her biological mother.

Stewart lay for some time unable to sleep, finally recognising that from now on he must stay well away from Marta if he was to keep his sanity intact. She seemed intent on creating a situation where she was going to force Wendy to side with her, or him, and he had no intention of allowing that to happen. He would stay at work for longer hours; it was only until his girls went off to uni in fifteen months. Surely he could cope with that. And hopefully they would be out and about in their Minis, removing any chance of mishaps and temptations from the equation.

He was dropping off to sleep when a smile flickered across his face. If he was brutally honest with himself, he had known it wasn't Wendy's body he was clutching at following the light kiss in the back garden; she wore a completely different perfume to the light fragrance his girls chose to wear. He had known it was one of them, he simply hadn't known which one. And he hadn't really cared.

30

Stewart felt permanently tired. The extra hours he was working were certainly showing in terms of his business. It seemed everybody wanted new blinds following an intensive advertising campaign using newspaper and magazine articles and an aggressive social media crusade that had brought orders rolling in from around the country. Being in the house with the girls was leaving him in a permanent state of fear; he felt he never knew what Marta might do next, and the way Ellie looked at him was almost with a sense of hatred. He couldn't wait for the day they left for uni, a day when he could begin to leave work a little earlier, relax a little more.

He could avoid the torments the girls portrayed. He had thought there was a gap between Ellie and Marta, but the last two years at school seemed to have drawn them closer together – and away from him.

He had spoken to Wendy about the possibility of her returning to the position she had held until they had decided to take on the task of fostering children, and ultimately the adoption process which they'd hoped would follow, but she had refused with a laugh. 'I have to get my girls safely off to uni now they've both decided that's where they're going, and I intend being at home until that happens. I don't want them to be latch-key kids.' She was firm about it.

'But they're nearly eighteen, they've got their own cars, and they're hardly of an age where we could call them latch-key kids.'

Wendy frowned. 'Are we suddenly becoming poor? Is that why you want me to go back to work?'

He laughed uproariously. 'Okay, I give in. I wanted you to come back to work because we've got so much damn work on, but I'll advertise the job and get somebody else in, some stranger who doesn't understand what they're doing, who I'll have to train...'

'My heart bleeds for you,' she said with a grin. 'You go off to work, my love, and I'll keep the home fires burning.'

He pulled her into his arms. 'I love you. You know I wouldn't have asked if I hadn't thought it was a bloody good idea, don't you?'

She nodded. 'It's not a good idea. Besides, I'm thinking maybe we should be looking at moving house, unless we really are poor.'

'We're definitely not poor.' His voice was firm. 'I was thinking the same thing. We can't get four cars on that front, we could do with something with en suites in every bedroom so our girls don't have to share the family bathroom and moan about us having an en suite when they don't, and maybe we could have a proper pool built instead of having to use this plastic one that kills my grass. I know they're off to uni soon, but they'll be home when they're not there, so we'll need the extra parking space.'

'I'll start looking this week.'

'Try to keep in this area. It's handy for the school, and handy for work, but it wouldn't be a deal breaker. If you find something that ticks all the boxes except location, we can definitely consider it.'

* * *

A week later, Wendy put the house search on a back burner. The lump in her breast scared her so much she waited a full week before ringing the doctor. He referred her to the hospital and said that in view of her history, it would be an expedited appointment.

The conversation with Stewart was tortuous; she watched as he fell apart in front of her, as he remembered the cancer that had resulted in a full hysterectomy; she saw the same fear in his face as she had seen all those years earlier.

'Have you told the girls?'

She shook her head. 'No, there's nothing to tell them yet, other than I have a lump. It may just be a benign cyst, and then that's a simple removal and they don't really need to know at all, but if it proves to be more, then I'll have to tell them. They're in the throes of exams, Stewart, I can't tell them now. It's the middle of November, and we've got Christmas coming up, let's not spoil it.'

He smiled at her. 'And then we have their eighteenth birthdays in January and February, so what excuse will you have ready for not telling them then? You're going to have to go into hospital, Wendy. They might just query where you are.'

'Let's wait until I have an appointment. It may not be as urgent as we think.'

He pulled her into his arms. 'I'm here for you, always. I'll go with whatever you decide, but if they start asking questions, I won't lie to them. Agreed?'

'Agreed.'

* * *

The phone call came the following day, and was unfortunately taken by Marta. She scribbled down the telephone number Wendy had to ring on her return home, then rang the number a minute later to hear it was the breast clinic.

When Wendy pulled up on the drive, Marta had been joined by Ellie, and they were both waiting for her to get out of the car.

'Hi, girls. Something wrong?' She gave a swift glance in the general direction of the two Minis, feeling a sense of relief that they seemed to be intact.

'You tell us,' Marta said. 'Is something wrong? Why do you have to make an appointment for the breast clinic at the hospital?'

Wendy felt a spasm of fear pass through her body. They'd already contacted her? It had only been two days since she had seen her own doctor.

Marta passed Wendy the slip of paper with the telephone number written on it. She looked at it then lifted her head. 'Let's go inside.'

* * *

Stewart arrived home from work to find his wife and daughters with tear-stained faces, drinking cups of tea seemingly by the gallon.

He glanced into the lounge and saw all of them, one daughter either side of Wendy, all clutching onto their teacups as if their lives depended on it.

Wendy looked across at Stewart and gave a gentle smile. 'They know.'

'But...' He felt out of his depth. Hadn't they recently had the conversation about not telling them until they had concrete proof of what it was?

'The hospital rang while I was out,' Wendy explained. 'Marta took the call.'

'You have an appointment?' She could hear the panic in his

voice, and hoped Marta and Ellie hadn't noticed the fear on his face.

She nodded. 'Yes. For tomorrow morning. I've explained what it could be, that it doesn't necessarily mean cancer, and they've both had a feel at the lump. I think Ellie wants to get the potato knife and cut it out right now, but I've explained that's not practical.' She smiled at her daughter, who inched a little closer to her.

'And you're all drinking tea!' Stewart knelt down in front of them. 'Okay, girls, we'll face this together. I'm relieved as hell that you know; I don't think we could have hidden it anyway. Tea?'

Marta and Ellie laughed, while still wiping away tears.

'It seemed the right thing to do,' Ellie said. 'I know we don't like tea, but... you know...'

'It soothes and comforts. I know. In fact, if I had two daughters, I'm sure one of them would immediately jump up and make a cuppa for their old dad.'

Ellie hugged his shoulders as she passed him. 'Sit on the chair, Dad,' she said. 'You're too old to be kneeling on the floor.'

'Minx,' he said. 'No sugar, don't forget.' He briefly raised a hand to his shoulder where she had touched him. He had forgotten what it was like to receive a spontaneous hug from her.

Marta was holding tightly to Wendy's hand. 'We'll go with you tomorrow, Mum. That okay, Dad?'

Stewart hesitated. He never knew how to take anything that Marta said, and he wasn't sure how to respond.

'You can't come anyway, Stewart. You've got four interviews lined up tomorrow for my job. I'll be fine with my girls.'

'You'll ring me after the appointment?'

She nodded. 'Of course I will.'

* * *

Stewart spent all morning prowling his office in between the scheduled interviews, waiting for the phone call from Wendy. Her appointment was for 10.15, and he couldn't believe he was still staring at his phone at half past two. His imagination soared, letting him think of all sorts of scenarios, remembering the horror of Wendy's previous diagnosis and the subsequent operation and recovery period.

When the call finally came, they were back home, and Wendy said they were all having cups of tea. 'We needed a cuppa,' she explained. 'I feel as if I've had a million tests, all with differing lengths of time for results, so I won't know anything concrete for around a week. Even the girls are knackered; they're having tea too.' She gave a brief laugh. 'I can't tell you any more, Stewart, because I honestly don't know any more. Will you be home early?'

'Bet your life I will. I've an interview at three, then I'm leaving. Save some of that tea for me.'

He sat down with a thud, staring into space. Only a week earlier, they had been talking about plans for the next part of their lives; the girls leaving for uni, moving to a new home, building a swimming pool, for god's sake. Now it felt as if they'd put that same life on hold.

His intercom buzzed. 'Mrs Johnson is here for her interview.' The disembodied voice of his secretary interrupted his thoughts.

'Thank you. I'll be there in five minutes. I have something to finish first.' He cradled his head in his hands and let his mind drift into a million what-if situations.

He swallowed the last dregs of his coffee, stood and left his office to head for the small meeting room reserved usually for staff meetings when they threw around ideas, devised new products and marketing strategies, and drank coffee and ate doughnuts.

Today the room smelt fresh and clean; he opened the door, extended his hand and introduced himself to Gemma Johnson.

An hour later, he was convinced she was the one to offer the extra help he needed, and he told her he would contact her the following day, after discussions of all the candidates with his wife.

She smiled and stood. 'Thank you, Mr Needham. If you need to ask anything else once you have talked through everybody's applications, then please ring me at home. On my part, I would love to work for your company.'

He stood as she left the room and knew she was his first choice.

* * *

'They've biopsied Mum,' Ellie said as her father entered the hallway carrying his briefcase.

'And?'

'Nothing yet. She has to wait for all the results to come through for the million or so tests she's had today, then they'll ask her to go back again.'

Stewart dumped his briefcase at the bottom of the stairs and listened for sounds.

'She's in the kitchen making lasagne,' Ellie said. 'It's like she's normal.'

He laughed. 'She is normal. We had our tears yesterday, now we've moved into the positive stage. Your mum is good at this. Where's Marta?'

'In her room. Mum said she didn't need any help, so she's gone upstairs to read.'

He detected a note of aggression, and pulled Ellie towards him. She stiffened, holding herself rigidly in place.

'Hey, come on. We'll all handle this differently. Marta isn't wrong to hide away from it, any more than you're wrong for clinging on to your mum. I've had a hell of a day not knowing what's happening, but I'm here now, and prepared to find my way through handling it. Leave Marta be, she'll be fine, as will the two of us.' He felt he couldn't care less how Marta was dealing with the current situation.

He gave Ellie's shoulders a gentle squeeze and they walked through to the kitchen together. Wendy was placing the lasagne dish into the oven, and turned to smile at the picture they presented; his arms around her shoulders giving her the support she needed right now. Ellie fixed the smile on her face for her mother's benefit.

'Let's have some wine,' Wendy suggested. 'I absolutely refuse to let this get me down. Nobody's driving tonight, are they?'

'Not with our English exams tomorrow, they're not,' Ellie laughed. 'We've both got a date with Shakespeare tonight, and I suspect Marta has a head start on me with it already.'

'Okay – make it the best wine, Stewart. I'm pretty sure we need it, but our girls are limited to one glass. It seems they need clear heads for William.'

Marta opened the kitchen door. 'Did I hear wine mentioned?'

Wendy laughed. 'Nothing wrong with your ears, Marta. I do love all of you, and thank you for all your support today. I couldn't wish for a better family.'

BOOK THREE
MARTA'S RETURN

December 2016 – January 2017

31

Christmas Eve was cold, and the day was spent with the final wrapping of gifts, preparation of sprouts, and general Christmas activities; Wendy remained on the sofa in the lounge, directing her troops and trying to keep her spirits as they should be in the Christmas season.

Her consultant had confirmed the operation to remove her right breast had gone well, and they were optimistic of a full recovery, although Wendy felt some degree of trepidation about his optimism.

She actually felt rubbish, and knew if it wasn't for her girls, Christmas would be a washout. She would simply go to bed and stay there until her world felt more normal. Her attempts to put off the operation until after Christmas had been met with the consultant's opinion that it needed to be sooner rather than later, and so mid-December had seen her in hospital.

'Medication time,' Ellie said with a smile, and handed her mum a small dish with three tablets inside.

'Thanks, sweetheart,' she said, and tipped them down her throat, swallowing yet more water.

'You want anything, Mum?'

'No, I'm good. Your dad has wrapped all the presents?'

'He has. Stop worrying, we're organised. There's enough sprouts to feed the entire city. The presents are all under the tree, and we're just chuffed that you're home in time for the big day. You don't need to do anything except be our mum.' She leaned over and kissed the top of Wendy's head. 'Love you, Mum.'

'Love you too, sweetheart. It'll be a very different Christmas this year, won't it?'

Marta caught the tail end of the conversation as she came through into the lounge. 'Too right it will; we're cooking the meal.'

'Well, it's time you learned how to do it,' Wendy said with a smile. 'Both of you are almost eighteen and all I can say about your cooking skills is that you're very good at beans on toast.'

'Well, tomorrow that all changes. For Christmas dinner, it's beans on toast with a side of sprouts. And for dessert, it's sprouts and ice cream.'

Wendy settled herself lower onto the sofa, and Marta tucked the blanket over her. 'Thank you, sweetheart. I'm going to have a little sleep while you plan a sprout cocktail with seafood sauce for starters.'

* * *

Marta and Ellie left the room and closed the door quietly behind them. They had no idea where their father was; he had simply said, 'See you in a bit,' and driven off; Marta felt relieved.

She couldn't escape the feeling of discomfort when she was around Stewart, but equally accepted her tormenting of him didn't help matters. It was almost as if she needed to tempt him, to take his obvious weakness for his daughters one step further. However, she knew that it wasn't just her father she felt uncomfortable around, she really didn't like anybody of the masculine sex being anywhere near her.

Tiny comments made by Wendy were slowly building a picture of Mother, and Marta suspected there was lots more she would discover over the next couple of weeks. However, the main theme was that Janette Gregson had been locked into a world where men played no part. Had Janette's genes simply passed straight on to her daughter? She guessed that part of her own story was hidden somewhere inside Wendy's computer, but that was something she could no longer access. The password had been changed, and it was clearly something very obscure as she couldn't even begin to guess it.

Information from Lorraine had completely dried up since the adoption had been finalised, no matter how hard she tried to steer conversations around to her early years. Fleur fell back on data protection laws every time Marta broached the subject with her.

Marta heard the throaty growl of Stewart's car, and ran upstairs to her room. Ellie could deal with him today; she needed thinking time.

Crossing to her mirror, she raised her finger to touch Child Two. 'Hi,' she whispered. 'You ready to go and have a look back home? Won't be long now.' Child Two nodded in agreement at the same time as Marta nodded. They exchanged a kiss, and Marta moved across to the window. It looked down upon the back garden, a garden with a large rectangular area of half-dead grass created by the May to September pool being on it; she knew it would be back as green as ever in the spring, but she sensed she wouldn't see that transformation come March.

She heard the ping of an incoming text on her phone and glanced at it quickly. Harry Banton.

Fancy meeting up over Christmas?

She gave a slight laugh.

No.

She knew she should really remove him from her phone, but something held her back from that action. Despite having left school to work with his father, he had remained on the periphery of the group who had stayed on to complete their sixth form studies, and frequently turned up if the crowd of friends met up for a coffee, or had a day in the library for study instead of working at home, and she knew she was probably the reason he was hanging on.

Ellie would have handled him so much better, and Marta felt aggrieved that since her first day at school, he had followed her around. Maybe he thought there was some kudos in being with somebody with such a strange past; it certainly wasn't because she was nice to him, because more often than not, she was quite acerbic and scathing.

She took Ellie's Christmas present, wrapped in pretty pale blue starry paper, from under her jumpers housed in her chest of drawers, and left it on her bed to remind her to take it down to put it under the tree. The delicate gold bracelet had a gold star with a tiny diamond on it at the halfway point, and she hoped Ellie would love it as much as she did.

To Marta, Christmas was still a revelation, and she had taken great care with her choice of gifts. She had bought a Burberry scarf for Stewart; for Wendy's gift, which had been ongoing for a couple of months, Marta had used a photograph of the four of them on a canal boat trip they had enjoyed, and had copied it onto a canvas before completing the picture in oils.

It had been while working on that picture that her thoughts had turned to life with Mother. There had been no pencils, no paper, no crayons, nothing that would have allowed her an outlet for the creativity squashed inside her. Now it was out and encouraged to develop. Ellie had asked her if there was anything special she would like for Christmas, and she had told her the name of a book showing advanced techniques in acrylics and oils, and she hoped Ellie had been able to get it.

She went in the back of her wardrobe for the wrapped oil painting and slid it carefully out – she smiled as she remembered thinking it was harder to wrap than to paint. Stewart's gift was in her bedside table, and she rescued that, then headed back downstairs carrying all three gifts, to see if Wendy needed anything.

She knelt down in front of the enormous tree standing in the bay window and carefully stood the painting at the back so that it was upright, then laid the other two gifts on top of the others already there. She smiled as she saw the package addressed to her – 'with much love from Ellie'. There was no disguising it was a book, and a large one at that.

'Stop looking.'

Marta turned and smiled at Wendy. 'You're awake.'

'I am, and if I had a dutiful daughter, she would make me a cup of tea, because I'm parched.'

'Then I'll be your dutiful daughter. Are you in pain?'

'A little, but I'm not due for more pain relief yet. It's manageable. Isn't it strange how healing hurts so much?'

Marta felt herself flinch. 'Yes, I remember it well.'

'Oh, Marta, I'm so sorry. How thoughtless of me to bring back the bad memories.' Wendy's eyes opened wide. 'And what's worse, I can't hug you to make up for my big mouth.'

'Hey, don't worry, Mum. That's all in the past. Nobody hurts me now.'

'No,' Wendy whispered. 'We love you too much to hurt you, or to allow anyone else to hurt you.'

'I'll get you a pot of tea. Are you comfortable? Do you need help to move?'

'No, I'm good. And I'm looking forward to tomorrow, it will be the first time I haven't cooked our Christmas dinner. Is the turkey big?'

Marta chuckled. 'It's massive. I don't think Dad considered it had to actually fit in the oven. We've got it ready, but we had to empty the fridge to put the prepped turkey back in it.'

A brief flash of worry crossed Wendy's face. 'You need me to supervise?'

'Nope. It's all under control. Dad says he's an expert, so really, what could possibly go wrong?'

Wendy groaned at the answer that flashed across her brain, and Marta left the room, saying she was going to make a drink for them.

* * *

Wendy was in bed before six, leaving Stewart downstairs with his girls. They had a game of Uno amid much hilarity, with Ellie becoming the eventual winner, and Stewart opened a bottle of wine.

He poured out glasses for all three of them, and carried the drinks to the coffee table. He pulled Ellie towards him, hugging her tightly. She flinched and turned towards Marta. Marta reached across and pulled her away from him, taking her towards the Christmas tree. 'Let's have a chocolate off the tree to go with the wine,' she said, and Ellie mouthed *thank you* in response.

Stewart raised his glass to toast his wife. 'To my Wendy. If love can make her better, then she'll be back on her feet in no time.' They lifted their glasses towards the bedroom above them, where Wendy was sleeping fitfully.

'What time we getting up, Dad?'

'Ellie, you ask the same question every year. I'm getting up at ten. What time are you getting up?'

'Six.'

'And you give that same answer every year.'

'Okay,' Ellie grumbled, with a smile on her face. 'So I'm predictable. We having Buck's Fizz?'

'We are.'

Marta stepped in. 'I like Buck's Fizz. How come we only have it on Christmas morning?'

Stewart thought for a moment. 'I have absolutely no idea. I'm not convinced it's sold any other time of the year.'

'Well, it's all wrong,' Marta huffed. 'I'll just have to drink Prosecco, then.'

'Can I point out, my lovely Marta, that you're not yet old enough to drink according to the laws of our land, and won't be for another two weeks or so, so stop whingeing.'

Marta's phone pealed out 'Rudolph the Red-Nosed Reindeer', and she glanced at the screen, smiling when she saw it was Lorraine.

'Hi, Lorraine. Happy Christmas.'

'And Happy Christmas to you, Marta. I just wanted to check everything was okay, but didn't like to ring Wendy in case she was sleeping.'

'She's in bed. We're all good, but Mum's not particularly comfortable. The three of us have taken over the kitchen tomorrow, so Mum doesn't have to do a thing.'

Lorraine's laughter was heard by the others. 'Oy, Lorraine Lowe,' Ellie shouted. 'We can cook sprouts, you know.'

'Tell Ellie I don't doubt her sprouts will be perfect. Please wish everybody Happy Christmas, Marta, but especially you, my special one.'

'Thank you, and the same to you and yours, Lorraine.'

* * *

Lorraine disconnected and stared around her. Her home was lovely, but empty. How she would have loved to be the one who had adopted Marta, but she had known Marta was with the right people from the beginning. She dreaded to think what would happen after Marta was given all the facts in just a few short days. The fifth of January 2017 was going to be traumatic for all of them, in more ways than one.

32

Christmas morning was a cold one. There was frost on the grass, giving at least the suggestion of a white Christmas, and Wendy cried as she opened the gift from Marta.

'This is so beautiful, Marta. I absolutely love it.' She stared around the lounge. 'If we move that picture of the Alps, we can put it there where we can all enjoy it. The Alps can move into our bedroom.'

Stewart groaned. Another item to add to his to-do list. He was drinking his tea and eating his bacon sandwich with his new scarf around his neck and reading the instructions for the swish new camera bought for him by his wife, before breast cancer stopped any further Christmas shopping.

Marta had finished her bacon sandwich, and was stroking the book bought for her by Ellie. She lifted it to her nose to smell it, and everybody laughed. 'Marta, my love, until you entered our lives, I'd never heard of people sniffing at books, but you do it with every one.' Wendy smiled at her daughter.

'In my defence,' Marta responded, 'I like the smell, and every one smells different.' She opened the book. 'Now stop laughing at me, and pass out the Quality Street chocs. It's Christmas, isn't it?'

* * *

Slowly Wendy improved as Christmas progressed, and Marta's room began to fill with pictures, some half-finished, awaiting inspiration to complete them, but others in a completed state, requiring framing. She tried many of the exercises suggested in her Christmas book, and made notes in the book as she discovered different ways of working.

And yet Marta felt on edge, as if change was imminent. She used her art as a way of separating herself from the world around her, and nobody bothered her, accepting that the new book had been inspirational, and she needed to enjoy it at her own pace.

Only Ellie was concerned; she wondered if maybe the hours spent in her bedroom producing the outstanding work were leading Marta away from her decision to go

to university. Would she simply finish her A levels, say enough is enough, and immerse herself in her art? Or was she copying Ellie's own way of dealing with a father with hands that seemed to want to touch all the time?

* * *

Even art was put on the back burner as the new year arrived, and on the fourth of January, Marta was taken on a surprise trip around the various art galleries in Sheffield, and her eighteenth birthday present from her parents was an original picture of her choice by Pete McKee, her favourite Sheffield artist. She avoided being by the side of her father by the simple slipping of her arm into Wendy's, giving her support when she faltered. Ellie seemed to feel the need to walk as far from him as possible, and Marta wished with all her heart that Wendy wasn't still in recovery, because they could have talked to her about the escalation of their discomfort when around Stewart. The two girls felt very much as if their only support was each other.

Later that week, Marta would think back to that day and reflect on how it had proved to be such a happy day, possibly the last one for a long time.

* * *

It snowed on Marta's birthday, but she didn't care. Today she would learn who she really was, maybe who she was destined to be. She dressed carefully, as befitted an adult and not the child she had been one day earlier, and Stewart drove her and Wendy into the city centre, where Lorraine was waiting for them outside Craigson and Marple, the solicitors. She had hoped Stewart would go into work, but it was not to be.

The four of them walked inside and were immediately offered coffee. All four refused; not one of them didn't feel nervous about the momentous day ahead. Stewart thought that maybe if they had been offered brandy...

Dominic collected them and led them through to his office. On his desk was a large banker's box. Marta drew in a quick breath at the sight of it, wondering how it would change her life, what it would mean for her when she opened it.

Dominic smiled and leaned across to shake all their hands. He held on to Marta's hand for a few seconds and said, 'Happy birthday, Marta.'

She smiled at him. 'Thank you.'

Once they were all seated, the solicitor moved the box to one side. 'We'll get to the contents of this later,' he explained. 'I now need to tell you of your inheritance. As there is no will, you inherit automatically as her only surviving relative. Now you are eighteen, it is all to officially be handed over to you.'

He paused and looked over at Marta. 'We were entrusted with taking care of the house, and Lorraine has kept a very close eye on the property for you. As far as we are aware, it is in good condition, and I happen to know that Lorraine does a regular flick around with a duster.'

Lorraine smiled at his words, and gave Marta's hand a squeeze.

'So, you're now an adult, Marta. I have some figures for you. We have had the house valued for you last week, and because of data protection, it is up to you to decide whether or not you reveal any of the following figures to your parents.' He pushed a small folded piece of paper across to Marta.

Everyone saw the flush of red appear in her face, but she took the paper and opened it carefully. There was a small gasp, but she said nothing, putting it carefully in her bag.

'This,' Dominic said, 'is a little more complicated. As per Janette's instructions that she gave us when Barbara Gregson died, we have monitored and managed her investments, the amounts we have paid for maintenance of the house, and any income received from insurance policies et cetera, and this sheet is a full accounting showing the amount in the current account, the amount in the savings accounts – there are three because your grandmother also features in this set-up – and where your investment portfolio stands at this time.'

Marta stared at him. 'My grandmother?'

Dominic nodded. 'Yes, your grandmother was quite well off, mainly because her parents left her a huge property and a healthy bank balance. She sold the large house, bought the one you've now inherited and invested the balance left. Your mother then inherited all of that when your grandmother died four or five years before you were born. All the exact dates are in here.' He touched the box lightly.

Marta glanced at the box and flinched slightly. During the long hours of the previous night, she had imagined being handed an envelope, maybe a key to the house she had always known would be hers one day, but this box, if it was full, held a lot of stuff.

Dominic pushed a second folded item across to her, almost a booklet, she thought, and she unfolded it. The first sheet was a summary of all the other attached sheets, and her gasp this time was almost a cry.

'You are a very wealthy young lady, Marta,' Dominic said, 'but I'm sure your parents will be beside you all the way, guiding you. Wealth brings its own problems and you're very young to have this much responsibility. I suggest you should now pass your investment portfolio on to somebody more skilled than me, and forget about it. When you're ready to decide on a career, you can make decisions, but that portfolio is very healthy for your future.'

'I don't pretend to understand all of this,' Marta said, speaking slowly while folding up the documents, 'but is there enough to fund a gallery?'

Dominic gave a gentle laugh. 'There's enough for five galleries, I imagine.' He pulled the large box towards him and untied the string holding on the lid. 'Now we come to your life.'

They all saw the panic flash across her face, but she didn't speak.

The first item out of the box was an envelope with a bank card inside it. He handed it to her. 'Pizza on you, tonight?'

Marta's hand trembled as she took it from him.

'The PIN number is on the sealed document inside that envelope. I officially handed everything over at the bank with effect from this morning, so they suggested I get you your bank card to assure the smooth continued running of the account for you.'

'Thank you,' she whispered. She tucked the envelope into her bag then looked around the office as if she wanted to plan her escape route. This was proving to be so much more difficult than she had anticipated.

'Okay, Marta, that's the bulk of the legalities dealt with. Our final bill for this year's work will need to be paid, and we'll send it when it's been prepared. I would advise you to have a solicitor, as your funds are substantial, and we would be happy to take instruction from you, but that must be your decision ultimately. Now, on to the box.'

He showed her a letter. 'It's not necessary that you read this at this moment in time. It's been in abeyance for three years, pending you reaching today, and it's a letter from your half-brother.'

They all saw the colour drain from Marta's face.

'My half-brother?' The question came out as a squeak.

'Yes. There are things I'm about to tell you that it was deemed sensible to keep from you. You had limited vocabulary when you were found, indeed it was limited everything. However, what I can tell you is that there are some definite facts. Your mother was Janette Gregson and she gave birth to you without anyone knowing. Until you were rescued, you had nothing. No birth certificate, no school admission, nothing. That is why you chose your own name and Lorraine organised your birth registration. We did have confirmation that it was 5 January 1999. And a man named Philip Hancock was your father. He never knew about you because your mother killed him after he had raped her.'

Despite her intermittent pain, Wendy pulled her daughter close. Marta's body was stiff, unyielding, as she tried to take in Dominic's words.

'Mother was raped?'

Dominic nodded. 'When she died, it was realised that some-where there was a child, and the house was searched. Your father's body was found in the cellar, as was the body of a second man. We believe, ludicrous as it may sound, that your grandmother was also raped and killed the man who did it, using the same heavy imple-ment to hit him on the head. Your mother knew nothing of this, as the first body was hidden round the corner of the cellar, and the room was unused. From the position of your father, we believe Janette simply tumbled him down the steps and locked the door, then sealed it with duct tape. There is visual evidence of this, which we'll get to in a bit.'

Marta was silent as she thought through what she was hearing. Finally, she sighed. 'And this half-brother is presumably my rapist father's son?'

'He is. He wrote to your home asking that you contact him, but we knew you had enough to contend with – you had just started school. I wrote to him and said I would pass on his letter when you reached eighteen. It's now up to you to decide what to do about it. You also have a half-sister, Olivia.'

'I can think all of this through? I don't have to do anything yet?'

Dominic shook his head. 'No, you don't. Get your A levels out of the way, then you'll have time to think. And if you have any questions, please ring. We're not abandoning you just because you're eighteen. There is something else we all have to discuss with you, though. The reason this box is so big is that, like you, I believe, your mother was an artist of extraordinary talent. She told the story of her life from the day she was raped, all in pictures, and although copies have been made of these by police and other rele-vant agencies, in this box you have her originals. They are outstanding drawings, all dated as if she was keeping a pictorial diary, but also very upsetting. I suspect drawing her feelings onto paper helped her come to terms with what had happened to her and also what she did to Hancock. Can you remember a dog?'

For a brief moment, a smile flashed across Marta's face. 'Billy, he sometimes used to sneak into my room with Mother.'

'Then know that there are good as well as distressing pictures in here, take comfort from that.'

33

'Do I have a key to my house?' They were all gathered in the kitchen, staring at the box which Marta had placed in the middle of the table.

'I have it,' Lorraine said. 'I thought I might take you down this afternoon if you feel up to doing that, and show you what's been done since you were last there. A couple of things had to be mended, but in the main, it's a good house.'

Marta gave a nod. 'Okay, I'll leave the box for now, we'll go and sort out the house.'

'You think you'll keep it?' Stewart asked. He'd remained silent throughout the meeting at the solicitors, but he felt he needed to let his daughter know she had his full support at this moment in time.

Marta stared at him. She had no intention of discussing anything with him about the house, she didn't want him anywhere near it. She dreaded to think what the outcome of a visit from him would be.

'I don't know. What I've heard this morning was all new to me, apart from the fact that Mother could draw, and now I know why you all knew that. I need to take in the atmosphere of the house, because don't forget the only place I have any memory of is that bedroom and en suite. I never came out of it. If I'd been seriously ill, what do you think Mother would have done? Got medical help or killed me off?'

There was a gasp from Wendy. 'Look, I know she wasn't the world's best mother, but she could have killed you at birth and she didn't. I believe that in her own strange way, she loved you.'

Marta gave a harsh barking laugh. 'You've got to be joking. If you love somebody, you don't hurt them in the way she hurt me, punish them for things that were out of their control, beat them with a slipper for standing and not sitting in the designated place on the bed – no, she didn't love me, she punished me for being alive.'

Marta stood and walked around the table. 'Shall we go?' she asked Lorraine.

'Of course. How do you want to do it? You don't know where the house is, and it's about fifteen minutes from here. Do you want to follow me, or shall I drive and bring you back after?'

Marta stared at the woman who had been her friend for such a long time, and destroyed that friendship in a few words. 'Tell you what, Lorraine, as you were party to the decision to tell me nothing, give me the address and the key and I'll go on my own.'

Lorraine's face became masklike, and she took the key out of her bag. 'The address is on the tag on the key.' She turned and walked out of the kitchen, and they heard the front door close as she left.

Marta picked up the banker's box, dropped the key into her bag and headed down the hallway.

She was inserting her car key into the ignition when her passenger door opened and Ellie slipped inside. 'I don't know what the hell is going on, Marta, but there's no way you're going in that house on your own. We're sisters, aren't we?'

Marta turned, unable to smile. 'Thanks. Just don't talk until we get there, and all will be okay. I just need to calm down.'

The journey was a quiet one, both girls deep in thought as to what they would find at the end of it. Marta pulled the Mini onto the driveway, and applied the handbrake. They sat in the car for a moment and looked at the house. It was clearly an extensive property, with large bay windows downstairs and upstairs at the front, both windows overlooking a paved area. To the left of the house was a garage, sporting a black up and over door, and the front door was the same colour.

'There's no colour.' Marta breathed out slowly. 'It's just black and stone.'

'If you decide to keep it,' Ellie said, 'you can add the colour. And we can stop the number two, which looks as though it's dead, from leaning to one side. It will probably only need a screw putting in to make the house number look like a twelve again. We can sort it all out for you, make it yours. Come on, let's get inside and check out this palace.'

Two steps led up to the front door. Ellie and Marta exchanged a quick glance, and Marta inserted the key. The door opened easily, and it was clear Lorraine had been earlier. Fresh flowers stood in a vase on the hall table, and a card had been placed in front of the carnations and roses, bearing Marta's name.

Marta ignored it, and walked slowly along the hallway. Halfway down on the left was a partially open door, and both girls walked through and stood looking around the lounge. 'Bit old-fashioned,' Marta said, 'but I can tart it up with some paint effects and make it look fab. Just look at that beautiful old sewing machine.'

She walked around the room looking at the pictures on the wall. 'These are signed by Mother,' she said.

Ellie saw a blank look cross her sister's face, and she reached to squeeze her hand. 'Hang on, don't let any of it get you down.'

'I won't, but why the hell couldn't she have been normal and shared this love of art with me? She could have taught me so much, instead of being brutal and cruel for the entire thirteen years we lived together. Janette Gregson must have been a very unhappy and bitter woman. I didn't even know her name until today. I only ever knew her as Mother, and when they said Gregson would be my surname, I didn't really connect it even then with Mother. I certainly didn't know her name was Janette because nobody, not even Lorraine, spoke about her. It's like she was a dirty secret, and I suppose that's exactly what she was. Let's protect this poor child from her memories. You reckon that was the plan?'

'Possibly. I know nothing of my early life, other than I was given up for adoption,' said Ellie. 'But I must admit it doesn't bother me. I've never known anything except Mum and Dad, I have no memories of anything that came before because I was too young. But you, you had thirteen years of hell, and it must have been truly awful for you.'

'Painful,' Marta said, and sat down on the sofa. 'I can see myself living here, Ellie. I'd always kind of imagined selling the place once the inheritance came through, so that I could fund my time at uni easily, but now I'm having a rethink. I wonder why nobody ever said anything about Mother killing the man. It seems very strange. Everybody at school knew I had catch-up to do in my education, and accepted it, but nobody breathed a word about her killing him. I can't remember his name, but I'm going to find out all I can. Yet again, it's like only having half a story of my life.'

'Look, reading between the lines, I think you'll know so much more when you've looked at your mother's pictures. I've only picked up oddments from listening to all of you talking, but it seems your mother drew everything, almost like a diary. Let's look round the rest of the house, send for a takeaway, and open the box. Pizza?'

Marta laughed. 'That's exactly what that lovely solicitor said when he gave me my bank card. Maybe we should christen it. Come on, let's find the kitchen.'

* * *

The rain was pattering on the roof of the conservatory as the girls investigated what exactly Marta had inherited. 'I could make this a studio, there's so much light in here.'

'You could,' Ellie said, 'but it's not very warm. I know it's January, but you don't only paint May to September, do you? It would definitely be worth putting some heating in here. But don't make any decisions until you've seen the entire house.'

'I wonder where Mother worked,' said Marta, leading Ellie into the dining room, situated between the kitchen and the lounge. 'Ah,' she said, staring around her, 'I think I have the answer.' There was an easel in the corner, with a half-finished oil painting on it of a dog. 'That's Billy.'

'He was lovely,' Ellie said, moving closer to the picture. 'You reckon she worked in here?'

Marta reached down and opened a cupboard in the sideboard. It held pencils, pencil crayons, oil paints, acrylics, paintbrushes – a cornucopia of artist's materials. 'There you are,' she said. 'All of this, and she never gave me so much as a pencil or a piece of paper to use. It makes me feel... worthless.'

Ellie was lost for words. She didn't know how to comfort Marta. They had discussed this day for so long, and yet it was turning out to be nothing like they had imagined. Marta's bad memories were surfacing, and there was no way of stopping them.

'Let's have a look upstairs, see if one of the bedrooms would be better for your studio, or at least warmer.'

The stair carpet was new, a neutral shade of grey, and it took a flashback of memory for Marta to realise why. When they had brought her downstairs to take her to the Children's Hospital five years earlier, there had been blood on the newel post and on the carpet. She suspected Dominic Craigson had authorised the purchase, ready for the eighteenth birthday of his wealthy young client. She must remember to thank him.

Marta had no idea which room had been hers, and she hesitated outside the first door, almost afraid to enter. When she did, she saw the most glorious quilt on the bed, and knew it was Mother's room. She walked in and touched the colours. The downstairs and outside might have been lacking in pigment, but this eye-catching bed cover left her in no doubt that Mother had understood tints and hues fully, and certainly knew how to blend the cotton fabrics together.

'That is stunning,' Ellie breathed. 'Your mother made your little quilt, didn't she?'

Marta nodded, still stroking the quilt. She lifted two of the corners before she found the label. It said *New York Beauty, made and designed by Janette Gregson, completed January 2012.*

'Is there a label on yours?'

'There is. It says *Quilt for Child*, but that's all. She didn't put her name or the date. It's somewhere in the back of my mind that she said her mother had started it, and she had finished it, but I'm not convinced I'm remembering that correctly. I think it's the only gift I ever had from her...'

'Oh, god, Marta, that's awful. So will this be your bedroom if you move in here? Or could this be your studio?'

'Oh, I will be moving in. I'd be stupid to sell this and have to mess about finding somewhere else to live. And this is a beautiful bedroom, with that huge bay window. I could have a small sofa in that instead of that huge dressing table.' She did a 360-degree turn, then nodded to herself.

They moved to the next door, and it was an almost empty room. Billy's dog bed was on the floor, but apart from the carpet, there was nothing else.

'I think this could possibly be the studio,' Marta said, 'but I'll check out the other rooms first.'

She paused outside the next door and felt the most incredible wave of anger wash over her.

'This is it, Ellie. This is where she kept me locked up for all those years, where she hit me with a belt buckle time and time again. Where she denied me a childhood and never said a kind word to me.'

Ellie took hold of her hand, and they stood for a moment. Marta grasped the round doorknob and turned it, half expecting it to be locked, but it wasn't. They walked into the room together.

34

Nothing had changed and Marta moaned, a long, low, strangulated moan that seemed to travel up her body and out of her mouth. She stood in the doorway with Ellie just behind her, and Ellie put a hand out to catch her, fearful she would fall.

Marta took a hesitant step into the room and looked around.

'It's the same,' she said, and tears rolled down her cheeks. 'It's just the same.'

She walked across to the wardrobe with the mirror attached to the door, and touched it with her finger. Child Two responded, and Ellie heard Marta whisper, 'We survived.'

Ellie walked across to the window, which had had the wooden board removed from it, and stared down into the garden.

'You said you'd never seen the garden before, but this room looks down onto it.' She turned to face her sister.

'The window was boarded up. It was always dark in here. I could have the lights on when it was a mealtime, but I got used to the darkness. She didn't want anybody to see me, or me to see anything of the outside world.'

'Well, it's not boarded now, and the garden from this angle is huge. It's mainly grass, but it's a blank canvas for your creativity, Marta. Somebody, probably Lorraine, has kept the grass down, so you don't have to think about this for a couple of months. From what I've seen, the house is in really good condition considering nobody's lived here for five years.'

'Oh, god, and I was awful to Lorraine earlier. I was so wound up and I felt as though people were still trying to control me, and—'

'Hey, come on. This is the start of the rest of your life, let's not get too down. Maybe this room could be the studio, it's amazingly bright.'

Marta shook her head. 'Not in a million years. I have plans for this room. I'm throwing everything out, buying new bedroom furniture and a new double bed to replace this poxy antiquated one, and I shall decorate it in pink for you.'

Ellie stared at her. 'For me?'

'This is your room. It doesn't have to be on a permanent happy ever after basis, but whenever you need to escape, this will be the place you can use as your hidey hole. You need to get away from him, don't you?'

Ellie flinched and looked at her sister. 'What do you mean?'

'I've seen him, Ellie. Seen the way he goes to touch you at every opportunity. He's settled on one of us – probably realised I didn't love him and wouldn't let him get away with it – and that "one of us" is you. I want you to always feel this is your safe place, and if you want to live here permanently with me, that's fine. If you want to be an occasional lodger, that's fine as well, but you have to distance yourself from Stewart Needham before he takes things a stage further. We only need to keep out of his way until September, and in that nine months, we can make this house exactly as we want it.'

'Pink?'

'Or blue, or purple, just don't ask for black.' Marta grinned at her sister, who was now looking at the room with its small en suite with new eyes. 'I'm right, aren't I? He is pushing harder?'

Ellie's head dropped. 'He is. I try to ignore it, but Mum spends such a lot of time in her room since the operation, and he knows damn well I won't tell her, not in the state she's in at the moment.'

'Mum will improve; she needs us less and less now, so he can take care of her. He can work from home, he's made that obvious since she came out of hospital, so we could be living here by the start of next week.'

'Or tomorrow.' Ellie spoke quietly.

Marta looked at her sister. 'He scares you?'

'I don't know if I'm scared, or wary. I'm almost eighteen, Marta, and I can't go running to anybody at school to tell them. Likewise, I can't tell Mum, she's too poorly. I had no idea you'd realised what was going on. I feel better just knowing you know.'

'Come on, and keep thinking about what you'd like in this room. We can get some paint and stuff pretty quickly, and get started, then maybe at the weekend go and look at the bedroom furniture. I want this room empty of memories as soon as I can. Let's go and order this pizza before doing anything else.'

* * *

Welcome home, Marta, I hope you feel I've looked after it well for you. It was done with love. Lorraine xxx

Marta had opened the card from Lorraine as they waited for the pizza delivery, and sat down with a thud to reread the words. She had been a proper cow with Lorraine, and she didn't deserve it. She held the card out for Ellie to read, and Ellie stared at her. 'Ring her. Do it now before we get the pizza. And grovel, dear sister of mine.'

* * *

Lorraine didn't know whether to answer the phone or not as soon as she spotted the name Marta on her screen. Tears hadn't been far away all day since the nastiness had spilled from Marta's mouth, and she dreaded hearing what Marta would follow those words up with. She hesitated, then accepted the call.

'Marta?'

'I'm sorry. I was such a little shit. I can only put it down to the stress of the day, and I feel awful for upsetting you. We've just ordered a couple of pizzas on my spanking brand-new debit card, so we wondered if you would come visit us at the house, and share it with us. It's just me and Ellie.'

There was a moment of hesitation before Lorraine spoke. 'I'll be there in ten minutes; pizza is better than a frozen shepherd's pie any day.'

* * *

There were hugs from both girls, and Lorraine handed over a couple of bottles of wine, but told them to save them for another day when they wouldn't be driving home. 'Housewarming gift,' she said, and hugged them again.

With the pizzas eaten and hands washed to get rid of the tomato sauce on their fingers, the banker's box was finally opened.

Ellie had seen nothing of the contents, and read the letter from Alex with interest. 'You going to meet him?'

'Probably, even if it's just to say stop mithering me and let me live my life on my own. Have you met him, Lorraine?'

'I've seen him, but not met him as such. I was required to attend the inquest into the deaths of the two men found in your cellar and Janette...'

Marta stared at her. 'Oh, my god. I've never even thought about that. We haven't seen the cellar yet; we've still got a bedroom to look at, all the outside – and the cellar, wherever it is.'

'It's the door opposite the lounge door,' Lorraine said quietly. 'Before you explore it, please be aware I've done a lot of work down there. After the forensic teams had finished, all the stuff pertinent to the two men was removed, leaving basically an empty room. I knew that one day you would be back here, so it no longer resembles a cellar as such. You wouldn't want to put coal in it or anything, because I've painted it white. I'll apologise now if I did the wrong thing, but I fell in love with little Marta, and I wanted nothing of the events of that time to be on show. Do you want to go down there now?'

'Is it scary?' Ellie's voice wobbled.

'Not at all,' Lorraine said, smiling at the young girl. 'It's nothing like it was. The cellar head, which is the space at the top of the stairs, is where all the cleaning equipment is – your vacuum cleaner, sweeping brushes, dusters, polish, all stuff like that, and I bought a couple of IKEA bookcases to stand in there for shelving.'

Marta moved towards the hallway, and came to a stop at the door they had ignored so far. 'This is it?' she asked, and Lorraine nodded. 'It's locked, and the key is on the jamb. Don't leave it in the lock; it hurts when you lean against the door and the key is sticking out of the lock. I would advise keeping it secured because there is a coal hole access from the side of the house.'

'Flippin' heck, it's like living in the Victorian era,' Marta said, her laughter sounding good to Lorraine's ears.

'It's a Victorian house,' the older woman pointed out.

Marta reached up and grasped the key, inserting it into the lock.

'Your mother drew a picture of her sealing this door up with duct tape. I feel I have to tell you that. Because when you start to look at the drawings, you're going to see for yourself. She never drew a picture of the cellar itself, just one of Philip Hancock on the cellar steps. She simply tumbled him down there, locked the door behind him and tried to get on with her life, until the smell of decomposition began to invade the house. That's when she sealed the door, and put a curtain in front of it. It's all documented. Ellie, are you okay?'

'If this is how blunt you have to be when you're an adult, I don't want to grow up,' she said. 'There's half a chance my pizza will come back up.'

Marta opened the door.

'Reach round to your left, there are two light switches. The first one is for the cellar head, the second one is for the bottom of the cellar steps.'

Marta clicked them both. The cellar head was pristine, glaringly white and stocked with everything she could possibly want for cleaning the house. There were two tins of white paint and a load of paint brushes, and Lorraine pointed to them. 'This is the paint I used for the cellar. One tin unopened, the other about two thirds used. I thought you might need it for any ceilings you paint.'

Marta stared around her. It must have taken Lorraine a lot of effort and time, and she had been an absolute cow to her. She stepped tentatively forward and looked down the steps. The walls were white, the steps black.

'The black paint is a special non-slip one. Go ahead, it's not dangerous.'

The three of them stood at the bottom, and Marta and Ellie stared around in amazement.

'This was for keeping coal in?' Ellie asked, her eyes wide.

'It was. This little corner here is where the second body was found, but there is no evidence of that now. This is a storage area for you. It's dry, it's secure, and at some time in the future, you may decide to do something with it. I had to change it for you, Marta, I couldn't leave it as it was, and have you walk into it knowing it had held the bodies.'

* * *

Lorraine, Marta and Ellie headed back to the lounge, where they drank a cup of tea before deciding to head off home.

'Are you free to come back here tomorrow, Lorraine, and go through the drawings with us?' Marta's voice was hopeful that Lorraine would say yes. 'I know you've seen them before, and I'm pretty sure some of them will need some sort of explanation.'

'Of course.'

'We're not due back in school until the twelfth, so we've six days to get used to the house, do some clearing out and stuff, so your help would be welcomed. And I'm really sorry I was such a bitch with you, after all you've done for me.'

Lorraine smiled, pulled the girls to her and hugged them. 'Safe driving; give my love to your mum and dad, won't you.'

35

This time, Lorraine brought buns. They sat around the dining table with coffees from Starbucks, and a boxful of assorted buns.

The top had once more been removed from the banker's box, and the pile of sketchbooks sat in front of Marta. They were arranged in date order, with the first one showing the agonised face of a woman who was clearly Mother, with a man on top of her.

'I'm dreading this,' Marta whispered, taking a sip of her coffee. 'I'm going to know so much more by the time I reach the end, aren't I?'

'Not really,' Lorraine said, squeezing Marta's hand. 'She's documented everything, how she hit you, when she hit you, all that sort of thing, but you knew about it anyway, you were the recipient of her twisted mind. You knew about Billy and there are quite a few drawings of him. Some of the sketches are quick ones, but some are really detailed, the ones that were emblazoned into her brain.'

Marta pulled the first one towards her.

'So this is Alex Hancock's father?'

'It is. She would have made a good witness; she depicted him very accurately. You'll see that even more on the next one.'

Marta studied the picture intently. Her first thought was what Mother had been like prior to this attack? Had she been normal? Possibly withdrawn, but normal?

'This is in the kitchen. What was he doing here?'

'Nobody can ever be sure, but at the time of his death, Janette Gregson had a dog kennelling business, and the police believed he used that as an excuse for being on the premises. According to the neighbours, who really knew very little, the dog owners were allowed as far as the conservatory off the kitchen, but not inside the house. Janette wasn't a big woman; it would have taken nothing to push her inside the kitchen and away from the view of the neighbours, before attacking her.'

'He didn't know her prior to this?'

'Not as far as anybody is aware. Don't forget the first time the police knew of this crime, Janette was already dead. They could only suppose, for the most part. What is definite is that she killed him.'

Marta turned over the first drawing and pulled the second one towards her. 'What's that thing she killed him with?'

'It's called a cobbler's last, or a cobbler's foot. It's made of cast iron, and people use them for door stops. It's not here now, obviously; it's a murder weapon and as such is safely tucked away in an evidence room. However, it was also the murder weapon used by your grandmother. The indentation on the skull of the older body matched perfectly with the indentation on the skull of Philip Hancock.'

Marta gave a sigh. 'Am I really old enough to be told such gory stuff?'

'I'd rather it came from me than from some other source who doesn't have the true facts.' Lorraine's voice was firm. 'When they found the older body, they worked out he hadn't been dead when he was tied to a chair in the cellar. I suppose it's pretty obvious, really, there would have been no need to tie him to a chair if he was already dead. It's believed he was unconscious, and your grandmother simply left him to die. Tough cookies, the women in the Gregson family, Marta.'

She stared at picture two for a while longer, noting the clearer face that Janette had depicted. Hancock was on his back, his face staring upwards, pools of blood around his head. She turned the page over, and began to make her way through the rest of them.

Ellie said very little, unable to comprehend fully the enormity of everything that Marta was seeing, and knowing it would be there for the rest of her life because of the pictures.

Lorraine was able to talk Marta through everything, and when it came to the dog pictures, Marta stroked her fingers down Billy's face. 'He was a nice dog, not a barking one. I hardly ever heard anything from him, but I suppose that's because nobody ever came to the house.'

'You don't ever remember hearing anybody at all?'

'Not a soul. But I don't suppose I would have called out for help, because I wasn't aware I needed help. Being locked up was a perfectly normal situation for me; I don't remember it ever being anything other than having to sit on the edge of the bed at all times, until a meal was delivered. Then I could sit at this little table here.' She tapped on the picture in front of her. The table had a drink spilt on it, and Janette was beating Marta with a slipper.

Ellie pulled the picture around so she could see it properly. 'I'm glad she's dead. She didn't deserve to live.'

'Does she have a grave?'

'It's a small plot where her ashes are interred. The solicitors dealt with it all, as there were no relatives other than you, and they had clear instructions to act on your behalf until you reached eighteen.'

'Will you take me one day?'

Lorraine nodded. 'Of course I will. But not yet. You have a lot to take on board and I think you need to get your head around the house first of all.'

'I don't feel any bad vibes from it, other than in the room where she kept me prisoner. It feels a nice house, even down in that cellar, and the bad bedroom will soon be a good one because it's going to be Ellie's room.'

'Painted pink, apparently,' Ellie said with a laugh. 'Pink, I ask you.'

Marta smiled. 'Okay, point made. You choose the colour, but that means you have to help with the work. Deal?'

'Deal.'

The next picture they pulled towards them had colour on it. It was the half-finished New York Beauty quilt, and Marta touched it with almost a feeling of reverence. 'This, in real life, is truly wonderful.'

'Even that has some facts behind it. We believe that quilt was in part responsible for Janette falling downstairs. It was thought that she had just changed the bedding and had put that quilt on as she had finished it. She gathered up the pile of bedding in her arms to carry it downstairs, and had a heart attack. It could have been brought on by the weight, because the quilt that had been on her bed was a heavy one, and she somehow caught herself up in the laundry and tumbled downstairs. She either died immediately or when her head hit the newel post, but either way, the quilt was never used by her. It's new to you, Marta.'

Marta nodded, not knowing how to respond.

They worked carefully through all the pictures, then sat back with a feeling almost of exhaustion. Emotions had been high in Marta and both Lorraine and Ellie had recognised it, allowing her the time and space to absorb everything she hadn't known about Janette.

Marta gave a small nod, as if she had reached a conclusion. 'As you know, it's always been my ambition to have a gallery where I can display my work, and also items produced by other artists. I will have one room dedicated to these drawings produced by Mother. They'll be uniformly framed and placed on the walls and it will be the Janette Gregson room. There'll be no explanations, just her name and the date of the picture on a small plaque. I think I understand her a little better now. I can't forgive her, but I can accept whatever talent I have came from her. Let that room be her legacy, and let visitors draw their own conclusions, as we have had to do.'

Lorraine stared at the young woman she had grown to love, and felt a little overawed by her maturity.

'They'll not be for sale?'

'Never. It's not just about Mother, is it, it's also about Child.'

'Well whatever you decide, Marta, you have my full support. Since the day I met you, I've loved you, and I hope you know I would do anything for you. Good luck with all of your plans, my lovely.'

* * *

The two girls were back home by mid-afternoon, to find that Wendy had taken herself off to bed with a good book, a cup of tea, and written instructions not to disturb her until the potatoes and other veg had been prepared for the evening meal.

Marta smiled at the note. Her mum had clearly taken advantage of the quietness of the empty house to do exactly what she wanted and needed to do, and that was to have peaceful rest while she continued to heal.

'Where's Dad?'

'He had to meet a new client, taking him for lunch, I think he said,' Ellie responded. 'I'm going for a soak in the bath to think things through. It's been a traumatic time going through those pictures. I was going to suggest you had them bound into a portfolio, but I think your idea of displaying them in their own room is much better.'

Marta nodded. 'I'm going to my room, then I can hear if Mum needs anything. I've a picture I'm close to finishing so I'm going to work on it. It's for my new lounge, I think.'

Ellie headed upstairs, and Marta heard the bath water running as she passed the door. Her picture was calling, and she opened her bedroom door, thinking she might use the same lemony yellow colour that made her smile every time she entered her room, when she decorated the room Mother had used for her bedroom.

She moved across to her easel, and stood for a while, simply looking. The picture was of her life, a chaotic splash of colour, with areas of more calming colours. She had used lots of red, knowing it represented the anger that was always just under the surface of her thoughts, and she realised maybe changes would have to be made to the picture in view of the morning spent looking at Mother's drawings.

Cadmium blue. She squeezed a little onto her palette and added a little of the crimson she had already used. She began to add the resulting colour, and the outside world faded into oblivion.

* * *

Ellie wrapped a towel around her hair, then picked up the bath towel and fastened it around her breasts by tucking one corner into the towel. She quickly washed out the bath, thinking how nice the bubble bath had smelt, then left the bathroom.

Stewart was standing outside the door.

'Hi, Dad.'

She saw the flush creep up his face. He reached up to the towel on her head. 'You're losing your towel,' he said, and moved it. She felt it drop onto the back of her neck, and lifted her hand to stop it from coming off.

Stewart flicked the wrap-over part of the bath towel, and it began to tumble to the floor. Ellie scrabbled around, trying to cover herself, and both Marta and Wendy heard her say, 'Dad, that's the last time...'

Wendy's door opened, and she saw her husband's hands as they moved towards Ellie's breasts.

'Mum,' she said, the desperation evident in her voice. 'Mum, for god's sake, tell him he's to stop this. He's to stop touching us.'

Wendy stared, taking in the sight of her semi-naked daughter, knowing she had missed something too important to have simply ignored. 'Ellie? What the hell's going on?'

Marta moved forward, and pushed Stewart out of the way. 'Pervert,' she snarled, and turned to her mother. 'How can you have not known, Mum? He's been watching and touching for years, but no more. Get dressed, Ellie. We don't have to stay here a minute longer. We've somewhere else to go now.'

Ellie sobbed, clutched her towels around her, and headed for her bedroom.

36

'Stewart?'

Wendy stared at her husband, daring him to deny what she had seen.

'Don't waffle and blag your way out of this one, Dad, you've been at it since the day we got the pool.' The anger in Marta's voice, the clenched fists, showed exactly what she thought of her father, and Wendy knew something had to be sorted before she could offer comfort to her daughters, and certainly before she lost her daughters for ever.

'Marta.' Wendy's voice was low. 'Can you leave me to sort this? I promise I will, but I need you to go back to your room for the moment. Or Ellie's room; she may need some comfort.'

Marta nodded, and knocked on Ellie's door before opening it.

Wendy stared at Stewart. 'Downstairs, now.'

Panic flashed across his face and he raised his hand.

'Just do it, Stewart. Just touch me once and see what happens.' The coldness in her voice froze him, and his hand dropped.

'Of course I won't touch you,' he mumbled.

'You reserve that for our daughters, do you?'

'It's only a joke, you know it is.'

'They're not laughing, Stewart, and neither am I. Wait – don't go downstairs, not yet. Pack a bag first, and get out of this house. If you don't, I will call the police, don't ever doubt that. These girls are my life, and I had actually thought they were yours, but how wrong could I be?'

She turned from him and headed downstairs. 'You have ten minutes, and then I want you gone. And don't go anywhere near those girls while you're upstairs. If you do, I ring the police.'

* * *

Wendy watched as his car pulled away, and wondered what else could go wrong in her life. The lounge door opened, and Marta and Ellie walked in, going towards their mother to hug her.

'We're so sorry, Mum. There's no way we would have told you, and definitely not at the moment, but he's escalated it now.'

'How long has it been going on, and just what is it that's been happening?'

'It's watching and touching, almost accidental, but he makes our skin crawl,' Ellie said. 'It became noticeable when we got the pool, because he couldn't take his eyes off us, but just now he actually pulled off my towel. Mum, he saw me completely naked.' The tears began to roll down her face and Wendy pulled her into her arms.

'Hey, shush. He's gone now. And why didn't you tell me you were uncomfortable?'

'How could we?' Marta said. 'He's our dad, and he was fine until we got boobs. What happens now?'

Wendy closed her eyes for a moment. 'I don't know, but I won't allow him anywhere near either of you again. I'm so sorry...' and she began to cry. Her girls stared at her with a feeling almost of horror – she never cried in sorrow, it was always with happiness. She was known for sobbing when anything pleased her, and Marta and Ellie both hugged her carefully, all too aware of the soreness she was still feeling following her operation.

'Where's he gone?' Marta asked.

'I've no idea. Since I said get out, we haven't exchanged a word. It almost feels like relief, and I know it shouldn't. I should be devastated, but for the past couple of years things haven't been right, and I actually think my diagnosis of cancer was almost the final straw for him, so please don't ever think this split was caused by you two. In my mind, but not Stewart's, it was on the cards, I fear. I just wish you'd told me before, and it wouldn't have happened like this.'

* * *

Marta sat on the end of Ellie's bed, hugging her little quilt. It was after midnight, and neither of them felt like sleeping. It seemed strange to be minus a father, but they were no longer looking over their shoulders in case he was anywhere near. They had made sure Wendy took a sleeping tablet, and a check a few minutes earlier had confirmed she was asleep.

'So what happens now?' Ellie kept her voice low.

'I'm still moving out as soon as possible. I don't ever want to see Stewart again, and there's always a chance he'll pop back to try and build bridges here. Well, he's not building one with me, the pervert. My house is only fifteen minutes away, and I can check on Mum at any time, but I think I knew the second I walked through the door of that house that I would be leaving home. And my offer for you to stay there as well will always be open, but I won't push for it, Ellie. It will always be your decision. And tomorrow I'm going to contact this half-brother that I seem to have acquired.'

'I agree. He is your direct family, and the only real family you have. And if you don't like him, you can tell him to piss off.'

Both girls giggled, stifling their laughter, all too aware of the sleeping person in the room across the landing.

'Okay, first thing tomorrow morning, I'll ring that mobile number at the top of his letter. It would be ironic if he'd changed his number, wouldn't it, now that I've made the decision to contact him?'

* * *

Alex hadn't changed his number, and promised to be with Marta by just after one, as he could take time out from his job at that point. 'Would you mind if I brought my sister along, if she's free?' he asked.

'Not at all. She has come round to the idea of having a half-sister?'

'She's said she'd like to meet you, which is a start. This is a massive day for me, Marta. And what a pretty name you chose. I've picked up little bits over the years, one of which was that you didn't have a name when they found you. Look, I'm just pulling up to my next stop in Chesterfield, so I'll go now, but I'm looking forward to talking later.'

'Sorry, I didn't realise you were driving.'

Alex laughed. 'I'm always driving. I'm an area manager for a betting company, and I visit our shops all over South Yorkshire. But at one today I'll be back in Sheffield, and knocking on your door.'

Marta said bye, and disconnected.

'Well?' Ellie was smiling.

'He sounds nice. You'll be with me, won't you?'

'If you want me there, of course I will. But what about Lorraine?'

'I'm not going to ask her. I don't think any of us would speak freely if a professional social worker was present, and I think we possibly do need to be open about stuff.'

* * *

Stewart woke early. He had had the worst night's sleep ever, wondering how the hell he was going to talk himself back into Wendy's good books, and how he could explain away what he had done with Ellie's towel. Wendy was clearly too angry with him to communicate at the moment. His late-night text telling her he was at the Premier Inn in Sheffield had generated no response, and his hope was that she had been asleep and not seen it, so would therefore text him her reply when she woke.

He went down for breakfast, then returned to his room, wondering what to do. Go into work? Act as if nothing had happened? Ring in and put Carl in charge for a few days, saying he had flu?

He decided on the final option, thinking he could persevere with Wendy without being distracted by roller and vertical blinds. Carl was more than capable of keeping everything running smoothly in the short term, and hopefully he would soon be back at home, having convinced Wendy it was just a single moment of silliness on his part. He had booked his room for three nights, but he knew it wouldn't take that long to sort out his marital issues.

He had no idea of the long conversation Wendy had had with her girls the previous night and the much shorter conversation they had had before leaving for Marta's house, when Wendy told them their father was currently living at the Premier Inn. They had left for the house, but only after extracting a promise from their mother that she would ring Lorraine and tell her what was happening, or at least as much as she could without breaking down completely. Lorraine would know what to do.

* * *

Alex and Olivia arrived in Alex Needham's very smart-looking Mondeo, and parked outside the house, having to leave it on the road as there were two Minis parked on the drive.

Olivia climbed out first, leaving Alex to finish his phone call with someone called Dee. She looked around, thinking how bland the house looked with its black doors. She felt more than a little out of sorts, quite put out that Alex had made the arrangement for both of them to meet this girl without actually checking she could do it. It also angered her that he knew she would find a way of doing it.

The wind was bitingly cold, and she tapped on the car window, mouthing 'hurry up'. He held up his thumb, and she watched as he disconnected the call, then opened his door.

'Sorry about that. I'm turning it off now; I'll get back to anybody who wants me later.'

'It's bloody freezing. Let's get inside.'

* * *

Alex and Olivia both felt a sense of surprise at how pretty the girls were. Marta led them into the lounge while Ellie went to make hot drinks for all of them. The house, after a couple of days of having the heating activated, was starting to warm up nicely, and Marta had been quick to point out there were throws if they felt cold. Five years without having heating on had made the soul of the house very cold, but it was certainly much warmer than the first time they had entered it.

There was some deliberately inane chatter as they spoke of where they were in their lives, but it was clear to Marta that Olivia was on edge. Finally, and with a slight tremble in her voice, she allowed her thoughts to spill out.

'So did Dad die in this room?'

Marta stared at her half-sister. 'No. No, he didn't. I wouldn't have been so cruel as to inflict that on you, but I'm not sure how much of the story you know.'

Olivia's cheeks flushed a bright red, as if she was holding anger in. 'We know very little. We know Dad supposedly raped your mother, and she killed him then hid him, but what I also know is that I've been without my dad for nearly nineteen years, and yet you, his other daughter, have had a dad. How would you feel, Marta, if somebody killed him? If somebody took your dad away from you, and you were kept in the dark about it?'

Alex leaned across and grasped Olivia's hand, but she shrugged him off. 'Leave me alone, Alex. Even now, we're not getting the full story. Where did he die, Marta? He was my dad and I know nothing.'

'Look, just for the record, Olivia, dads are a bit fleeting in all our lives. Stop saying I have a dad, because currently that feller you think is my dad is living in the Premier Inn in Sheffield. So pack it in with the missing father bit. They did wrong, they've gone.'

Just for a fleeting moment, Marta considered telling both of them to leave, but one glance at Ellie's face, the shock caused by the caustic tones in Marta's voice, told her this wasn't going to go away, and if they didn't reveal everything in the story, it would eat away at the brother and sister sitting on the sofa. Marta stood.

'Come with me,' she said. She led them into the dining room, where the banker's box stood in the middle of the dining table. She lifted it towards her and removed Janette's drawings, each sketch-book now slipped into a plastic folder to preserve it.

Marta took out the first book, and told Alex and Olivia to go through the book. The pictures were all dated and all in order.

'Mother kept a diary. An illustrated diary; she used very few words. This was how the police could piece everything together, once they got into the house. It's how they found me, how they realised that somewhere in the house there was a child. You see, you may have been without your father, Olivia, but I was without everything. It wasn't just a name that was missing in my life. She called me Child from the day I was born. I was a nonentity to her, and I honestly believe if I had been a boy, she would have thrown me down the cellar steps to be with the man who gave me life. Your father. And why do I believe that? The fourth picture is a naked baby, making it very clear it is a girl. And on this one, she used three words. *Change of plan*, followed by the date. I was one day old.'

37

Olivia didn't try to deny it was her father in the first three pictures. 'This is the kitchen in the picture?'

'It is. The police reconstruction showed he came into the small conservatory which Mother used as an office to book in the dogs she kennelled here for owners who went on holiday. She was a supremely private woman, never spoke to the neighbours, hardly ever spoke to me, and they believe your father pushed her through into the kitchen, and raped her. The cobbler's foot which she hit him with was within reach of her hand, and she used it. The pictures tell you the full story. Your father was then pushed down the cellar steps and wasn't found for thirteen years. They don't know how he knew Mother, but they believe he probably used the excuse of needing a dog putting into kennels for her to allow him into her office space.'

'Our father,' Olivia said.

'What?'

'I said our father. You keep saying your father did this, your father did that, but he was our father. The three of us.'

Marta nodded. 'He was. It's hard to think of him like that.'

'Can I see the kitchen?' Alex spoke quietly.

'Of course. I've only had the house a couple of days, as you know, so the kitchen is exactly as it would have been. Mother never had workmen in the house, so I'm pretty sure nothing changed anywhere.'

Brother and sister followed Marta through to the kitchen, with Ellie standing close by in case Marta should need her.

Alex and Olivia's eyes immediately dropped to the floor, and it was obvious they were imagining the body of their father lying there, blood spatter everywhere, caused by the blow or blows from the cobbler's foot.

Olivia knelt and touched the floor. 'Why, Dad?'

Alex moved towards her, but Marta held up a hand, and shook her head.

'You wouldn't have hurt a soul. Why did you do this?' And finally Olivia's tears came.

* * *

Alex and Olivia had departed by three o'clock, and Marta and Ellie sank back onto the sofa.

'Well, that was a doddle, wasn't it?' Ellie said.

'Sarcasm doesn't become you,' was Marta's heartfelt rejoinder. 'Alex seemed to accept what his father had done, much easier than Olivia did. I was dreading showing them the cellar, but after the kitchen, the cellar was a bit anticlimactic. Have you checked Mum is okay?'

'Yes, while you were doing the cellar tour. Apparently Dad keeps ringing and texting her, but she's ignoring him.' Ellie frowned. 'I hope she's not considering letting him come home.'

'Well, if she does, we're out of there for good, and we're in here.

We can decorate and refurnish while we're living here. That okay with you?'

The look of relief on Ellie's face said it all.

* * *

The girls planned to cook a pasta bake once they arrived home, aware that Wendy had seemed a little spaced out when they had left earlier that day.

'You have to eat, Mum,' Marta said. 'Chicken pasta bake okay?'

'It's fine, but I'm not really hungry. And you can tell me all about your half-siblings while we're eating. As you're both in a good mood, I'm assuming everything went well.'

'Eat a little, eat a lot, it doesn't matter as long as you eat something. And Ellie is ace at pasta bake. The meeting was good, we chatted a lot, and I'm sure we'll not drift apart now we've taken this step.' Marta smiled at her mother, aware of how poorly she looked. 'I'll tell you more later.'

'Oy,' Ellie said, 'this is a joint effort. Come on, let's go start it.'

Wendy returned to her seat in the lounge, carrying her phone with her. She didn't want her girls to see just how many times Stewart had messaged, or how many calls he had made that she had ignored. And the final one that she hadn't ignored, answering it more in desperation than anything, wanting him to stop the incessant harassment. That was the phone call in which he had tried to explain it was all the fault of the girls, that Marta and Ellie had flaunted themselves in front of him, and he had found it hard to resist.

Wendy forced some food down her, aware of two lots of eyes on her checking she was eating something, and after everything was cleared away, the girls disappeared, Marta to work on her painting and Ellie to do some English revision in preparation for the imminent A level exam. Life still had to go on, Ellie felt, despite her world imploding at the moment.

Wendy watched something mindless on television for a while, then switched it off and picked up her Kindle. She was almost at the end of a book, and keen to finish it and start the next one in the series.

She headed upstairs just before nine, popping her head round Ellie's bedroom door to wish her goodnight, reminding her not to work all night, before heading to Marta's door. The picture was close to completion and Wendy drew in her breath. It was a large canvas, and colour flowed out of it. 'Oh, Marta, that is wonderful.'

Marta turned, smiling. 'You like it? It's for my house, for the lounge. It could definitely do with some colour in it. Will you come with us one day, Mum? Come and see the house?'

'I'd love to. I've not mentioned visiting it because I need a bit longer to feel well enough to do anything, but I will call in, I promise you. I'm off to bed now, and I've taken a sleeping tablet, so two pages of this and I'll be in the land of nod. Don't stay up too late, sweetheart.' She waved her Kindle around.

'We'll not disturb you. I'm tired as well; it's actually been quite emotional and a little bit frustrating meeting Alex and Olivia today. I think Alex accepts what his dad did was wrong and justice probably happened, but that's not the way Olivia felt. She was really pissed off that I had landed on my feet and had a father, while because of Mother, she had had to do without one. If only she knew...'

'You didn't tell her?'

'Not in detail. I just said my father, the man she was going on about, was currently living in the Premier Inn, not at home with us, and things weren't always black and white. I left it at that; it's nothing to do with her.'

Wendy nodded. 'Okay, sweetheart, goodnight and God bless. I'll see you in the morning.'

Marta worked for a further half an hour, had a quick shower and climbed into bed. She made a half-hearted attempt at doing some of the revision she knew had to be done, and finally cancelled the idea, the papers scattered across the small quilt. The thought that took her into the late evening of a day where she appeared to have acquired a brother and sister, although somehow she felt the sister wasn't going to be a long-term relationship, was that life felt so much better without Stewart around.

* * *

Ellie studied until almost two, flitting in and out of her bedroom as she collected a glass of milk, a bag of crisps, a couple of satsumas, all at different times, and all in a vague effort at keeping her concentration going.

It didn't work. She fished under her pillow in the end, found her Kindle and opened it. A good murder or two was just the right thing to let her drift off to sleep. She didn't read for long; her eyes closed, the Kindle hit her on her nose, and she gave in to sleep.

Nobody in the house heard or saw anything unusual. The long day had blessed them all with tiredness, and they slept. Until nine o'clock the next morning.

* * *

Wendy had just finished drying her hair when she heard the peal of the doorbell. She felt so much better. Not taking a sleeping tablet was the best thing – she didn't feel tired and drained when she woke, and she thought today might be the day to visit Marta's house. She knew her girls thought she needed the small white tablets at the moment, but she had felt a little white lie the previous night had been justified. And necessary.

She opened her bedroom door and called the girls, hoping one would respond and say they'd get it, but there was no sound. She slipped on her dressing gown carefully, aware of the still healing wound, and headed downstairs. She could see two people through the glass, so she guessed it wasn't the postman.

She pushed the door chain into its housing before opening the door.

'Fleur! Alan! How lovely to see you!' She closed the door, removed the chain and welcomed them in. 'Coffee?'

'Alan will make one for all of us. I need to talk to you. Are the girls around?'

'They're in bed. Busy day yesterday. You need them?'

'I think it would be for the best.'

Wendy stared at her friend. 'What's wrong, Fleur?'

'Get the girls, Wendy, and we can talk.'

Wendy went upstairs, and opened both bedroom doors. Marta was lying in bed reading. Ellie's bedroom appeared to be a bit of a picnic area, and she had to shake her youngest daughter to wake her.

'Fleur's here. She wants to talk to us.'

* * *

Alan had now risen to the rank of Detective Sergeant. Wendy was congratulating him on his promotion, and also Fleur on her rise to Detective Inspector, when the two girls entered the kitchen. Alan handed them a coffee each, and they sat down at the table.

'Well, it's lovely to see you both,' Marta said, rubbing her eyes. 'But you're not here because it's something nice to do, are you?'

Fleur shook her head. 'No, we're not. Wendy, Marta, Ellie, I'm sorry but a body has been pulled from the canal, in the canal basin, actually. A man, and he's been identified as Stewart.'

'Stewart?' Wendy's face had drained of all colour. 'My Stewart?'

'Yes. His wallet was in his pocket, with his driving licence in it, a couple of credit cards in his name. And obviously I identified him. We now need to investigate why he was there, and who hit him on the head with something pretty solid, maybe a brick or a rock, causing him to fall into the basin that's next to impossible to get out of. Can you help by filling in missing parts?'

'Not really.' Wendy was struggling to hold back the tears. 'We haven't been getting on too well and I told him to go. He messaged me to say he was staying at the Premier Inn in Sheffield; I received the text yesterday morning when I woke up, but it arrived at some point during the night. He sent me lots of messages and rang several times yesterday, but I didn't want to talk to him.' She slipped her phone from her dressing gown pocket and passed it across to Fleur. 'You can see for yourself what sort of a day I had.' She opened the phone by putting in her code.

Fleur thanked her and scanned through the messages, noticing the increased desperation in the tone of them. She moved on to the ignored calls, and realised Stewart's day must have been spent entirely on his phone. Clearly a man determined to speak to his wife, intent on putting right whatever was wrong.

The last call, timed at 16.32, had been answered.

'You answered the last call?'

'I did. I was cheesed off. And that's basically what I said, although a bit stronger language may have been used. He didn't ring again after that.'

38

'So, you were... where? Last night, I mean.' Fleur stared at the three women, with whom she would at any other time be sharing a laugh and a joke. 'Wendy?'

Wendy closed her eyes momentarily, attempting to remember the time scale of what had happened the previous evening. 'The girls arrived home around fiveish, I think it was, and then they made a pasta bake for our evening meal. I don't feel recovered enough to tackle anything like that just yet, so they are looking after me. As you can see from my phone, I'd spent the day fending off Stewart's attempts at communication with me. That in itself was truly exhausting. We ate at around sixish, the girls went upstairs to work, and I watched a bit of inane television, took my sleeping tablet, read a little bit until I knew I was falling asleep, and then went to bed around nine. I said goodnight to both girls, and that was it until about an hour ago.' She hesitated and fixed her eyes on Fleur. 'I can't believe this is happening. Do you know when he died?'

'We don't have pathology results yet, but he left the Premier Inn around ten last night, asked that they stock up on tea and coffee for him as he'd used up the first lot, and headed out. He said he was going for a walk, and would be back in about an hour. He didn't return, and one of the workers in the canal basin reported a body in the water at around six this morning. We're treating it as a suspicious death, as there is an obvious head injury. I'm so sorry, Wendy.'

'Our split was very recent, Fleur. I've been with Stewart for many years – we met at school when we were only fourteen, so I've loved him for a long time, still do now. But things had changed recently, and we... I... decided to call it a day. But I would never, ever, have wanted him dead.' And she burst into tears, apologising for not being able to hold them in any longer.

Marta passed her the box of tissues, saying, 'Do you need anything? Are you in pain?'

Wendy shook her head, smiling up at Marta. 'No, I'm okay. This is the worst possible news.' She turned to Fleur. 'Can I see him?'

'Possibly tomorrow. Although I identified him, we do need a formal identification from a member of his family.'

'Then let me know,' Wendy said, 'and I'll be there. I'm sure my brother will come up to go with me; he lives in Worcester.'

'The girls can accompany you...'

'No, I won't ask that of them.'

'So there's nothing else you can tell us, Wendy?'

'No, it seems while he was leaving us altogether, I was fast asleep.'

Fleur nodded. 'We'll get your statement typed up and ask you to sign it when you come in tomorrow.'

'Do we need to make statements?' Marta asked, indicating both her and Ellie, who sat there, staring into space.

'If you can go through everything you did last night, it would be helpful.'

'Okay, we were at my house most of the day, then came home

for about five o'clock. I can't be accurate on that, but it seems Dad was still alive at that point anyway.' She heard a stifled sob from Ellie, and put her arm around her sister. 'Hey, come on. We can cry later.'

'And you and Ellie cooked the meal?'

'We did. After we'd loaded the dishwasher and tidied the kitchen, we went to our rooms. I'm working on a painting for my house, and it's nearing completion, so I wanted to carry on with that. Ellie is the bright one, she went to do some revision for the exam we have next week.'

'You weren't together?'

'Not all night, but I did take her a hot chocolate at one point, maybe around half past nine, and she was sitting on her bed surrounded by paperwork and books – oh, and chocolate wrappers. Made me feel a little guilty, if I'm honest.'

'And where was your mum?'

'She'd said goodnight to both of us, telling us not to be late in bed when she saw what we were doing. But I do have to add that's standard conversation when Mum pops into our room to say goodnight.'

Wendy gave a brief smile of acknowledgement that she had indeed said those words.

'So you didn't go back out after returning from your house, you were in all evening?'

'We were together all evening, and that's more to the point,' Ellie finally spoke. 'My statement will match Marta's because we left the kitchen together, we chatted a couple of times during the evening, and we both saw Mum at nine when she went to bed. And believe me, when she's had a sleeping tablet, she's out for the count. And I can probably quote fifteen or sixteen parts verbatim from *A Midsummer Night's Dream*, all of which I learnt between seven and two, just to prove what I was doing. Fleur, I know you have to question us, but really! As if any of us would kill the man who rescued us from a life of children's homes, who gave us a happy stable childhood, and who took on Marta with all her teenage issues as well as her other issues. For goodness' sake, Fleur...'

Fleur reached across and grasped Ellie's hand. 'Hey, I know. It's my job to prove innocence as much as to prove guilt. I just have one more question.'

Ellie nodded. 'I'm sorry. I'm a little stressed.'

'Okay, now this is to all of you. Did anyone else apart from you three know he was staying at the Premier Inn? It seems his late-night walk took him down to the very picturesque canal basin. Either it was a totally random attack by a stranger for reasons unknown, or he was followed, or someone made an appointment to meet with him. In this day and age, it could very easily be the first reason. He may have looked at somebody a little bit wrong, and paid the ultimate penalty. But we can't take that as gospel, I have to check all possibilities. So, did anyone else know where Stewart was staying?'

'Yes,' Ellie said, and shuddered. 'Yes, we told Marta's half-brother and half-sister yesterday, just an aside, really. Olivia was saying how unfair it was that she had lost her much-loved dad at the hands of Marta's mother, and yet Marta had landed on her feet and hooked herself a nice dad. We said things weren't always what they seemed, and he was currently residing in the Premier Inn. But we certainly told nobody else; he'd only been there overnight, and I don't think we'd even spoken to anyone else, not even Lorraine.'

'I told Lorraine,' Wendy said quietly. 'She called round about fourish to leave you some things for your kitchen, Marta, because she was in the area seeing a client. There's a carrier bag in the cloakroom, I completely forgot to tell you about it. She didn't stay long, we had a cuppa, I shed a few tears and told her about Stewart, then she went home.'

Alan was making notes. 'So apart from you three, three more people knew where Stewart was? Have I got that right?' he asked.

'It seems like it,' Marta said. 'We didn't know Lorraine knew. I'm glad she does, though, she's kinda part of our family, you know?'

Fleur picked up her coffee and drained it. 'Please, once again, accept our condolences. I have assigned a family liaison officer to you, and she will be around within the next hour to introduce herself. She will keep you fully informed, although our relationship over the years means you'll probably hear anything new from me first. I just have to stick to the correct procedure. Now, obviously I have Lorraine's contact details, but I don't have them for the Hancock family. Do you?'

Marta nodded. 'Olivia is still at home with her mum and stepfather, so I don't have that one, but it's apparently the same house they lived in when Philip Hancock went missing, so you'll have it somewhere. Alex has a different address. I'll get it for you; he wrote it on the back of his business card.'

Marta headed upstairs, leaving a silence in the room she had vacated. It seemed they were all talked out. The card was tucked into her purse, and she retrieved it and headed downstairs, handing it to Alan as they stood in the hallway waiting for her.

'Look after your mum,' Fleur said softly, as she opened the door. 'The enormity of it will eventually hit her, and she'll need you two to be the adults. I know this couldn't have happened at a more difficult time, with exams looming next week, but you're both going to have to put it to one side while you deal with your futures. Time to grieve later.'

Marta nodded. 'We'll be okay. Do we need to go somewhere to sign the statements?'

'I'll let you know. Your mum can sign hers when she comes in to identify your dad. Marta, was he ever violent towards you or your mum?'

'No, not violent.' She held back on any further comments, closing the door as they left, and leaning against it to collect her thoughts. Only six people had known of Stewart's whereabouts. She hoped and prayed the police came to the conclusion it was a random act of brutality that had taken his life; the other suggestion was unthinkable.

* * *

Olivia was still in bed when Fleur and Alan knocked on the door of the house they had visited so many times in the past. Nothing seemed to have changed except the Rhus tree in the front garden had grown bigger – it had been a newly planted tree the first time they had called to discuss the man who had disappeared without explanation.

Theresa Hancock opened the door, her hands and the front of her apron floury. 'Fleur? Goodness me, I expected you to be an Amazon driver. What can I do for you?'

'We're here to speak to Olivia, if she's in.'

'Oh, she's in, all right. She's still in bed. Come in, I'll go and rouse her. Excuse the flour, I'm baking bread. Can I help? Or does it have to be Olivia you see?' She waggled her fingers as if to emphasise her current activity, and Fleur smiled at her.

'Thank you. We won't keep Olivia long, she can go back to bed after we've gone.'

Theresa opened the lounge door with her elbow, then went upstairs, still holding her floury hands in the air and away from any objects that she didn't want covered in the stuff.

They heard her tell Olivia to get her arse out of bed, the police were here to arrest her, and she came back downstairs, laughing.

'She says she can't be arrested for perving over our dishy new neighbour, and she hasn't done anything else wrong. She'll be five minutes; she needs a wee and to brush her teeth. Her words, not mine. Can I get you a drink while you're waiting? And maybe a scone? I did the scones before I started fancying some homemade bread.'

Alan answered before Fleur had even opened her mouth. 'That would be lovely, thanks, Theresa. Tea, no sugar, for both of us.' He grinned at Fleur. 'You have to get in quick with your answers when people mention scones.'

39

The tea, scones and Olivia all arrived at the same time. She'd managed the wee and the teeth-brushing exercise, but not quite stretched her morning routine to brushing her hair. It stuck out at many angles, and she was attempting to flatten it down a little as she entered the room.

'Hi, Fleur, Alan,' she said. 'What are you arresting me for?'

'Ogling the neighbour and having a bad hair day,' Fleur said, trying to look serious.

Olivia held out her wrists. 'You want to cuff me now? I'm guilty on both counts.' She sat down and picked up a small plate and a scone.

'We just want a little bit of information, really,' Fleur said. She smiled at the grown-up Olivia, who had been a somewhat gauche twenty-year-old or thereabouts the last time she had seen her. Five years on, and she had matured into a beautiful woman, albeit with currently spiky hair.

'Can you tell me what you were doing, and where you were last night?'

Olivia's surprise showed on her face. 'Last night? I was here.

Mum and Brad went to the cinema, then for something to eat after-wards. They got home around eleven, but I was in bed by then, watching Netflix. I was babysitting the puppy.'

'He's asleep at the moment,' Theresa explained. 'He's only nine weeks old, seems to spend most of the time asleep. Little Cavachon we've called Albert.'

Alan was taking notes and at the side of the word Cavachon, he put several question marks. What the hell was a Cavachon? 'So you didn't go out at all?' he asked.

She shook her head. 'No, not even when our neighbour went into the back garden. I figured he wouldn't want to see me with my Winnie the Pooh PJs on, so I stayed in the kitchen. He had a bit of a bonfire, so I enjoyed the sight from afar.'

'He's a bit of all right then, this neighbour?' Fleur smiled as she asked the question. It was hard to be formal when you already knew the person being interviewed.

'Dishy. Think he'll be gay?'

'Possibly. So, I take it your mum is aware of your visit to Marta and Ellie yesterday?' Fleur brought the conversation back to where it was supposed to be.

'Yes. I can't say I was impressed with my half-sister, although I could see a strong resemblance to Dad – his eyes were her eyes, and the way she smiled made me think of him straight away. She just seemed a bit...' – there was a moment of hesitation – 'hard, I suppose is the word I want. She opened up a little when she was showing us her mother's pictures, because I got the impression her world is all about art. She spoke of one day having a gallery for selling artisan goods and her own artwork, and she specifically mentioned having her mother's pictures on display, not for sale, in a separate room of their own. I didn't feel too happy about that, but they're her pictures and there's nothing we can do about it. I think Alex liked her, but Alex isn't me, he likes everybody. What's this all about?'

'I can't go into details, but we have a dead body and we're treating it as a suspicious death. It happened last night, and you're on the periphery of it.'

'Who's dead?'

'I'm sorry, I can't reveal that as there are other family members to consult. Did you speak to anyone last night? See anyone apart from the dishy neighbour who didn't see you? Did anyone ring you on the landline?'

She shook her head. 'I sent text messages to a couple of my friends but that doesn't really help, does it? I could have been anywhere doing that.'

'Can I look at your phone, please, Olivia? We can have your phone number checked to make sure it was in this area, and that would clear you of being anywhere else, so it's good that you sent texts. It will corroborate what you're saying is correct.'

Olivia handed her unlocked phone to Alan, and waited until he had the information he needed. She retrieved it and slipped it back into her dressing gown pocket. 'Is that it?'

Fleur and Alan stood. 'For the moment. We know where you live if we need to speak further with you. Thank you for the drink and the scones, Theresa, hope your bread rises successfully.'

Theresa escorted them to the door, wondering where all the flour had gone that had been on her hands but now wasn't. 'I never properly thanked you for your kindness when you came to tell us Philip had been found. I know I'd moved on, but Philip was always in my heart. He isn't now I know what he did, but even so, you were very good to us, both of you. So thank you. You will probably need to ring Alex if you need to speak to him, because he'll be out and about, could be anywhere, he's got a big area to cover now he's area manager. Have you got his number?'

'We do, and his address. Marta Needham gave them to us. Thank you, Theresa, please give our regards to Brad.'

She smiled and closed the door. They exited by the front gate and Fleur turned right. 'I just want to check with the neighbour, make sure he did have a fire last night. Olivia's a charmer, and she could be bamboozling us with this.'

She walked up the neighbouring path, and knocked on the door. To her surprise, it was opened, and reasonably fast. She had half expected him to be at work as it wasn't even midday.

They held up their warrant cards, and she apologised for intruding. 'I just need to check if you had a bonfire in your back garden last night, and what time you had it.'

'Oh my god, have I broken some relic of a bye-law or something? And does it really merit a visit from CID?' He looked shocked, his deliciously brown eyes clouding slightly in panic. He ran a hand through his equally delicious brown hair. Olivia was definitely correct in her visual assessment of the neighbour.

'No,' Fleur laughed. 'You did nothing wrong. We're just checking whether somebody else did something wrong. So what time did you have it, this bonfire?'

'About nineish. Can't say with any more accuracy than that. I've just moved in, and I had a load of paperwork I don't need any more, plus cardboard boxes that I knew the recycling people would grumble about taking, so I burnt some of them. It was out by about ten, because I came in as the BBC news was starting. My neighbour can confirm, because I spotted her in their kitchen, and I'm pretty sure she saw me. Is she the one who said I'd had the fire? Am I in trouble?' Suddenly he stopped talking. 'I'll shut up. I've done nothing wrong.'

Again, Fleur laughed. 'No, you haven't. Thank you for your help, you've actually confirmed an alibi. We won't trouble you again.'

Alan got into the driving seat, and waited until Fleur had belted up before starting the engine. 'Olivia was telling the truth, then.'

'Seems like it. We'll get her phone triangulated and then we can write her off. But somebody killed him, Alan, and we've already discounted four of the six people who knew where he was staying. We've only got Lorraine and Alex left. I'm not leaning towards a random attack. I think he went out for a walk to meet somebody. I have no idea at the moment who that somebody could possibly be, but we're eliminating, we're eliminating. I'll ring Alex Hancock now and see where he is. We'll track down Lorraine later.'

* * *

Alex wasn't surprised to receive the phone call; he'd already had one from Olivia telling him of her wakeup call by the Feds.

'The Feds?'

'Well, whatever they're called. I don't know who died, Fleur wouldn't tell us, see if you can find out. She said I was on the periphery. Got to go, I need to get ready for work. Late shift today. Ring me, brother dear, as soon as you know anything I don't know.'

She disconnected, and ten minutes later, he received a call from a number he didn't recognise. He arranged to meet Fleur and Alan at his home address, saying he would take a late lunch break, but he had to be on his way by three o'clock.

* * *

Alan paused to admire the silver Mondeo with the very new number plate, jotted it down into his notebook underneath Olivia's registration plate number and waited behind Fleur while she knocked. It was a small terraced house in an upmarket suburb of Sheffield, and Alex invited them in with a flourish. 'Good to see you again,' he said, 'although I've no idea what you can possibly want. I didn't meet Marta until yesterday, and it's something to do with her, so my sister informs me.'

'We won't take up much of your time, Alex.' Fleur stepped forward and Alex had no choice but to invite them in.

'You lived here long?' Alan looked around, taking note of the new furniture, and the cardboard boxes stacked in one corner.

'Two weeks,' Alex said with a laugh. 'I'm slowly working my way through a box a night. I work long, stressful hours, but I'll get through those damn boxes eventually. Would you like a drink?'

'No, thanks,' Fleur said, before Alan could even open his mouth. 'We're all tea and coffee'd out today. The next drink I have today will be something with a bit of tonic added.'

Alex invited them to sit down, and Alan took out his notepad.

'So, Alex, that ten-year-old little lad grew up. I understand you're an area manager, but I don't think anyone said what of.' Fleur smiled, trying to put him at ease. He seemed a little nervous.

'A major betting office chain. My area is South Yorkshire, and I get that super-duper car outside as a definite perk of the job. Although Olivia would argue with that; she loves her ancient little Beetle. Love what I'm doing now, and I have Marta to thank for that. Three years ago, I realised I needed to make something of my life, and as a betting shop manager, I was going nowhere. I felt that if I ever met my half-sister, I didn't want her to look at my home and think how awful it was, so I approached my superiors, told them I wanted to climb higher, and they helped. Next step is regional manager, but I'm happy where I am at the moment. The increase in salary helped me buy this house, and it's somewhere I would be proud to bring Marta and Ellie.'

'You got on with them?'

'I did. Maybe more with Ellie, if I'm honest; Marta felt a little abrasive, but it was our first meeting. She would have been as nervous as I was. She didn't hold anything back, whatever we asked she answered, and she showed us around her house. It'll be beautiful when she gets it sorted. It was hard, particularly for Olivia, seeing where Dad died, but I didn't feel the same emotions as Olivia did, I'm sure. She actually knelt down on the kitchen floor and touched the area where he would have drawn his last breath. I never got on with my father, he was strict, controlling, but he certainly loved Olivia. More than he loved me, anyway. But that's not why you're here, surely? That's many years ago now, and I think we've all more or less let it go. Well, maybe Olivia hasn't, but Mum and I have.'

'No, it's about a suspicious death we're investigating, and as I said to Olivia, you two are on the periphery of being acquainted with the dead person. I just need to know where you were last night, between, say, eight and midnight.'

Alex actually blushed. 'Why?'

'You need an alibi,' Alan said.

'Shit. Do I have to name names?'

'You do if you don't want locking up.'

There was a pause in the conversation, then Alex looked down at his feet. 'I went out for a meal with a friend. Then we came back here, and my friend stayed over.'

'Is she married?' Alan was puzzled by Alex's reticence.

'No. She's a he. And I'd rather my family didn't know yet, if that's okay with you.'

40

They left Alex alone with his embarrassment and took a break in Sainsbury's café while they waited to see Lorraine. They had an hour to kill, and ordered a panini and a large latte each.

Alan took out his notebook and collated a list of the car registrations he had gathered from Marta, Ellie, Wendy, Olivia and Alex, and looked up at Fleur.

'I don't suppose your super brain knows the car reg for Lorraine Lowe's car?'

She thought for a moment. 'I can probably find it for you.' She took out her phone and scrolled through her pictures.

'There,' she said. 'It's a jeep, and we went in hers for our Christmas lunch at Wentworth, because I wanted to get my Christmas tree. Her car is bigger than mine. Father Christmas delivered it to our car for us, so I took a picture.'

She handed him the phone and he burst out laughing. 'You're both kissing him!'

'Too damn right we were. We were trying for his naughty list last year. Anyway, you can see her registration quite clearly.'

He added it to his list, trying not to laugh, then took out his own phone. 'I'm texting these in to Tamsin. I'll ask her to feed them into ANPR for the canal basin/Hilton Hotel area, between nine in the evening and two in the morning, for last night. She might as well be working on that, and that's one thing crossed off our list.'

'Strange case, isn't it? Usually with a murder we're ferreting around for suspects, but there were literally only six people who actually knew where Stewart Needham was staying.'

'Seven. Possibly.'

'Who?'

'He probably rang his company to tell them he wouldn't be in. I'm not saying he would have told them where he was, because they didn't actually need to know, he had his phone with him. But he might have said...'

She stood. 'I'm going to the ladies'. Ring Wendy and get the number for his second in command at work.'

She came back several minutes later, and handed a Dairy Milk bar to Alan. 'We might need the sugar,' she said, in explanation. 'I've spoken to him, he's called Carl, and all Stewart said was he was taking a couple of sick days, because he had flu. Carl thought he was at home, so didn't say anything other than he hoped it would soon pass. Wendy did ring him earlier to tell him about Stewart's death, and to ask him to carry on doing whatever Stewart would have needed, until they could sort things out. So we're back to our six. I've sent the list to Tamsin, and got back a text saying "On it", so now we sit back and wait. And eat chocolate and drink coffee.'

'I don't think we'll be long at Lorraine's; of all the so-called suspects on our list, she's the one who's the gentle soul,' said Fleur. 'She's seen some bad stuff with her job, neglected kids, abused kids, teens who've run as soon as they could... and she's stayed sane through it all. I know she was badly affected when we found Marta, and I did think at one point she was considering applying to adopt her, but Marta soon became settled at the Needhams' and Lorraine stuck to her mentoring role. We both fell a little bit in love with Marta. We still are really, never miss a birthday, Christmas and birthday gifts for both girls. Lorraine was the one who placed Ellie with the Needhams, so she's known them a long time.'

'So really we're looking at the ones who we've already interviewed,' said Alan. 'Is that what you're saying?'

'Oh, I don't know. My head's going round in circles. I can't see how it could be any of them. Are we really looking for some random drunken idiot who came across a lonely man on the canal side, hit him with something and pushed him in the water? Is that what it's coming down to?'

'Shall I ring and see what was used to cause that head injury? And if it was that weapon that killed him or he drowned?' He ate the last of his chocolate bar before taking out his phone.

'Yes, be polite because they might not have got round to Stewart yet. I don't want them to think...'

'What? That you're pushing them?' He laughed. 'Every case we've ever had, you've wanted sight of the forensic results before they've even set up the tests.'

'Don't be cheeky, DS Jenkins. Am I really like that?'

'Noted for it, boss.'

Alan rang the morgue, and waited patiently. 'Good afternoon. Can I ask a quick question about the body of Stewart Needham, found in the canal basin in the early hours? It's DS Alan Jenkins, asking for DI Fleur Lavers.'

He waited for the usual explanation about how they were rushed off their feet and had only been working on it for a few minutes, then interrupted. 'I only want to know if you've managed to ascertain what caused the head injury. And did it kill him, or did he drown?'

He held the phone away from his ear as the pathologist carried on explaining that anything he could tell them would have to be verified by fool proof testing, and then he said, 'But you can tell that young whippersnapper Fleur that it was a hammer that was used, and he did drown. He was alive when he was either pushed or rolled into the water. It wasn't a brick as we first thought – the indentation, once cleaned up, showed it to be a sizeable hammer-head that was used.'

Alan thanked the man, and turned to Fleur with a smile.

'He called you a whippersnapper.'

'It's because he likes me. We went on a couple of dates a few years ago, but then he was transferred and it fizzled out. When he returned to Sheffield in our most senior position, he was married. So whippersnapper I'll always remain, I suppose.'

'Anyway, it was a hammer, with a large hammerhead. And it didn't kill him.'

'He drowned?'

Alan nodded. 'He did. He would have been unconscious from the blow, so unable to save himself.'

'Shit way to go. We'll keep this to ourselves until we do the briefing tomorrow morning. One thing I'm getting surer of is that it wasn't a random killing. Nobody carries a hammer around, certainly not a large one, looking for some stranger to bump off.'

'I agree. Maybe we should have pushed for more information on why suddenly there is this major split in the Needham family. But even so, they all had alibis.'

'Between themselves, Alan, between themselves. Nobody outside that close family group can confirm they were all in that house, all night. What had he done that suddenly upset Wendy that night? If it had been a split that had been coming for some time, he would have planned to have a home to move into, so it must have been sudden. He just upped and left.'

'Tried it on with one of the girls?'

'That thought hit me at exactly the same time as it hit you. Hundred quid says that was the reason for the sudden departure. And I can't tell you how much the thought of that upsets me. These girls were adopted from rubbish situations, and for their adoptive father to have possibly tried that... doesn't bear thinking about. If it is true, and I will get to the bottom of it, I'll take a hammer to him myself. Marta's been a huge part of my life, as has Ellie since Marta went to the Needhams'.'

Fleur's face had suffused with colour, and her breathing was ragged – the anger was evident. 'Get me a bottle of water, Alan, will you? I need to cool down.'

He looked at her, and immediately stood, returning a minute later with two waters. 'I first saw Marta as a scared little girl, certainly didn't look thirteen, and with very little vocabulary. She's turned into a stunning young woman, personable, and I suspect she's taken the lead in the Marta/Ellie relationship, protective of Ellie. Suppose it was Ellie who was hit on by her father? What would Marta do?'

Fleur briefly closed her eyes, as she put herself into Marta's shoes. 'Marta is no stranger to violence as a punishment. Please, please don't send my mind in that direction. If you – or, heaven forbid, a judge – asked me if I thought Marta would be capable of physical punishment that could potentially end in death, I would have to say yes. Until she was thirteen, that was all she knew. Regular beatings for even something as trifling as being in a standing position instead of seated merited a slap across the face, but the belt beatings must have been unbearable. Oh, yes, Marta understands excessive violence as a means to an end.'

'We have to ask the right questions, Fleur. We need to talk to Lorraine, get her written out of the scenario because I think both of us know this is a close to home crime, and then have Wendy and the girls brought into the station to be formally interviewed. Separately. They were all together this morning, backing each other up, but something's not right. We'll have to get an appropriate adult for Ellie, because she's not eighteen yet, but Marta is. And I don't think we should ask Lorraine to be the appropriate adult. I know that's one of her roles for us, but not in this case.'

'You're right. It seems that our case is hinging on why Stewart left the family home that evening with no forewarning or planning, and until one of them breaks and tells us the truth, we're not going to progress. At least then we'll have a motive, if not the killer. We do have to be aware that Wendy is recovering from major surgery, and needs to be treated gently, but we need to know if she is capable of driving, with the operation site making movement somewhat limited at the moment. And she was the last one to speak to Stewart from that family, so did she plan this?'

Alan drank from his bottle, and stood. 'I'm going to the gents' before we leave for Lorraine's house. Just to confirm, we say nothing of our thoughts to her?'

'No, but take your lead from me. If she says anything that Wendy or one of the girls may have said to her, I'll make a judgement call on it. I'll wait at the car for you.'

He handed her the keys, and Fleur gathered up her bag and notebook, which contained the words bread, milk and cornflakes. It seemed Alan was doing any note-taking they needed for the case, and she realised that once again she hadn't done her shopping, which had been the plan when they chose Sainsbury's for their lunchtime meal.

She headed out into the bitterly cold air, and felt snowflakes touch her cheeks. 'No, no, no,' she said, and an elderly gentleman entering the store turned to her with a smile.

'And it's going to settle,' he said. 'Best get out the sledge.'

She crossed to Alan's car, pressed every button on the fob until it unlocked, and eased herself into the passenger seat. He joined her a minute later, brushing off the snowflakes before getting in the car.

'Love snow,' he said. He began to sing 'Winter Wonderland' and she hit him with her bag.

'See, that's how easy it is to turn to violence. Now stop singing and drive; let's get this bloody awful day over with.'

41

They arrived at Lorraine's home ten minutes early, and remained in the car, watching the snow slowly building on the windscreen wipers.

'Why the hell is it snowing?' Fleur asked.

'Well, see, when the clouds reach a certain height, and the warmer air meets the freezing air...'

She hit him again with her bag.

'Just trying to lighten things. You're getting lines of worry etched into your forehead.'

'It's because I know we have to bring in Wendy, Marta and Ellie. That family is so important to me. If there was one case that will remain fresh in my mind until the day I die, it's the day we found that little girl, and almost everything she said was *please don't hurt me*, or *will it hurt?* I've never kept away from them, whether I was supposed to or not, and I was there at the celebratory meal for her adoption into the Needham family. How the hell can I now be bringing them in for questioning about the murder of their husband and father?'

'I know exactly what you mean. I did the tidy up, the dealing with the bodies in the cellar – how Marta has gone back to that house knowing what went off there, I'll never understand.'

They watched as a jeep drove slowly towards them, and a flash of headlights and the left indicator told them it was Lorraine. They waited until she had pulled onto her drive, before climbing out of the car and hurrying across to join her in her hallway.

'Shit weather,' Lorraine said. 'Do you wanna build a snowman?'

'No, but I am kind of frozen,' Fleur countered, carrying on the joke.

'Crackers, the pair of you,' Alan said. 'We going through to the kitchen?'

'Yes, it's the warmest room,' Lorraine said, and waved in the general direction. 'Sit at the table and I'll make us a drink.'

* * *

With their hands grasping the mugs of coffee, the three of them shared a quiet moment until Fleur moved the conversation on to the previous evening.

'I have to do this to rule you out of the investigation, Lorraine, but can you tell me where you were between 9 p.m. and 2 a.m. last night?'

'I can. I watched TV for a short while but nothing took my fancy, so I did a bit of cross stitch until I ran out of a particular colour and then went to bed. You suspect I killed Stewart?'

'No, it's only the fact that there are a very limited number of people who actually knew where Stewart was staying, and you're one of them. You're the last one to be seen about it, and everybody has an alibi. Did you speak to anyone last night? Can they corroborate what you're saying? Somebody ringing you on your landline around tenish would be really good,' Fleur said with a smile.

'Sorry, can't oblige,' Lorraine said. She sipped at her coffee, staring into the distance as she gave the issue some thought. 'I didn't call anybody, and nobody called me. Couldn't the killer simply have been some drunken lout who took offence to a well-dressed man out for an evening walk?'

'Of course you're right. The killer could be anybody, and it may well be that something shows up on CCTV that will help us with that. It's been collected from the little artisan shops on the canal wharf, and one or two of the canal boats have CCTV set-ups, so by the time we get back, there could be further information to help us.'

'Well, thank goodness for that. This is the first time I've been interviewed formally by the police. Crap, isn't it?' Lorraine tried to smile.

'It is, and I'm sorry we had to do it. Sometimes my job can be really rubbish, but just occasionally it gives me perks like the entire Needham family, and you. You must feel the same about your job. I bet you have a fair few acquaintances who come into your job life, and remain as friends. Am I right?'

'You are.' Lorraine sighed. 'And Marta, I would do anything for. Ever since the day I saw her face for the first time, and knew she didn't know how to cry. I've come across one or two children in my job who were afraid to cry. If they did, they were punished. That was Marta. The first time I saw her laugh was when I read the Marta book to her. I don't think she had ever laughed before.'

Alan's phone pealed out with the *Star Wars* theme, and he pushed back his chair after glancing at the screen. 'I have to take this, it's the station.'

The two women heard the front door open and close, and both took a drink of their coffee.

'Is that it?' Lorraine asked. 'You're not having me measured up for bespoke handcuffs?'

Fleur laughed. 'You can't build snowmen in handcuffs. We'll

pass on them, I think. Speaking of snowmen, have you looked out the window? It's quite deep already.'

'I know. It might be a smart move to get on your way. It won't look good if Sheffield's finest end up sleeping on my sofas because they're stranded by snow.'

They heard the front door open then close, and Fleur turned her head, her eyebrows already raised in query. 'Everything okay?'

Alan looked at her, then sat down to take a drink of his coffee. 'It's getting very deep out there. That was Tamsin, back at the station, boss. She's sending you a text with some information on it.'

Fleur gave a brief nod, and drained her cup. 'We really ought to be going, Alan. Or does your car turn into a sledge?'

The ping on Fleur's phone gave her a reason to move away and she stood in the hallway to read it. She had guessed from the way Alan had given her no information after his phone call that something was wrong.

Five of the vehicles requested for ANPR coverage show no movement through ANPR camera sites. The sixth one, registered to Lorraine Lowe, was confirmed in the canal basin/Hilton hotel area at 9.58 p.m., then returning at 10.22 p.m. No further sightings.

Fleur stood for a moment, then went back into the kitchen. Alan didn't move; he guessed there was much more to follow.

Fleur was now thinking on her feet. There had been contact between Lorraine and Wendy during the afternoon when Lorraine had called to see her friend, and to drop off some things for Marta. During the time Lorraine would have been there, Wendy had taken the decision to answer Stewart's call. Or had Lorraine suggested she take the call and arrange to meet her husband that night?

Fleur's head was swirling; the direction her thoughts were

taking her was definitely not the path towards a random killer, but more towards a close friend killer. She took a deep breath and walked back into the kitchen.

'Lorraine, something's cropped up. We need a couple more answers from you. And just to protect you, I need to caution you. Lorraine Lowe, you do not have to say anything, but it may harm your defence if you do not mention, when questioned, anything which you later rely on in court. Anything you do say may be given in evidence.'

Fleur watched Lorraine's face as she registered what was being said, and it went from shock to acceptance in about thirty seconds. She said nothing, simply waited.

'Lorraine, we've had information from our ANPR system, and your number plate was seen last night in the canal basin area. When I asked you earlier, you said you didn't go out at all. Did anyone borrow your car last night?'

Lorraine shook her head, and Fleur stood. 'Lorraine Lowe, I am arresting you on suspicion of murder. I have already cautioned you, but it will be repeated in the interview room.'

'I'll get your coat,' Alan said. He went to where they had all hung their coats, collecting Fleur's as well as Lorraine's. He handed them to them, and when they stepped out into the ever-deepening snow, Lorraine still hadn't said a word.

* * *

Marta and Ellie clung to each other as they watched Wendy being helped into the back of a police car; Marta felt numb, but Ellie was heartbroken. Marta softly stroked Ellie's hair, trying in vain to reassure her sister that their mother would be home later.

'But she's ill,' Ellie sobbed, 'surely they can't do this.'

'If she needs a doctor, I'm sure they can get one quicker than we can,' Marta said, a touch of bitterness in her tone. 'How on earth they can think she had anything to do with Dad's death, I'll never know. She can't lift her arm up high enough to bash him with a brick or anything else.'

The police car pulled away from the kerb and Marta blew a kiss, hoping her mother could see them standing at the front window. The snow had completely covered the garden to a depth of at least four inches, and Marta knew it would be a struggle to drive later to pick up their mother; neither of the girls had so far had to drive in snow.

'Come and sit down,' she said to Ellie. 'We need to talk.'

* * *

Wendy was led into an interview room, mildly warm and painted in a truly miserable shade of grey. She was immediately asked if she needed a doctor, and she shook her head, saying all she needed was to go home to her daughters, and be allowed to grieve with them as they mourned the loss of their father.

Fleur and Alan watched her for a moment. 'We'll take Wendy first?'

Fleur nodded. 'I think so. After we've got her statement, it may be all a bit irrelevant for Lorraine, who I think is on the verge of telling all anyway. It's to do with the girls, I'm getting more and more sure of it by the minute.'

They waited until a PC had finished providing Wendy with a cup of tea, and then entered the interview room.

They logged in on the recorder, and asked Wendy to log in.

'Wendy, I understand you don't want a solicitor?'

'No, thank you. You seem to think I've done something wrong, but I haven't, so why would I need a solicitor?'

'Okay. You can change your mind at any time. Wendy, you

stated earlier that you had a visit from Lorraine Lowe yesterday afternoon.' Fleur felt mildly shocked that it really was only the previous afternoon. 'Can you tell us why she called to see you?'

'Of course. She brought some kitchenware items for Marta to take to her house. We had a cup of tea, a chat, and she left.'

'What time was this?'

The first hesitation was apparent. 'Around four.'

'Thank you. While she was there, did you answer a phone call from your husband?'

And now came the second hesitation. 'I did.'

'You had ignored his calls and his texts all day and yet you suddenly answered one when you had a visitor. Strange...' Fleur looked down at her notes. 'Can you remember what you and your husband spoke about?'

'Yes, I asked him not to come back to the house.'

'Did you make arrangements to meet him somewhere?'

'No comment.'

Fleur laughed. 'Oh, Wendy, you've watched far too many crime programmes. Let's try again. Did you make arrangements to meet Stewart Needham at the canal basin, a short walk from the hotel he was staying in, last night around ten o'clock?'

'No!'

'Who did meet him, then? Let's think about this, shall we? Let's go back to when you threw out your husband the previous night. The night when he ended up at the Premier Inn because he had no idea he would need to organise a place to stay. What had he done that caused you to throw him out? Did he force himself on Marta? She's a very curvy girl, just the sort to appeal to men of a certain age. Beautiful face, wouldn't you say, DS Johnson?'

'Definitely. Stewart must have felt the odd twitch every time he looked at her...'

'Stop it!' Wendy screamed out, covering her ears with her hands. 'It's obscene. He took off her towel...'

'He took off Marta's towel? With her permission?'

'No.' Wendy was sobbing now. 'It was Ellie's towel, and she just stood there, not knowing what to do. My Ellie.'

'Where was Marta?'

'She was in her room. She came out, as I did, when we heard Ellie yell out. She was standing there, totally naked, trying to get to her towel, which was on the floor. Her head towel had been loosened by him, and was covering her face. She was so frightened. What else could I do but tell him to go?'

Fleur pushed the box of tissues across the table towards Wendy. 'Did you tell Lorraine?' she said gently.

'I told her everything. Marta, Ellie and I sat up late and talked everything through. He'd been touching Marta as well, it wasn't just Ellie. He took advantage of Ellie being on her own as she came out of the bathroom. Ellie said he tugged at the head towel, which started to fall off, so she grabbed at it, and he flicked her towel off that was around her body. He thought I was asleep, Fleur, he thought I was asleep.'

Fleur slowly unscrewed the top of her water bottle, and watched as Wendy tried desperately to recover.

'Wendy,' she said quietly, 'did you arrange to meet your husband at ten o'clock in the canal basin, knowing it wouldn't be you going to meet him?'

Wendy nodded.

'Please answer for the tape, Wendy.'

'Yes.'

'And who did go to meet him?'

'Lorraine,' she whispered. 'Lorraine asked me to answer the next call from him, and arrange to meet him. She said she would go instead, when I said I wasn't well enough to drive yet, and we didn't speak again after that.'

* * *

Lorraine Lowe was arrested later that afternoon, after signing a full confession, and charged with the murder of Stewart Needham. Wendy Needham was charged with aiding and abetting a murder, and Fleur made the horrific journey through the deep snow that was still falling to the Needham home.

Fleur knew the girls must have been watching for their mother coming home; the door was opened before she even reached it. She stamped her feet on the doormat and stepped into the hallway.

'Where's Mum?' Marta sounded aggressive, and Fleur put an arm around each of the girls.

'Let's go through to the lounge.'

* * *

By the time Fleur was back in her car, she felt exhausted, drained to the point of despair. She had left her number with them, asking them to put it into their phones so they would always have it, and arranged for them to be collected the following day to be taken to make statements at the station.

She felt awful having to tell them they wouldn't be allowed to see Wendy, but what had made things so bad was hearing how long they had been tolerating the unwanted actions of their father. Despite a slightly rocky start to their relationship, the two girls seemed to have bonded remarkably well, and she felt they would be each other's rocks.

Marta, shy, non-verbal little Marta of five years earlier, had grown to be the strength for Ellie, and they talked long into the night, making decisions, crying, knowing two days had changed their worlds.

That night, after she had lent Ellie her little quilt for the very first time, Marta took out a new sketchbook and began to draw.

Her own diary would start now.

EPILOGUE
ONE YEAR LATER

The candle was standing wedged inside a puddle of its own wax, and within a silver foil mini apple pie case. It did not look classy, but with all the candle holders packed away, Ellie had been forced into being creative.

She faced Marta across the kitchen table, surrounded by Chinese takeaway containers, but they had managed to rescue two plates out of a box. Plastic picnic forks were their cutlery.

Ellie held up a plastic beaker filled with wine, and waved it in the general direction of Marta. 'Happy birthday for tomorrow, my lovely Marta. We'll eat first. And then I'll give you your gift.'

Marta smiled. 'Will it be as good as last night's gift?'

Ellie blushed. She had no difficulty sleeping in the same bed as Marta every night, she just had difficulty talking about it.

'You may not find it as exciting as I did...'

Marta reached across the foil dishes and grasped hold of Ellie's hand. 'I will. If it's just a packet of Liquorice allsorts, I'll find it exciting. I love you, Ellie, and because of that, everything's changed.'

Ellie returned the squeeze and picked up her fork. 'Well, this is proper luxury. Sweet and sour chicken balls, what could be more elegant than that?' She laughed. 'But I guess tomorrow it will be pizza in the hand while we're walking around trying to find a place for everything.'

'It's truly happening, isn't it?' Marta's eyes were shining in the candlelight. 'Tomorrow we're leaving here and locking it up until Mum finishes her sentence and comes home. Our house is finished apart from looking a little bare of furniture, and we can start our lives properly. I am so glad we took a year out to decide what to do next, and while I know I won't be going to uni, I don't want you to rush to make your decision. You know we can make the gallery a joint project, but I won't ever push you on that.'

Ellie smiled. 'I know, but for you to continue to make your artworks, you need somebody up front, managing the rest of the business. I've almost come to the decision to take five years out, help you establish the gallery, and then possibly go to uni as an older student.'

Marta paused with her fork halfway to her mouth. 'You'd do that for me?'

'I'd do anything for you,' was Ellie's simple and straightforward answer. She reached down by the side of her chair, and picked up a small package wrapped in Christmas paper. 'I couldn't find birthday wrapping paper.' She smiled. 'Happy birthday, Marta.'

Marta opened the gift, and stood it on the table. 'Oh, my, it's a Chinese brush holder.'

'I believe the name for it is bitong, but it's Ming dynasty. Do you like it?'

'Oh, god, Ellie, I love it.'

Ellie's smile grew wider. 'Do you have any idea how difficult it is to buy something for the girl who has everything?'

Marta pulled Ellie close to her, and kissed her. 'I have everything now.'

* * *

They cleared a couple of boxes off the sofa and sat side by side, both grumbling about the food babies they now carried thanks to being a bit over-enthusiastic when they rang in the order for delivery.

'Mum didn't look very well last time we saw her.' Ellie frowned as she brought her mother's face to mind. 'It's rubbish that she had to go to prison as well as Lorraine. I'm sure if we'd thought it through properly...'

'We couldn't have done it any other way.'

'I know. Deep down, of course I know. But we also know how easy Mum and Lorraine are to manipulate, and I can't help feeling we took advantage of that.'

'We did.' Marta smiled at her. 'As soon as we told Mum about the different times Stewart had touched us, or simply ogled us, and how scared we were to be in the house alone with him in case he took it further, we both knew she would talk to Lorraine about it; she's programmed from years of childcare to do that. And let's face it, of all the people in this world, Lorraine loves me more than anyone else. I've always known that, and she's always said it, so hearing about Stewart from Mum was the only trigger we needed to pull, albeit from afar.'

Ellie smiled. 'I did notice we had to work hard at looking surprised when they told us he was dead. Wonder if it's classed as patricide by remote control?'

'Whatever it is, Lorraine is in it for a long holiday, Mum not so long, but long enough. I didn't want them in prison either, you know. But somebody had to pay for his death, and let's face it, Lorraine did do it, and Mum did tell her what was going on, knowing Lorraine would chuck him in the canal or something. The main thing we have to think about is that neither of them would have let us be sent to prison, they would have taken the blame anyway.'

'So we're virtually orphans.' Ellie smiled at the thought. 'Think anybody would want to adopt two nineteen-year-olds?'

'Nope, we're on our own, and happy to be so, I reckon. Come on, let's go to bed, it's got to be comfier than this, and when we get up, it will be the first day of our lives properly together. And won't Mum and Lorraine be surprised by that!'

ACKNOWLEDGMENTS

This book was a pleasure and a delight to write. That it has reached the stage of being readable is entirely down to the amazing team at Boldwood. I have so many thanks to give to Tara Loder for her edits and advice, and marketing thanks have to go to Nia and Claire, who answer my daft questions with such patience, and special thanks go to Candida Bradford for her excellence in proofreading.

Thanks also go to Lorraine Lowe for the loan of her name – thank you so much, Lorraine, I hope you love the role you played.

I have to talk about my team of Beta readers, who offer such sage advice when they get a copy of the book a long time before it sees an editor – Marnie Harrison, Tina Jackson, Alyson Read, Sarah Hodgson and Denise Cutler, thank you so much for all your input. And I extend those thanks to my forty strong team of ARC readers, and their very welcome reviews posted on launch day. Absolute stars, all of you.

And my friends – Judith Baker (J A Baker) and Valerie Dickenson (Valerie Keogh) who support and encourage me on the dark days when I'm thinking the book is rubbish, I'll never get it finished by deadline day, it won't have enough words, and every other silly thought that goes through my head. Thank you for keeping me sane, and being part of my world.

I can't ignore my family – they wouldn't let me anyway. So here they all are, the ones who encourage, tell me they didn't want a character to die, and am I sure this word is spelt correctly? Dave

Waller, Matt Waller, Richelle Waller, Siân Dawson, Anthony Dawson, Kirsty Waller, Brad Waller, Beth Machin, Katie Waller, Melissa Waller, Dominic Kitchen, Lucie Davison, Cerys Kitchen, Lyra Grayson, Isaac Grayson, Lily Taylor and Elle Taylor. And the cutest of them all, our great grandson William Kitchen, who at eight months can't read yet, but I'm sure one day he'll pick up one of Nanny Neet's books and marvel at just how many people his great nan has killed off. Thank you all for your unswerving support, I love you.

Anita Waller

Sheffield 2022

ABOUT THE AUTHOR

Anita Waller is the author of many bestselling psychological thrillers and the Kat and Mouse crime series. She lives in Sheffield, which continues to be the setting of many of her thrillers.

Sign up to Anita Waller's mailing list for news, competitions and updates on future books.

Visit Anita Waller's website: www.anitawaller.co.uk

Follow Anita on social media:

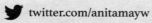 twitter.com/anitamayw
facebook.com/anita.m.waller
instagram.com/anitawallerauthor
tiktok.com/@anitawallerauthor

ALSO BY ANITA WALLER

One Hot Summer

The Family at No. 12

The Couple Across The Street

The Forrester Detective Agency Mysteries

Fatal Secrets

Fatal Lies

THE

Murder

LIST

**THE MURDER LIST IS A NEWSLETTER
DEDICATED TO SPINE-CHILLING FICTION
AND GRIPPING PAGE-TURNERS!**

**SIGN UP TO MAKE SURE YOU'RE ON OUR
HIT LIST FOR EXCLUSIVE DEALS, AUTHOR
CONTENT, AND COMPETITIONS.**

SIGN UP TO OUR NEWSLETTER

BIT.LY/THEMURDERLISTNEWS

Boldwood

Boldwood Books is an award-winning fiction publishing company seeking out the best stories from around the world.

Find out more at www.boldwoodbooks.com

Join our reader community for brilliant books, competitions and offers!

Follow us
@BoldwoodBooks
@TheBoldBookClub

Sign up to our weekly deals newsletter

https://bit.ly/BoldwoodBNewsletter